Posthumously

Bob Pappert

POSTHUMOUSLY

COPYRIGHT 2017

Make inquiries to the author Bob Pappert or Trash Publishing Co.

ISBN 978-0996911801

Acknowledgments

For a first novel I want to thank all of the people that made this possible, and in thanking everyone I am sure that I would leave an integral person off my list. So I am not acknowledging anyone.

Not my wife Shauna, who has been so supportive. Nor my children, Josh and Kaitie, who have inspired my life. Not Kaitie's husband, Ryan Lewis, who suggested the title.

Then there is the family, Owen and Henry, Sarah and Zooey, Lorelei and Isla and Ryan and Kaitlin, Taylor and Brendan and Jameson and Blake. Obviously, too many to thank.

And those thousands of students over the years whose stories I have listened to, Alex and Ron and Rachel and pick a name and there is a story. Way too many names to mention here.

Geri McClure and her husband Mike, and loyal friends like Dan and Jeff and Stu, even if he doesn't read, should be listed, but they won't.

Best not to acknowledge anyone. Thanks.

Posthumously is based on a bunch of true stories (at least the people claimed they were true). The characters and events, though, are all fictional.

Posthumously

Part I - 2004

Chapter 1

She was wearing don't-fuck-me-flats. The cuffs of her jeans revealed little more than a snippet of her ankle, and the gray oversized sweatshirt, devoid of lettering, was as gloomy as the dimly lit room. Under the California Angels cap hiding her eyes, her brown hair twisted like a tornado. The glass of untouched house cabernet remained within reach of her hand as her head tilted to see the weatherman theatrically reveal a warming trend. Behind the bar, a white towel was drying the inside of a wine glass.

"Can I interest you in a lemonade?"

Kristen turned with obvious displeasure toward the voice. The black eye softened her inner turmoil for a split second. This was definitely not a person humming, "Somewhere Over the Rainbow." He was wearing his usual wardrobe of "nobody's gonna ever have sex with me" Levis and a black Billabong tee shirt, and a body and face that were a few steps from enlisting in the Salvation Army. He climbed, without grace, onto the bar stool next to her.

"What happened to you?" Kristen asked, reaching for her wine.

"Lemonade," said James toward the bartender.

"Sprite is as close as we come," answered the man, pulling the taps as he poured a patron's beer from the spout.

"Just one." He raised a finger looking inquiringly at Kristen as she contemplated his eye. "My girlfriend hit me."

"You probably deserved it," answered Kristen, a little bothered she had started this conversation, but from the looks of him, he was as dangerous as a tadpole in a drying pond.

The Sprite slid in front of him.

"I don't think so. It's a long story."

"All stories are long, even the short ones," Kristen replied. Kristen found her starvation for conversation being fed, even though she had come to Scully's to think and be alone on this Friday night. Besides, his voice had a pleasing cadence. Kristen needed this. Needed conversation. Conversation. The nutrient that keeps the body and mind healthy. The liquid of ideas poured in the air to be swallowed and savored. The ideas that let feet stand strong on the ground. The chance to travel with words to places and understanding that you never expected. Where a few pleasant words can turn into forty years of delight. But if conversation is withheld or not allowed. A permanent stop sign to the freeway of the future. A poisoning silence that devours the credibility of who you are. The blocking of exchange, the heart to heart, that never has a chance to flow. The wrapping of who you are into a box that is never opened. Kristen needed this conversation.

"I had a girlfriend. Do you know how old I am?" he continued.

"What, twenty-five?"

"Almost thirty. In about a month." He took a sip. "I hope I'm not bothering you. But you know how some guys are good at math, know the quadratic formula like the pledge of allegiance,

7

know physics so well they could tell you when a leaf should hit the ground after falling off a tree or can name twenty-five mountain ranges in the world, everything from the Rockies to the Aravalli Range in Western India?" James was hoping he was making sense. His last conversation hadn't ended the way he had expected.

"Yeah. I get it. I got good grades," said Kristen. She had never heard of a mountain range in India.

"Yeah. So did I. I got good grades in everything except for girlfriends. I flunked out. But two years ago I met this girl, Molly. Some guys got Ds and Fs in school. They couldn't multiply nine times five without a calculator or phone. They didn't know how to put a period at the end of a sentence... but they knew how to find a girlfriend. They would have a new girlfriend every three months. They could care less that the capital of Norway is Copenhagen."

"It's Oslo, not Copenhagen," answered Kristen, inserting a touch of smugness into the conversation.

"I mean these guys have been touching girls for years, and every year in school, I'm touching computer keys and textbook pages and ballpoint pens and my library card, while Timmy Numbnuts doesn't even look at the bright, bold, red fifty-seven percent written on his test. No, he is looking at Rachel with the tight sweater and short skirt, and she is looking at him and smiling. And he is not going to fail with Rachel."

"Your black eye?" asked Kristen, now more than a little interested in what he was saying.

"I just wanted a girlfriend. I was like the Gobi Desert."

"I believe the Gobi is in Asia and Mongolia," responded Kristen.

"Damn." James was impressed, quite impressed, by this dressed-to-the-ones young lady sitting on the barstool next to him. "Yeah, I was drowning in sand. A girlfriend drought that should have ended a long time ago. I mean, I'm twenty-nine and the rains of girlfriends should have flooded the plains of the Serengeti, but

8

I had been in a prolonged drought, and then somehow, don't ask me how, Molly falls in love with me."

"And how did that happen?" Kristen wanted to know.

"We worked together at Aerodynamics R Us, quite a childish name for a big company. She asked me to dance at the Christmas party, and I almost broke one of her toes, and the way she held my hand when the dance ended must have forced my voice box to actually speak and I asked her out, and she actually said she would love to go out. Those were her actual words. 'Would love to go out.' 'Would love.' That was pretty sweet."

"So why did she hit you?" Kristen was trying to pull the story toward an ending, but at the same time enjoying a mind that could tell a tale. The black eye next to her was shining a light through her that hadn't been switched on lately.

"I mean we're having dinner and movies and, get this, s-e-x. Life is finally good. I'm not going to my grave a virgin. But I don't know how to be a boyfriend. I've failed for fifteen years, so you can't expect me to get it right on my first try," explained James, wondering if he should take his foot off the gas of this story.

"Is the Sprite good?" asked Kristen, as she raised a finger to the bartender to ask for a Sprite.

James decided to keep his foot on the gas. "So I'm a man, and Molly, my girlfriend, needs to know I'm a man, so I do a couple of macho essentials, get stoned with my buddies and don't call her. Tell her I'll meet her for dinner and show up an hour late. The topper was when I didn't know how important her sister's baby shower was." James opened his hands to show how he didn't have a clue. "Man, I took a sledgehammer to that day. For every five things I did right ... Well, let's just say I will never make the honor roll in dating.

"You were pretty stupid," Kristen chimed in.

"Yeah, in capital letters. But the ship was still sailing smoothly after going through the rough waters and hitting a couple of icebergs at the beginning, until last week when I saw Green Day

9

in concert. They played for three-and-a-half hours. It was awesome." Kristen could see in his unblackened eye, the enjoyment the concert must have given him.

"I take it you didn't take her. You didn't think she would enjoy something that you might like?" wondered Kristen.

"She never liked Green Day. She thinks 'Good Riddance' you know that 'I hope you had the time of your life' song is the worst song ever written. 'A pile of marketing crap' she calls it, so sentimental it makes you want to puke. She wanted me to stay and watch a movie and not go with my friends. Green Day. Stay home and watch a movie." James gestured with both hands as if they were the scales of justice. "It didn't seem like much of a decision. I mean I'd had the ticket for two months. But I thought I had made some inroads to maturity when I told her I'd see her after the concert by midnight."

"That's pretty early for a concert. I take it you weren't there by midnight. Let me guess. Three AM, puking on the couch?" Kristen sipped her Sprite, forgetting the anxiety that had brought her to Scully's. Forgetting her own problems, while remembering what it felt like to be entertained. To talk. To laugh.

"I knocked on the door, real quiet, by 12:30, and pushed open the door… Ya know, all I have done is talk and talk and talk," James offered, knowing he hadn't heard more than a sentence here and there from her. "By the way, I'm James," he said, not knowing if he should reach across and shake her hand.

"No, keep going. I'm Kristen," responded Kristen, taking a longer drink. The nine o'clock news was ending on the television above the bar. "I like this story." She sat back on her bar stool, her arms folded comfortably.

"So, when I got to the door, I reached down to untie my shoes," James began again. "I knocked quietly, so I wouldn't wake Molly, and then I opened the door carefully and stepped inside and then a right cross knocked me onto her doormat, followed by a barrage of incoherent anger with every cuss word known to mankind."

10

"She hit you for being thirty minutes late?" Kristen laughed, picturing the punch that knocked him flying". James was shaking his head.

"You know how those concerts are. Somehow we made it to the floor, thanks to some guy freaking out on an usher. You gotta take those opportunities when you can to get closer to the stage. Joints are being passed around like candy on Halloween. We're jumping and dancing like idiots. Elation. Pure elation for the whole show." James paused for a second, understanding the elation he felt just talking to this delightful person he was next to. Who she was he had no idea, but in the ten minutes they had been talking, he already felt a connection. Something about her was the draw of a magnet, the current of the ocean, the moon pulling the tides. No cliff to fall over. No crevice to disappear into. No crack starting to form, where you know a separation will soon follow. No. This felt natural. Felt good.

He went back to the story, his hands talking as much as his mouth. "We leave. Hop on the freeway. Quarter to twelve. I think I'll call Molly to tell her I'll be a little late. She'll know how much I care. But I can't find my phone. Nokia, my friend driving, tries calling me to see if maybe I left my phone in the car. Nothing. I must have lost it and like a fool I don't borrow Nokia's phone to call Molly. I'll only be a half hour late. How bad can that be? After the punch Molly throws me down on the couch, and I can finally make out what she's yelling. Man, chicks can be pretty strong when they're pissed. So she's yelling at me. I can censor this if you want."

"This is too good to be censored," smiled Kristen, now thoroughly enjoying her night.

"So she's screamin,' 'So I'm a cunt, huh? My ass is so big it is only mercy sex? You wish my tits were like this?' And Molly holds up her phone in front of my face, and there on the phone is a picture of someone's breasts. There was some other stuff but I don't remember."

"I don't get it," remarked Kristen, a little puzzled.

11

"Someone who found my phone at the concert decided to have some fun at my expense. Seems Molly texted me and whoever found my phone texted her back. Not very cool. They kept texting back and forth. She thought it was me, of course. Most expensive fucking concert ever."

"That was good. Really a good story. So why Scully's?" asked Kristen.

"I thought I'd give the walls of my apartment a break. Walls aren't very good at conversation. When I turned twenty-one, this is where my brother took me for my first beer, legal or otherwise. Where I decided I would never have another drink. Where I play pool sometimes, chalking my stick, without wetting my throat."

"So you ordered a lemonade?"

"My first time with beer when I was twenty-one didn't work out so well. Baby steps. I need time for my wounds to heal. There's some history there also," James said, knowing it was time to listen to Kristen. "But enough about me. What brought you to that stool?"

"I'm engaged to Ken."

"The doll or the man? Sorry. That wasn't very nice."

"Actually, the doll. Waxed always. His Porsche. His body. His clothes. He's a lawyer. His name and his father's name are on the building. They have more money than is in the Bank of America. And a body," Kristen's eyes looked up at James. "No offense, but every time I look he makes my body tremble. Six-pack abs that really are a six-pack and not the big gulp from 7-11," said Kristen, shaking her head.

"And the problem is?" asked James.

"I might as well be a couch. He'll lay on me every once in a while, but I think he likes the refrigerator and his new fifty-inch plasma television, and his elliptical machine more than me. I'm just another piece of furniture. For two years I've been his accessory. He takes me to the fanciest restaurants, the fanciest hotels. Do you know what it's like to eat at a restaurant and the

12

waiter has more to say than your date? I almost struck up a conversation with my lobster. But then I look at that dimple and that smile and that body and I tremble. I want to take that drug, but I know it is no good for me," said Kristen, looking to James for confirmation.

"He looks that good, huh?" responded James, his head tilted toward his Sprite.

"Everyone says I'm the luckiest girl in the world. The wedding is in three weeks. Twenty-two days to be exact."

"So you're still with him. It sounds complicated." James cringed at the stupidity of his words.

"I didn't dress like this to find my Mr. Right. We were supposed to go to the game tonight. I'm freaking out. Right at this moment my feet are pretty cold!" She moved off the stool and dug her fingers into the pocket of her jeans. The glare from the diamond she pulled from her jeans could have blinded a stadium filled with fans.

"Sweet Jesus. You could feed a country with that thing," James blurted.

"I know. My parents know. My sister knows. My friends know. The fork in the river is getting close. Too close."

"If it doesn't work, you will be a rich woman."

"I don't need the wealth, just the health," sighed Kristen.

"Sounds like a rap song. I just want a girl that can't throw a punch."

Kristen laughed at his wit. "You asked if I wanted a drink pretty boldly. Weren't you afraid I might throw a few jabs in your direction?"

"Many years ago I would have ducked as soon as I asked the question. Actually, many years ago, I never would have opened my mouth. Would have run in the opposite direction. I would have done anything not to take a step in the direction I wanted to go, but Myra Brighton cured me of that once and for all."

"Who is this Myra Brighton?" asked Kristen, delighted that the avenue of conversation was dotted with green lights. James had a way with conversation that was like an adhesive band aid, soothing whatever bruises one held inside.

"On my first day of high school, I was this nervous little freshman hoping I wouldn't be lost or thrown in a trash can. I finally found where you picked up your schedule so you could find your classes. The line was about six people long, under the "B's," when I noticed this beautiful blonde hair a couple of people in front of me. Anyway, she turned to wave to a friend and the smile on her face turned me into a wanton puddle of helplessness."

"You were wanting her," continued Kristen.

"Yeah, but since I was a freshman, I didn't understand much. All I knew was I was mush."

"So what'd you say to her that made you realize…?"

"I can't get to the punchline yet. We still have a few streets to go down to get there," interrupted James.

"Start driving," quipped Kristen, happy with her own wit for a change.

"She is in my very first class," continued James, not missing a beat, "and I am in love with her but too scared to say a word to her. I mean, what if she says to shut up or won't even say anything?"

"Most girls aren't like that."

"I didn't know that. I was a fourteen–year old freshman. Checking the mirror every day to make sure a zit hadn't grown to the size of Mt. Everest. I didn't know anything," emphasized James, his hands showing the raising of a mountain on his face.

"Mt. Everest huh? Your head could explode." The elation that Kristen felt was unmistakable. She pushed some of her tornado hair from her eyes toward the bill of her cap. Secretly she wished James could see the way she really looked. She looked at her don't-fuck-me-flats and inwardly shook her head. *Why did she look so bad?* she wondered. The evening was not supposed to turn out like this.

14

"So my whole freshman year I was obsessed with her. I found out her schedule just so I could watch her walking from English to lunch with her friends. Found out her locker just so I could watch her take her books out. I was pathetic."

"It's O.K. You were a freshman," comforted Kristen, who desperately wanted to touch his shoulder in support, to touch his hand, to touch his forearm, to touch his warmth instead of the cool glass of Sprite.

"My sophomore year, the same thing. By my junior year my mind was working twenty-five hours a day, engineering ways that Myra and I would meet and talk and fall in love. One scenario had her walking by the tennis court when a ball my opponent hits knocks her to the ground and for a second she passes out until I administer mouth-to-mouth and, oh... It's so ridiculous and absurd." James shook his head in embarrassment.

"Kind of like in *Sandlot* where the kid gets mouth-to-mouth from the beautiful lifeguard," giggled Kristen.

"Yeah. That was it. One of my favorite movies, by the way," admitted James. "In my senior year, she is in my English class. She sits right next to me. I still haven't said a word to her. Over three years and I haven't said a word. The first essay I write in this class, I pour my heart onto the paper. I usually write a good solid three-page essay, but this time six-pages fly out of the computer. I confess my love for her, despite the fact I have never talked to her."

"Pretty brave to write about your obsession. Was the teacher a man?"

"No. Just a woman who loved to laugh and teach. She made me feel I mattered. So, two days later she passes out the essays, except for mine and says she wants to talk to me after class."

"You're in trouble?" asked Kristen, wondering how the story was going to end.

"No. She tells me it's a good essay, and that I have to have the courage to talk to her, that I can't move forward until I

15

take a step. But when I tell her she is in the class and that I sit right next to her, she can't believe it. Then this little smile comes to her lips and she says, 'James I'll take care of this.' " James paused to take a sip from the Sprite, lonely and forgotten on the bar.

"So what did she do?" Kristen eagerly wanted to know. She would have to be married to Ken for thirty years, she thought, before he would ever be able to engage in such a gratifying conversation.

"She didn't do anything. When she said she would take care of it, at first I was kind of relieved. She had taken the pressure off of me. But then I kept waiting and waiting and nothing. Finally, it was a month before we were graduating. It was May 16, I remember the day, and Myra has on a really short black skirt and a white blouse, and she looks awesome. I mean awesome. And then I hear a 'Myra and James, can I see you for a minute?' I'm shaking like a leaf, as we walk to her desk. 'I need these posters taped to doors and stapled on the bulletin boards around the school,' she says, and she hands us this stack of posters and a stapler and some tape."

"So did you end up taking your dream girl to the senior prom that year?" asked an excited Kristen.

"For the next half hour, all I hear from her is negative. 'That's not straight. You're using too much tape. Why does she want us to do this?' I even ask her if she likes Saturday Night Live. I mean, who doesn't like that show? But no, 'It's so stupid.' I figure after four years of obsession I have to give her a little more, so I ask her what she is into, and all she wants to tell me about is the car her dad is getting her for graduation, and about how immature the boys around here are and how she can't wait to get to college."

"You found the only girl in the world that doesn't like Saturday Night Live," said a grinning Kristen.

"After class I waited and thanked the teacher. Told her I was so stupid. I wasted four years on fool's gold. She told me it

16

was only four years, and I had another seventy or so to make other mistakes. She said, 'Don't wait so long to screw up next time.' Obviously I haven't lost my touch," he said pointing toward the eye that had been recently blackened.

"I guess my Myra story is in the form of a softball. For six years I was obsessed with softball," said Kristen.

"Did you play in high school and college?" asked James.

"I played my first year of high school, and then I traded in my bat for my school work and dreamed of going to Berkeley. My history teacher had protested in Oakland during the Civil Rights Movement of the sixties and had graduated from Berkeley, and I wanted to follow in his footsteps. But when I was in the fourth and fifth grade, I used to sleep with my bat. I didn't have a lot of power, but I could lay down a bunt that would stop halfway between third and home and beat the throw every time. I was always lead-off when I played. I thought I was hot stuff. I dreamed of making the Olympics back then and singing the Star Spangled Banner as I was receiving my gold medal. I loved bunting on the very first pitch of the game and taking control of the situation right out of the box." Kristen's voice tailed off. The somersaults in her stomach took a break. "Times have changed." The image of her situation with Ken appeared before her. In three weeks her control of the situation would be a memory of the past.

"Did you go to Berkeley?" asked James.

"No. Never made it." The mirth of the evening had been broken.

The bill of Kristen's cap pointed to the ceiling, as she gazed at the television in the corner. "The Laker game has been over for a while. He'll be walking through the door in about an hour." The avenue of conversation had hit a speed bump. She took a deep breath as she dismounted from the stool. She was still enormously grateful for an evening of enjoyment, her first in a long long time. "Thanks for the fresh air, James. The third party. No dog in the fight."

17

"Not in your fight anyway," answered James, returning some of the light atmosphere that Kristen had breathed in easily. "I met some knuckles I never imagined would have flown on a one-way ticket to my eye."

James reached into his pocket and pulled out the slimmest of wads. Finding a twenty- dollar bill in the folds, he raised his glass of Sprite and secured the bill underneath.

"The last of the big spenders."

"You don't have to."

"Three Sprites and a ...I think I can handle it. Steak and lobster and Russian Caviar from Moscow or Kiev, though..."

"That was the best conversation I've had in two years. I guess I owe thanks to whoever found your phone," Kristen laughed.

"Sorry if I'm not laughing," James answered, opening the door of Scully's, as Kristen walked past. "Maybe we should meet here every Friday night?" James added, halfheartedly.

Kristen laughed, smiled and nodded her head.   "I'll try to have two eyes the same color," James added with an ounce of confidence. "Can I get you a cab?"

"No, I drove. Right over there." She pointed to a metallic BMW, shining in the darkness of the moonlit night.

James walked her to her car. The Angels cap, the oversized gray sweatshirt, the faded jeans, the don't-fuck-me-flats. The conversation. His eyes never left her and followed her BMW out of the lot and up Olive Avenue, until the taillights slowly dimmed in the distance and then disappeared. He wondered if he would ever see her again. Wondered if he would recognize her if he did see her again. Wondered what she looked like. Wondered why it had taken him almost thirty years to have a conversation that felt so comfortable, so real, so free. Would she really be here next Friday? Both eyes, although one had a depth of darkness, now stared at a deserted street.

Chapter 2

The front door opened with the energy of a sloth, slow and quiet. Kristen turned from the couch and as the pointing stick of the weatherman predicted clearing skies, the entering body tingled her senses and confused her mind.

"Get me a finger of scotch," Ken muttered mechanically, as he ambled to his desk. "The traffic was terrible."

Kristen reached above the counter for a 1939 Macallan, a wildly expensive bottle of scotch, worth over five-thousand dollars, a gift from one of Ken's clients. *How can one bottle of booze be worth that much?* wondered Kristen. She remembered her first year in college when Top Ramen was king, and she had to stretch one hundred and twenty dollars for two weeks, and the pride she felt every other Thursday knowing she had done it. She worked ten hours a week at the school library with under fifty dollars take home pay, which left steak and Haagen-Daz and all other extravagances out of her shopping cart. As she poured Ken a drink, she thought the Macallan didn't even smell good, but what did she know?

As she placed the three-hundred-dollar ounce on the edge of this month's Forbes Magazine, Ken's eyes never moved from his computer screen, actually larger in size than Kristen's grandmother's television of yesteryear. The mouse zigzagged furiously across the pad, like a basketball point guard trying to break a man-to-man full-court press. She placed a hand on his shoulder as she journeyed to the bedroom.

"Can I have the scotch?" he asked.

"It's already there," she managed.

His eyes went back to the red and blue lines of the graph, as his fingers brought the scotch to wet his lips. He drank one hundred and fifty dollars worth and then the whole three hundred before returning the emptiness to the center of Forbes.

Kristen knew he wasn't coming to bed. The room was quiet as she slid under the warmth and richness of the sheet. The click of the lamp was the only sound made, besides the clearing of her throat. The pressure of her thoughts made the sheet heavy upon her. A night spent in conversation. A night spent away from the isolation of the house, from her role as an understudy to Ken, to a brief appearance on the stage of life at Scully's, where the lines she uttered had an audience that listened. A night where the bubble from a two-dollar Sprite had lifted her spirits more than the amber jewels of opulent scotch.

The one or two times a month that Ken wanted sex were always only sex. She loved running her fingers over the taut muscles of his abdomen. She loved the strength of his shoulders and the piercing gaze of his dark brown eyes. But the glass was never full. She wanted sixteen ounces of lovemaking, not the shot glass that lasted two minutes at best. She had told him she needed more, told him she loved the feel of his fingers on her skin, the feel of his biceps as his arms wrapped around her, the pleasure of his kisses, of his mouth on hers, but it was a recording that he wasn't listening to. He touched his Porsche more than he did her and he made sure the hum of its engine was always finely tuned.

When they first met, she was overwhelmed by his wealth. She had been an intern at a law office, filing and flirting, as youth often does, until this strikingly elegant vision of power and strength had caught her with her mouth agape. Where had this Adonis come from? The suit and tie. The brown eyes. The dimple. This was more than a woman, any woman, could stand. And the Christmas party was when it all began. One too many or just the right amount of alcohol, depending on one's perspective, brought her arm around his waist at the bar.

Embarrassingly, she worshipped this idol, "God, you're beautiful." The alcohol had erased the timidity of her actions.

"Then it might be time for us to leave." The beautifully handsome face had spoken.

She was too mesmerized to think of anything but nodding her head, slipping her hand in the crook of his arm and following. When the valet slowed the Porsche next to her and Ken opened the door, the luxury of love, the wealth of love, consumed her. He could have asked for anything and she would have tried to give him more. The piñata was opening and she was the one grabbing the riches. She didn't feel she deserved to be so close to the pavement zipping underneath the chassis of such a well-tuned machine, sitting next to another chassis so well-toned that his chiseled chin was not the only thing sculpted.

She felt like a lottery winner, aglow in her secure position of the bucket seat, held tightly, strap across her chest, buckled in. Ready for the ride, the acceleration, the speed. Next to the man a few feet away, maneuvering through the turns and straightaways, knowing where he was going, knowing what he wanted, knowing what to do. The song on the radio was the only sound, "Somewhere Over the Rainbow." Not the Judy Garland version of finding a better life, but the soft romantic version that melted Kristen into the seat. A once strong, determined lady turned to butter.

If melted butter can throb with excitement, that was Kristen. Her mind tingled with anticipation. Somehow she spoke.

"Where are we going?" she asked. Not the most original of lines. Her eyes still gazed at the road ahead, as her hands fumbled for a mirror and lipstick.

"My place." His words were assured but not forceful, as the vein on his hands bulged when he downshifted into second.

She kept her gaze ahead, imagined his strong arms around her, imagined being picked up like a feather and placed softly on a bed of dreams. She rationalized that everything she had been taught by her mother and grandmother did not apply to this situation. She was a grown woman, twenty-seven. She knew that Kyle, her hometown high school steady of three years, whom she reconnected with after earning her college degree, was not the one she was meant to spend the rest of her life with. She knew he was only a testing ground and a comfort food that she could stomach, but not forever. She knew Kyle would inherit his father's frozen yogurt business and knew she wanted more than small, medium and large for a future.

The Porsche started climbing up Country Club Drive like a horse returning to the barn. Past the magnolia trees planted along the sidewalks. Past sprawling front yards hidden behind established hedges. Above her, the stars were pinheads dimly shining, as the Porsche downshifted with a purr and turned left at an iron gate, the car's headlights glaring through the slats as the wrought iron opened to a long driveway and a house more massive than a herd of elephants. After parking in the garage, they walked into the backyard, which sprawled above the lights of the city. They walked past the ten patio tables with umbrellas wrapped tightly, the six barbecues, and lounge chairs too numerous to count. Kristen was always a half step behind Ken, his hand never reaching for hers when the door opened to a mahogany cabinet over a polished marble kitchen floor. He disappeared behind a bar and quickly became visible again; two glasses and a bottle of wine dangled from his hand.

That was the beginning of two years where she was the gem he adorned himself with. She was wined and dined in places where hundred dollar bills, Franklins he liked to call them, flowed like a swollen river out of his suit pockets. His plastic cards were made of gold.

Every few days she tested the beauty of mirrors with additions to her wardrobe, placing a shoulder underneath a dress made by designers who most could only dream of hanging in their closet. But, behind the glamour of her life, she still had a mind and an ambition that continued to toss the coin of her future into the air, landing on heads, landing on tails, or just spinning on the hard surface of the table.

She thought of James and his voice of an hour (was it that long?) in a bar. A stranger who had made her laugh. Had made her laugh. A constant conversation for sixty minutes, without judgment, without bias, without resentment, without having to pick the right word off the shelf, hoping it would fit. She had walked across the floor of Scully's and hadn't broken any eggshells. Kristen sighed with contentment and closed her eyes.

The next morning Kristen heard her ringtone echoing and hurried to find her phone next to her toothbrush in the master bathroom. She saw it was her sister, Kathy.

"Hey, Kathy."

"Only three weeks before you are Mrs. Ken Anderson," oozed her sister Kathy's voice. "I can't wait for the wedding. Your dress is so beautiful. You are going to look like a million dollars."

"Twenty-one days and four hours to be exact," said Kristen, finding a chair to sit on as she moved into the kitchen. "And a million isn't so much anymore."

"You don't sound right," stated Kathy.

"I don't know what it is," lied Kristen, knowing exactly what it was.

"I think everyone has a few of these feelings. Nothing to worry about. But I am puzzled because of all people, you really have nothing to worry about. Ken is awesome."

"Kathy, it was weird. You know how Ken went to the Laker game at Staples the other night? Well, I decided to just get out of the house. I dressed like a slob and went down to Scully's for a drink, and this guy comes in with a black eye, dressed like someone who should be on a skateboard, maybe, or coming from band practice in a garage, and he asks if he can buy me a lemonade." Kristen could feel the butterflies in her stomach landing softly on the branches of her organs.

"Sounds like a total loser. Was he drunk?" Kathy's voice squashed the butterflies.

"No, he wasn't drunk. He was funny. Really funny. I haven't laughed that much in two years."

"There is more to life than laughter, Sis. I'll tell you what, though. You take this guy with the black eye. I'll take Ken. And I'll see if Unicef will take Frank as a donation. Just kidding. You know I love Frank. Most of the time anyway. How was your trip to Atlanta? Did you make it out to where Martin Luther King Jr. was born?" Kathy continued.

"Atlanta was fine," Kristen answered, knowing she couldn't plug her outlet for truth into her sister. And her sister was right. Laughter doesn't put a roof over your head or food on the table. And she definitely wasn't going to trade Ken, no matter how bad he might be, for Frank, Kathy's high school sweetheart who had turned as sour as three-month-old buttermilk.

"You wouldn't believe what a parent requested today." Kathy began her lecture of what it was like being a high school teacher. Kristen caught the words Disneyland and Mickey Mouse before her own predicament overwhelmed her thoughts. When the pause arrived in Kathy's voice, Kristen landed back on earth and covered up her disinterest.

Kristen threw her support toward her sister. "Every parent of a fifteen-year-old thinks their kid can do no wrong, and if he does, they will search the earth for the cause of the problem instead of looking in the mirror. That's the first place they should look."

"Isn't that the truth. So, what new present did Ken shower you with this week?" asked the jealous Kathy.

"His secretary picked out a pretty cool dress from Desigual, a Spanish clothing brand from Barcelona to be exact. Red and white, triangles and diamonds. I kinda like it. She has good taste."

"You are so lucky." The green of envy colored Kathy's voice brightly.

Kristen had to admit she was indeed lucky.

Chapter 3

James was putting the finishing touches on the latch of the gate of the wrought iron fence that had been ordered and promised for tomorrow. One would think that a degree in biology from UCLA would have led James to a distinguished career, but despite spending a year working in an office with Molly, he had followed in his father's footsteps and become a welder. Making that everlasting bond between things was always appealing, and the punch in his eye had solidified his decision to weld. No more offices for him. His father was right about the freedom of welding and the satisfaction of a job well done.

His father now lived in Chicago, and James rarely saw or spoke with him. He was a troubled man. James wasn't sure of his dad's third wife's name, Elizabeth or Judith or Meredith, something with an "ith," he thought. His father, a skilled craftsman, who was dubbed one of the best welders by his colleagues, lacked the basic mettle for a solid relationship.

When James' father, Charles Brand, married his first wife, Loretta, James' mother, he thought marriage would be the television image of family he had watched every day from 5 to

5:30, the family of *Leave It to Beaver* and the perfect wife and mother, June Cleaver. The show was ingrained as truth for thirty minutes each week, until his father started watching *All in the Family,* another half-hour show, and then the Cleaver family of perfection soon became pure fiction.

When James was born, Charles didn't resent having a son. He just didn't understand what it meant to be a father. Diapers filled faster than a gutter during a storm. Crying was a musical symphony of bad sound, depending on the score of hunger or lack of sleep or irritation from a new world of tangible objects. The constant sterilization of feeding equipment... But the most important feeding accessory, the human breast, the beautiful breast that could be touched and tasted, was now off limits, only to be touched by the baby's lips and a pump. The sexiness of life left quickly for James' father. After enduring a nine-month vacation for childbirth, the desert sands of his son's early months left the taste of sand between Charles' teeth. Charles Brand wasn't programmed to be a father. Looking for companionship, Southern Comfort was quick to warm his heart and take away the sting of a cool bedroom.

When Charles was drunk, if chicken pieces flew from the high chair or grapes were dropped like bombs from the tiny fingers of James, the inner turmoil of having a child disappeared. Life became a matter of simply cleaning the battlefield. His own slurred words were not too different from his son's. They both said "path" for "patch." And neither could say "enough." James was too little to attempt "enough" and his father coughed out "euf." Charles felt a car seat was an inconvenience and an accessory not really needed. The kid would be okay even if Charles couldn't walk a straight line, balance on one foot, or touch his nose with his index finger.

Charles thought life should be orgasms and excitement. Grab all the gusto and the moans you can. You only have one chance to jump into the abyss before you disappear. Forget looking before you leap. This might be your only chance to jump.

27

But it was James' dad who repaired his bicycle when it was broken. When the neighborhood bicycle jump, a piece of plywood and concrete blocks, turned into bruises along the right side of James' body and injuries to his bicycle that seemed fatal, his father welded the frame and handlebars back in place. And when the coup de grace, the seat, was the last part to be fixed before his bike was complete again, his dad put a mask like Darth Vader's over James' head, his welding helmet, and for the first time passed his acetylene torch to James, to secure the bike seat. When the weld was set and James had flipped up the mask, the edge of his father's lip curved almost to a smile. It was a moment James tried to recapture with a soccer ball, with a tennis racket, with grades beyond reach, but his father's lips remained set.

James hoisted the finished gate off his bench. He holstered the torch and stepped back and admired his work. The five pointed flourishes in the middle of the gate, some would call them stars, had been his first attempt at this type of design and the symmetry of the triangulation was pleasing to the eye. Working with metal or iron or aluminum was easier than the flesh and blood one had to deal with in relationships. James wondered if he was a coward for not trying to reach into his heart and explore what made it so vulnerable, to understand why answers were so hard to come by, to respect the uneasiness and uncertainty that love always carried in his back pocket. A gate or table couldn't take a swing at you if you made a mistake, couldn't cause you to replay every step you had taken in your mind. It wouldn't strike back no matter how much you twisted or burned their surface. But a gate also couldn't whisper in your ear how your touch could turn a calm afternoon into the sizzle of arms and legs entwined in passion. No amount of welding could hold and connect, like arms around your waist and eyes locked together into a musical symphony of love. James thought of Friday night and Kristen and the chance meeting of two elements, neither in their prime condition, and wondered if she would be the material, that alloy,

28

that purity, that could weld his life together. Maybe she was the one.

James looked out of his open garage to a leaf from a liquid amber tree in the driveway. The leaf, a bright red, its fingers pointed toward James, rolled once, rolled again, and then fled with the next breeze. A mostly green, almost antique, Honda Civic rolled to a stop across the street.

Nokia Carson, his friend from Mrs. Peters' fourth-grade class, hair askew, plaid shorts and a Kraft mac and cheese tee-shirt, walked up the driveway where the leaf had just been. In Mrs. Peters' class, Nokia's nickname became a reality. Joe Carter sat in the front row; Moe Kazlewski sat in the back of the class; Bo Carpenter and Bo Dissinger sat in the middle next to each other, one a boy, the other a girl, and Nokia sat in front of Moe. Nokia soon joined the ranks as "Noe." Joe, Moe, Bo, Bo, and Noe. Quite a class.

"Dude, you don't answer your phone?" approached Noe.

"Hey. It's a new phone. Not really that thrilled with the whole phone business these days," said James, lifting the gate onto a rag on the floor and then bumping knuckles with his buddy.

"What kind ya get?"

"Noe, who cares?"

"The phone you carry is important. You don't want your phone status to be a wrong number, if you know what I mean. I mean if you get the wrong phone, you might need to find a new best friend."

"Twenty years of friendship is probably enough. Might not be a bad idea," countered James.

"You forgot about the blood pact we made when we cut our pinkie finger at the bike racks in the sixth grade and then made a lifetime oath of loyalty and love forever," reminded Noe, stepping away from James needing a new best friend. Maybe he had stepped over the line with that comment.

"Noe, we never did that," smiled James.

29

"Yeah, but I still think it would have been cool if we had. Wanna go get a slice from Biagio's?"

"I'm starved. Good timing."

Twenty years of friendship had traveled through some rough terrain. The divorce of Noe's parents when he was in the eleventh grade brought years of playing the "if only" game for Noe, who shouldered the loss. If only he had gotten better grades, especially in Spanish; his mother insisted that fluency in two languages was necessary for success. If only he had made the varsity tennis team; his father had been all league when he was in high school, and his son's forehand was never as aggressive as he felt it should be. No matter how many lessons Noe had taken from Thomas Scott, the tennis pro at the club, he never felt his heart beating to the rhythm of racket and net. If only he had dated Mary Anne, his parents' best friend's daughter. But he had known her since the second grade when they were forced to sit next to each on the Disneyland ride, "It's a Small World," which always made him resent her and the stupid song. Through it all James was there, sturdy and loyal, silly and serious, kind and caring. Twenty years of friendship isn't a leaf that blows onto the driveway, only to be gone with the next wind.

"Are you ever going to get this seat fixed?" asked James, already knowing the answer, as he slipped into the front seat of Noe's Civic.

"The eye's looking better. Almost not black anymore," countered Noe, not even listening to what James had said for the hundredth time about the condition of his car. "Have you heard from Molly?"

"Not a thing," said James, adjusting one foot on the dashboard. "Not even a text," he kidded.

"I know she'll call you. She has to. You can't just punch some guy when he wasn't responsible."

"Well, she did! Hey, I met this girl last night."

"What? You already met someone else? A little quick don't you think, unless she was smokin' hot," said Noe, cruising

30

at three miles below the speed limit, maybe the slowest driver under thirty in the world.

"That's just it. I have no idea what she looks like. She had on a huge sweatshirt, a baseball cap, beat up jeans, not the designer ones with the holes in them, just some raggedy ol' jeans. And some flats, that looked like she wore them in the Girl Scouts."

"Was this some homeless chick?" wondered Noe.

"She was at Scully's."

"What were you doing at Scully's? Going to play pool without calling me? You don't even drink since that legendary day at twenty-one."

"Yeah and I usually don't get punched in the eye. Thought my life was going to shit. I figured it was time to give drinking another try."

"You said you were never drinking again. Remember?" said Noe.

"Everybody breaks promises. That's why you make them."

Noe edged the car into a parking space at Biagio's. "What about your dad?" Noe knew how much James despised his father's drunken antics. "What if it is you someday prowling the sidelines at your son's soccer game drunk as a skunk, yelling shit that makes your son so embarrassed he wants to hide in the soccer goal?"

"I know, but I'm not done. When I walk into the bar I see this mess of a girl sitting and figure maybe I can talk to her without her thinking I'm trying to hit on her, so I ask her if she would like a lemonade."

"If she would like a lemonade? In a bar? That's a good one. She try to hit you but you ducked out of the way?"

"She didn't throw a punch. Didn't look me up and down and vomit. So I'm feelin' pretty good. I ended up talking to her for a couple of hours."

"And you don't know if she's hot?"

"There's more to a woman than the way she looks."

31

"Since when?" responded Noe quickly. Noe was still without a serious girlfriend. He did have ten notches in his belt for previous girlfriends, but he courted each one less than a month, except for Laura. Laura was six weeks minus the five days she had the flu.

James reached for the wooden triangle of a handle to enter Biagio's as he had a hundred times before. Biagio's, the little hole-in-the-wall Italian Restaurant that everyone wants to find, the one the locals know about, where the meatball sandwich, the vegetarian lasagna, the Chicken Marsala, and the Fettuccini Alfredo are much better than the pizza, but even the pizza is five steps beyond any chain around town. Most of the locals had already departed when James and Noe entered. The sixteen-year-old granddaughter of the original Biagio escorted them to the in-need-of-replacing Naugahyde booth patched with duct tape.

"She poured her heart out to me," voiced James above the menu he was holding, knowing before he even left the car that their meatball sandwich, not a slice of pizza, would soon be in his stomach.

Noe also took the cue of familiarity. In a restaurant one reads a menu and then orders, but reading Biagio's menu was like reading the same book again and again and expecting different events to take place. To have Moby Dick swallow Ahab instead of being lashed to his side, to have Daisy say yes to Gatsby and leave Tom Buchannan, to have Hester Prynne and Reverend Dimmesdale conceive three more children and live happily ever after, to have Tom Sawyer paint the fence himself. It won't happen. Slowly Noe lowered the menu. "I'm probably gonna have the meatball. So what'd she say?"

"Said she's supposed to marry this really handsome, really rich guy in three weeks," answered James, figuring this was the right time to put the napkin in his lap.

"Not to be too stupid, but you… or this really rich guy. She sounds pretty weird. No disrespect, of course."

32

"That was my first feeling too. Come on. Black eye and me," said James, dousing any flame that could be ignited.

"You're one of the smartest fucks around, but somehow you like welding shit together," responded Noe. The light blue apron of the waitress approached the table and walked away with the gained knowledge of two cokes and two meatball sandwiches with extra cheese.

"Did you tell her about your eye?" wondered Noe. "That's a good one."

"Yeah. Told her all about it," said James.

"Man, you did have a conversation. I think the longest I've ever talked to a chick was ten minutes, and I might be stretching it some."

"But you'd had like ten girlfriends and lost your virginity before I even knew what virginity meant," said James.

"Yeah, I just don't say too much."

"Maybe that's why you've had so many girlfriends." The sandwiches arrived. The red marinara sauce dripped over the toasted French roll, as the meatballs found a moment of respite before consumption.

"So, you gonna see her again? I mean what's the difference between a million dollars and driving through El Pollo Loco for dinner?" questioned Noe sarcastically.

James held his sandwich suspended in air. "Maybe love likes chicken more than diamonds. A real long shot, but I'm going to Scully's on Friday just on the outside chance. I know it is a real longshot, but look what just happened. I mean, the Red Sox were down three games to zero to the Yanks. The Red Sox, who hadn't won a World Series since 1918, and then, well, you know what happened. So, long shots do happen. I mean, after a TKO, it's good to get off the canvas."

"Yeah, to ready yourself for more punches. And don't keep reminding me about the Red Sox. You know, you can talk and eat," offered Noe, taking his third sloppy bite of meatball nirvana.

James dropped from his daze and started inhaling his lunch. "I don't think she wants to marry this guy. I mean, she's three weeks away and has questions. Raise the red flag of surrender already."

"I thought it was a white flag for surrender and red flags were for questions or fire danger or something like that."

"Well there's some red flags going on with her, that's for sure. She says this guy just doesn't pay any attention to her," added James.

"A bunch of my girlfriends always said that about me. Hmm. Maybe it's important. But I want to make some money first, before I have to worry about mortgages and diapers and two hearts beating as one. I'm too young. I'm nowhere close to being ready to settle down."

"How was everything? Any room for dessert?" cooed the young blue apron, as she cleared the empty plates. Noe shook his head "no," and the white ceramic plates headed for the dishwasher.

"I'm ready. The punch knocked some sense into me. I want to find someone I can talk to. I'm ready. Now it's just a matter of time. I don't need a white picket fence. But some kids. A great woman. I'm ready. Hope I don't have to wait eighty-six years like the Red Sox did," said James, nodding his head with conviction.

"Well, I'm not ready. I'm still holding out hope for Jennifer Aniston. She and Brad are all the rage now, but you never know, maybe he has a really small one and she wants a real man like me," said Noe, puffing out what there was of his chest. "I mean, I'm happy for her that she found Brad. Man it would suck if you never found someone. All you want is to grab the brass ring, but you practically never get a chance. Like living on an island with only a volleyball to keep you company."

"Wilson, I love you," mocked James as they laughed about Tom Hanks' love for his volleyball, Wilson. Scooting away from the table, James picked up Noe's ten and replaced it with a twenty. They waved to Mr. B, the owner and maker of the meatballs, on their way out.

When James reached for the front door, it pulled open to reveal a gorgeous young lady, brown silky hair, a chiffon salmon dress that matched the softness of her face and sunglasses dangling from her hand. Her brown eyes met James' gaze, and with her lips curved and her eyes smiling, she whispered, "Excuse me." She edged past James, the hem of her dress brushing against his knee, as he held the door open to let her pass.

"Excuse me," he repeated, nodding his head toward her, and then boldly walked two steps toward her. "Have we met before?" he asked, as she turned and stared directly into his eyes.

"I don't think so," she answered, with a reluctant shrug of her shoulders and a twirl of her sunglasses.

The boldness of his steps toward her fell quickly into shambles as he didn't know what to say next. "I thought, oh, never mind," and he turned and left opportunity where she stood before him.

"What was that all about?" asked Noe.

"I thought that might have been her. I guess maybe I was hoping. No. I know I was hoping. The truth is, I don't know if I would recognize her if I did see her."

"Obviously your first attempt wasn't very good. I hope you get another chance," supported Noe. "And I really hope Jennifer Aniston calls me someday."

Chapter 4

Kristen gazed wistfully out the bedroom window to the dusk settling over the Valley. In a couple of hours, the dim lights would brighten as darkness settled in. In the galaxy of her mind, her wedding stars were in constant motion, an everlasting orbit of emotion that was now only two weeks and one day from splashdown. She would be handling the controls, the last details, of her wedding-to-be for the next two weeks and she was worried about the entry of her spaceship, of herself, into the atmosphere of "til death do us part." When Kristen first said, "I will," to the diamond glaring in her eye, the ship departed happily from the launching pad, but now, Kristen felt strapped to that decision, unable to hit the eject button, knowing in her gut that it would be the right decision to leave the cramped quarters of the cockpit now.

The finishing touches of the wedding and reception were almost all in place. Sarah Vutton, designer and friend, had worked for a month on her dress and the five-foot train of Venetian lace that would follow behind. The dress hung in her sister Kathy's closet, two weeks away from the unveiling. Franklin, better known as "Za Who" in the club industry, was still a source of contention, as the hired deejay. Za Who reeked of marijuana when Kristen and her mother hired him. Kristen was adamant, though, as she knew the dance floor would be jammed with his ability to mix the hits that made feet, usually stuck quietly under tables, leave the protection of the carpet and stomp and twist on the dance floor. Her mother was against braided hair on a man's head and feared that the respectable, mainstream favorites of The Beatles and Sinatra, of the Eagles and Michael Jackson, would be discarded for the gutter sounds of Jay Z and Kanye West, the only two contemporary names known to her mother.

Kristen's mother had visions of her sister Martha and brother-in-law, Uncle Bill, walking out with their Bibles raised high in their hands, as the first rap song gyrated through the room. Kristen was in no mood to jump off her horse for her mother's worries about the music at the reception. Being invisible to Ken was bad enough, so Kristen wasn't about to step off her mark. Za Who would rock the house whether her mother liked it or not, and if Uncle Bill and Aunt Martha wanted to part the seas of the dance floor on their exodus, so be it.

Kristen's last seven days with Ken had been remarkable. A conversation of thirty minutes had taken place. A ray of sunshine through the darkness might be too strong of an image, but a flash from a camera illuminated the room, however briefly. Ken galloped for half-an-hour about the speakers he wanted installed in their living room and where they should be located. At one point he even asked Kristen for her ideas, but she soon realized that nodding her head were the words he understood much more easily than those spoken. The height of the speakers on the wall, and the distance each speaker was to be placed from the corner, and why the ceiling speaker shouldn't be close to the light fixture, and how the easy chair in the corner might distort the bass, and the importance of setting the treble correctly were enough to make Kristen shiver. But the fact that he was talking and she was in the room listening to something other than, "get me a drink," was maybe a first step to an actually meaningful two-way conversation. To listen to his voice, quite pleasant actually, speak about sound and the science of its waves, was mystifying since the sound of music rarely made its way into the four walls of their living room, and nothing musically upbeat could be sung about their relationship.

Ken needed to fly to San Francisco that afternoon for a fundraiser that one of his associates was unable to attend. The fundraiser was a client's attempt to dissolve the problems of the homeless in the city by the bay. The client, Liquid Plumr became a client when an ad the company almost aired was deemed beyond the limits of good taste, and Ken and his associates had saved Liquid Plumr's rear end from clogging their financial drain. Ken had hurried out of the house to get to the Burbank Airport for his 4:00 flight to San Francisco without even a nod of his head or a goodbye. Just the actions and no words. Oh, how Kristen missed the words.

Kristen looked from her window to her mirror. In fifteen days she would be forever tied to Ken. Kristen had found herself thinking of James and his black eye more than once during the week. She had tried to tell her sister Kathy, but that had fallen in the dumpster, and she knew she would never say a word to her mother. She wished her grandmother was still alive. She was someone she could talk to without being judged. She would never tell her what to do but would tell her a story instead, like she did when Kristen was in the third grade and thought that her best friend was Jennifer. She knew after the story, a story of apples and oranges eating lunch together, that Jennifer wasn't her best friend, and, in fact, that Jennifer wasn't a friend at all. She remembered going to sleep that night reassured, with her blanket wrapped around her like her grandmother's arms. She knew if she could only talk to her grandmother, the woman who suffocated her with hugs and kisses and wisdom, that she would know if the foundation she was standing on was about to tilt or crack or suddenly open and swallow her chance at a wonderful life.

Kristen nodded to the mirror, as she pulled her sweater up over her head. A glass of cabernet at Scully's last week had led to an evening of interest and entertainment, of warmth even, of no physical contact, but rather lungs filled with laughter, and the sweet taste of dialogue, a delicacy of imagination, a gourmet of shared memories, a dessert to be savored. She might as well, she thought, see if serendipity was ready to take the stage again. Another glass of cabernet couldn't hurt. One can only be alone for so long, and even in Ken's presence she still felt alone, even during the thirty-minute conversation, if one could call it that, of speakers and wires and decibels and bass and woofers.

She opened her closet, walked in, looked up and shook her head at the stupid and ugly sweatshirt she had worn to Scully's a week ago. Her hand moved over the hangers until she pulled out the navy blue dress, the thirty-nine-ninety-nine bargain she had found on clearance at Macy's three years before. Clearly, her Grandmother's influence once again. The blue dress was always accompanied by compliments and turned heads. Since she had been with Ken, she hadn't worried about the way others saw her, but now she reflected on her reflection in James' eyes, both the black one and the good one. She wondered if he would notice the two-inch heels and her legs, if he would be aware that her don't-fuck-me-flats were nowhere to be seen. She would never go there, to a bedroom, never again so quickly as that night two years before when she was mesmerized by Ken, his body, his eyes, his car, his aura erected completely by her own mind, losing herself completely. She meditated whether James would even be at Scully's tonight or if she would be alone there, nursing a glass of wine for an hour, deflecting a couple of hits from the typical male trolling through the bar, and then return to her bedroom window, the view dazzling with the lights of the city.

Her eye was only inches from the mirror. With the sure strokes of an artist, she painted the pale skin above her eye a subtle Sedona bronze, a shade that opened her eyes and her soul to the possibilities churning in her heart. She finished the last touch of beauty and stepped away with confidence. She knew she looked good, knew she would turn heads, knew she was a woman. Kristen grabbed her purse, no bigger than a softball, and left the lights on, as she opened the garage door.

The drive to Scully's started with one of the new favorites, seemingly played every hour, Outkasts, "Hey Ya." The only lyric Kristen knew besides "shake it, shake it," was "shake it like a Polaroid picture," that camera from long ago, before the Vietnam War, she thought, when you took a picture and the photograph slid out of the camera, so blurry you couldn't tell what it was, but by holding the white edge of the picture and waiting for a few seconds, everything finally came into focus. She had been with Ken for two years and still couldn't see a foot in front of her. She had known James for less than two hours but even then the horizon looked more defined. The branches of the trees were filled with fruit. The mountain range was silhouetted perfectly before her. She could see the dips and peaks in the range, the summits to reach and the valleys to climb out of. A life. A hand to reach for if she stumbled. A voice to encourage stepping into the unknown. Arms to hold her like glue and a heart to pulse freedom through her veins. Thoughts raced through Kristen faster than the thirty-five-miles an hour her car crawled down Olive Avenue toward Scully's. Past city hall. Past Olive Recreation Center with the old fighter plane in front. Past NBC studios, until the parking lot of Scully's coaxed her BMW into an unoccupied space.

The bar was lined with the usual suspects, two with ties loosened over starched white dress shirts, sleeves rolled up, two empty Coronas with limes deserted on the bottom, and two fresh bottles alternating between swallows and the business of the day. Three young ladies, about thirty, slim, medium, and large, filled with a weekend's enthusiasm, danced with their arms to Gloria Gaynor's "I Will Survive" that boomed from the relic of a juke box. A couple of men well past fifty found the security of a glass in their hands more comforting than a human relationship, waiting, always waiting, for that beautiful woman to come along and see what no one else had ever seen, their charm, their intelligence, their likability. At the end of the bar stood three empty stools, the olive green cushions ready to comfort another soul reaching for a few ounces of strength or confidence, reaching for a few ounces of memory obliteration, reaching for the liquid capable of more destruction than the bomb dropped over Hiroshima.

As Kristen seated herself and raised a finger toward the bartender, one of the men mentally left his cocoon of depression and flapped newly formed wings, as if he could fly like a butterfly and land on the flower that was Kristen. Like so many other moments of his past he never took flight, still glued to his stool, and soon found himself once again staring into the almost empty glass of vodka, a cheap vodka.

The bartender toweled the area in front of Kristen and placed a napkin down as she ordered a Justin cabernet. The Justin, a taste she had recently discovered and savored, was warm and smooth. The change of mood was immediate, a calming, a confidence, a red liquid, soothing and massaging.

Kristen discreetly scanned the bar. Besides "fifty something" attempting to be noticed, there was nothing unusual about the setting. A few couples and groups of four or five engrossed in the whispers of the evening, sat around tables. A couple at one table dipped fried green beans in a chipotle mustard sauce, and an order of onion rings as high as a mountain, traveled with a waitress to a landing spot on another table, but as Kristen continued looking, there was no sign of the man with the black eye.

Kristen took a pen from her purse and decided to make the best of this time, procuring a napkin to make a list. She had almost finalized the seating arrangement of the wedding tables, of who would sit with whom and who needed to be separated by a referee or put into a ring with gloves on so they could settle their differences once and for all. Ken had two-hundred guests who were "critical" to be at the nuptials, while Kristen's forty-four were more than she had counted on. She knew to separate great-uncles Murray and Jeff but didn't remember which one gave the other the insider trading tip nearly twenty years ago that had turned more sour than milk left in a refrigerator for a year. Kristen tried to remember the two aunts, one was maybe Delores, who had a boyfriend stolen from her during high school. They were seventeen when it happened. Delores, if it was her, was his steady, even had a ring on her pinky as proof, but when Delores had brought him to a Cinco de Mayo party, he was found kissing someone, Kristen couldn't think who it was, in the backyard behind the sycamore tree. Even thirty years later, her aunt still held on to her anger as if it had happened yesterday. The boyfriend involved had died five years ago, an early death at fifty-nine. He was a husband, father of three, who had moved out of state his senior year of high school, only months after the fifth of May incident. None of that mattered. It didn't stop Delores or whoever it was, from wrapping herself, like a cloak, in bitterness.

James spent Friday contemplating the best time to go to Scully's. His eye had almost healed. The deep purple and red had subsided to a lingering dull yellow that now surrounded the eye. From early afternoon he had been working in the Hollywood Hills, a place off Los Feliz, not far from the Greek Theater, for an eighty-year-old matron, as nice as a summer day. She wanted a change in her backyard scenery by having James replace the straight barred wrought iron fence, first installed in 1969, two days after Neil Armstrong had set foot on the moon. James learned a great deal of history from his constant companion of the afternoon, but his mind was restless, ricocheting the moves he desired to make, if, just by luck or whim or fate or destiny, the young lady of the week before materialized at Scully's again. What a terrible word, *materialized*, he thought. The week before he had arrived at Scully's a little after nine, but he thought arriving closer to ten, this time, would make more sense. The early bird might get the worm, but the second mouse would get the cheese.

"Young man, would you like some lemonade?" the lady asked, as James' hand held a hammer and his mind spun with anticipation.

"Yeah. Thanks." For a few seconds James was back on earth, but then take off commenced once again. On the other hand, he thought, if she were to arrive at nine, maybe she would already be gone by ten. There would be no worms and no cheese. How would he recognize her? What would she be wearing? What should he talk about? How much money should he bring? Should he ask her out if everything went well? What should he wear? Questions lingered without the time to imagine any answers, only the contemplation of what might be.

After finishing the job and listening to one last story about how the American people never understood the good that President Nixon had done, James hopped on the freeway to fight the Friday evening rush hour traffic. Up the Five past Griffith Park and off at Buena Vista he drove, his mind fighting traffic of its own. When he finally made it home and his mind cleared he entered his one-bedroom apartment, as if someone were watching. His phone rang before he had a chance to close the door.

"Dude. What you doing?" asked Noe. James didn't even have a chance to say hello.

"You don't like to text, do you?" asked James, ready for a shower and some food.

"If anybody doesn't like texting, it should be you," declared Noe. "I mean, it only got you slapped around like a little girl."

"Hey, it wasn't me," James reminded him.

"Yeah, but it was your mug that felt like Mike Tyson had just pummeled you with a flurry of punches."

"So what's up?" asked James, trying to see if this conversation had more merit than friendship.

"Thought you might want to shoot some pool after the rendezvous with the mystery woman," stated Noe. "I was thinking Shakey's or Sarducci's. I know you don't like drinking."

"Sarducci's is good. I'll text you," answered James, hoping he would be holding something other than a pool cue in his hands that night.

"What time you heading to Scully's?" asked Noe.

"I think about ten."

"Yeah, if she's there before you, you have got to make her wait, that way you know. You know what I mean?" advised Noe

"Yeah, I hear ya," answered an oblivious James, not understanding one word of Noe's advice.

"Make sure ya put on cologne. Chicks dig cologne. And don't say too much," offered Noe with a real depth of care and a real shallowness to his own ideas.

James knew better than to listen to too much of Noe's pitch, no matter how sincere it was. Most of his pitches were wide of the plate, and if you swung at them, you would strike out, but once in a while an idea was a grooved fastball that you could connect with and circle the bases, arms raised with triumphant wisdom. Today, his pitches were nowhere close to the plate.

Was this the night James would take his first drink since the regrettable night at Scully's when he turned twenty-one? Was this another footprint of many to follow his father's path through life, drinking and stumbling and fumbling every opportunity handed to him? James' mind raced with ideas, as he circled the block that inhabited his apartment, keeping a steady thirty-five miles per hour in his Ford 150, as he made right turn after right turn after right turn after right turn. He was going in circles, like a plane circling above an airport, readying for a landing.

James was still a little unsure, still a little cold, waiting for his truck to warm his confidence and deliver him to Scully's. He was still not ready to hit the main road that led directly there. He hit 102.7 on the radio and Britney Spears sang "Toxic." He quickly hit another button, 106.7 where Eminem rapped about "One Shot," one chance, one opportunity. That was better. Tonight he thought might be that chance. Might be that opportunity. He contemplated the first sip of wine that would

44

warm his core of love and togetherness, and of sharing that delight with the sweatshirt and shoes of the week before. Jesus had worked a miracle turning water into wine; maybe tonight would be his miracle, one that would bring him a woman whose heart could comfort him forever. Would she be there? His hands tightened around the steering wheel. His finger switched back to 102.7 and the Black Eyed Peas sang, "Let's Get It Started." James smiled as he rerouted his landing pattern of right turns, and he guided his truck straight toward Scully's, a known road that could send him on a new path. He couldn't see through the windshield to where this new path might ultimately lead, but it was time to get it started. He pulled into Scully's at two minutes after ten. A parking place opened as he drove in, the bright lights from the car leaving, blinded him for a second, before James paralleled the truck between the white lines.

James opened the front door unsure of what to expect, as the unmistakable aroma of Scully's was tasted. James knew the smell of Biagio's, of pizza cooking, knew the rugged scent of his father's garage when he was twelve, knew the rich smell of his mother's kitchen in the morning, bacon or pancakes, knew that his nose was an instrument of security, and as he took another step inside Scully's, he felt at home, felt he was where he belonged, felt like he could be himself. Here was the setting of one pool table in the back, the light hanging low to the green felt table, the shelf along the wall where his elbow found comfort. Tonight he didn't care about eight balls or corner pockets or the little cube of blue chalk. He glanced around the bar for a sign. He didn't want to stare, to be too obvious, to give away a clue of how deeply he wanted to see the young lady whose words had opened his heart.

The same three women of the week before, he was almost sure, were sitting at the bar, laughing loudly, especially the one who was overweight. But then James second guessed himself and wondered if maybe she had brought a couple of new friends with her, and he tried to see if one of the other two could be the woman of mystery. One tilted her head toward James and just as quickly

45

broke into laughter, returning her gaze to her friends. No, they weren't Kristen.

At the end of the bar, a young lady was making notes on a napkin, her mind absorbed in her activity, obviously waiting for her boyfriend to return, as a margarita and barstool were both unoccupied next to her. James heart skipped a beat at her beauty, a beauty that made words superfluous.

The tables surrounding the bar were mostly filled with three or more persons, all in tune with those around them. James' heart fell into reverse. He wasn't getting anything started. His plan had fallen through the floorboards into the never ending abyss of the basement below. He was sure that she had arrived about nine and left before he had walked through the door. Noe was an idiot for encouraging him to make her wait. But maybe, he thought, maybe she had other plans and wouldn't be getting to Scully's until after ten. Maybe she wasn't coming at all. Maybe it had been one great night the week before, a chance to unload the baggage of his heart, releasing feelings he wouldn't have to carry around anymore. Maybe that night had given her a chance to let the steam out of the pressure cooker, given her the chance to write a new recipe of how to love the man she was to marry.

James walked to the last seat at the bar, the one next to the beautiful woman's boyfriend. He would be able to watch from there, in case Kristen did walk through the front door. She would see him sitting at the end of the bar and then run to him with arms outstretched and tears running from her eyes and tell him that he was the one. James laughed to himself that he watched too many romantic movies. The beautiful woman didn't immediately look up as James eased onto the stool. She put the pen to her chin in thought and then raised her head.

It was her. James could see her eyes. The same blue eyes that had stared across the table from him the week before. A tidal wave of exultation swept over him. A volcanic eruption of hope spewed through him. Oh my God! It was Kristen and she was a knockout.

46

"Excuse me, but is the man you are supposed to marry in a couple of weeks sitting here?" asked James, hoping like hell that the answer was no.

As Kristen smiled and faced James, his body tried to return to normalcy. The tidal wave was slowly dissipating and the volcano tried to return to dormancy, but he was still drowning in happiness.

"Not that I am aware of. Should we try to grab a table and find him?" she said with a laugh, pushing her brown silky hair behind her ear. "Good to see you." Kristen slid off the stool, her navy blue dress a couple of inches above her knee. James ejected from his barstool and landed a few feet from her.

"How 'bout that table over there," he said, pointing to a corner table just being cleared by a waitress. He let Kristen pass and then followed her, as the waitress' towel made a last sweep across the table's surface.

"Would you like another glass of wine?" offered James.

"Another cab would be delicious. Thank you," she answered, and the sound of her voice was like the waters of the ocean receding from the sand.

James went to the bar, next to the laughter of the three friends, and ordered two glasses of cabernet. His father couldn't touch him in the presence of such beauty, and if a glass of cabernet was her desire, he would break from the feelings that had followed him since he was ten and take a drink in a new land, a new continent that he was ready to explore. This was an adventure where he had no idea what lay ahead, but every step would be filled with opportunity.

Kristen, happy to have a few seconds to make sure there wasn't a raisin stuck between her teeth or lipstick on the tip of her nose, quickly took her mirror from her purse as James headed to the bar. Within a minute of seeing James, the happiness of dialogue was dancing through her veins, a departure from the tiptoeing she was used to doing around Ken. Kristen understood these feelings of joy. With every other boyfriend she had ever

47

had, those first few times spent with them were always the best, thinking this guy is the guy, this is the man who will give me goose bumps, this is the man who will set the butterflies free, this is a man who is not like any other man, one of devotion and loyalty and care and understanding and passion. She was sure James was that man. She wanted to feel the heat of passion burning through her body, a thirst needing quenching, a hunger needing to be fed. She stretched her fingers, turned her neck, and shrugged her shoulders to her ears to soothe her emotions, which were running an obstacle course of excitement through her body. The happiness could dance through her veins, but the excitement needed to be calmed.

"It is really nice to see you," said James, handing Kristen her glass of wine when he returned to the table. He was surprised by the calmness of his voice. "I was looking for a sweatshirt or parka or serape or…" his voice trailed off.

"Your eye looks like it's healing. Or is that makeup?"

"The black eye turned the corner to a dull yellow. Makes coordinating my outfits a little more difficult; yellow is just not as easy to match as black." James' stomach was doing somersaults of joy.

"Maybe that's been my problem all along. The color of my eyes," added Kristen, feeling that he was two parts hydrogen and she was oxygen and together they made water. The chemistry was definitely there.

"Let me ask you something. You know how Jack dies at the end of the *Titanic*? What if he doesn't die and they make it back to port. What do you think happens?"

Kristen had no idea where this question was coming from. It seemed to arrive out of left field, but she was happy not to be talking about the wedding or anything else too personal yet. "They'd get married probably. They'd have a couple of kids. Her parents wouldn't be too happy about it, but they would finally see what a great guy he was. Maybe." She brought her lips to her glass and sipped from the nectar of the gods.

James couldn't help but see her lips caress the glass and feel the desire for his lips to trade places with the glass. "I don't think so."

Kristen smiled inwardly with his response. A man willing to share ideas. A slight shiver shook her. "Why not?"

"Well, look. He wins the tickets to get on board. He's a hustler. Jack of all trades. Paints her when she's naked right? I mean, they've known each other less than a week and he has already convinced her to take her clothes off. In what year? 1912, I think. You've seen what their bathing suits were like at that time."

"They loved each other," answered Kristen, her eyes staring directly at him above the tilted wine glass.

"In a week? I don't think so," replied James, immediately realizing he was talking to a woman he had known for only a week, actually for only two days, and felt as smitten as he had ever been. He quickly changed direction. "Jack is not a good guy. He's a scam artist. He gets back and they get married and have a couple kids. Do you really think he is going to be a good dad? Or is he going to find some other chick to convince to take off her clothes and model for him? I mean look at Picasso. He changed wives, like four times, always looking for someone new to model for him."

Kristen studied James' hands as he spoke. Strong and rugged, with slight bruises on two of his knuckles and a small callous on the pad of his palm. She wondered what he did for a living but didn't want to take this tangential conversation down the natural road of most conversations. His brown eyes and brown hair were of no help in determining how his ideas traveled to the surface and spilled over the table. His body wasn't the physical specimen of Ken's, but his style made him too delicious ever to think of punching him in the eye. Kristen searched for the next thing to say. She wasn't about to agree with him and end the discussion.

"I think you're wrong. Jack has seen some of the world and scammed his way through, but to survive a tragedy like the Titanic would change a person. Jack would have made a great husband," responded Kristen, breathing a large gulp of air as the word husband leaked from her breath unexpectedly. She quickly continued before husband became an issue. "What about *Harold and Maude*? Did you ever see that?"

"Oh my God. Did I ever see *Harold and Maude*? My English teacher in high school made us watch it and write an essay on it." The blood was singing "Hallelujah" through James' veins. Beautiful and interesting and has seen *Harold and Maude*. Too good to believe.

"Well what do you think happens if Harold gets Maude to the hospital in time to pump her stomach and save her?" asked Kristen with a smirk on her face and lips as luscious as the question.

"I don't think Maude would marry him. The thought of marriage would be too restricting to her. She knows her time is over, and she has made Harold into a man."

"How is she going to tell him no? That she doesn't want to be with him?" Kristen asked, leaning towards James. "She will destroy all the lessons she has taught him. His confidence will once again be shot, won't it?"

James knew she was right. "Yeah, but if she lives, then you and I aren't here talking about the movie because no one wants to see an eighty-year old woman gettin' it on with some eighteen-year old kid. People would have been throwing up in their popcorn boxes if she hadn't died at the end. The movie would have lasted only a week before teenagers would have protested around the world. They would have burned the film. She had to die."

James and Kristen were in a movie of their own. The three ladies from the week before, small, medium, and large, had laughed their way out the door, their stools readjusted under three forty-somethings. The two men in ties who had earlier screamed

50

at the television for a half-court shot made at the buzzer at a Laker game, exchanged exiting high fives with the bartender, as they stumbled out the door toward their waiting taxi. One of the trolls made his scheduled, every fifteen minutes, lap around the bar, checking the surroundings for wounded females. Neither James nor Kristen had spent a second gazing off the stage of their setting.

For the next two hours, conversation flowed like the Mississippi River. Mark Twain would have been proud. They navigated their way through music and elementary school, through friends and vacations. Through the unusual incidents, like when James was caught cheating on a test in sixth grade even though the answers on the paper were not for the test on *The Bridge to Terabithia,* but his study sheet for history, or when Kristen was not allowed on the bus for a field trip to Catalina in the fourth grade because the teacher was a germaphobe and Kristen had been sick the day before the trip. Kristen's grandmother almost had the teacher fired over that one. James felt the satisfaction of wine and conversation and beauty. He realized how many times he had been at Scully's and chalked a pool cue, leaning over a green felt table, analyzing angles and spin and combinations, hoping that with one stroke, a ball would disappear down a pocket. A game he had played. As he looked across at Kristen, his heart wasn't playing. His heart was speaking a language he had never heard before. He could see Kristen's lips moving, but he was too enamored, too engulfed in this arena with exhilaration and passion to hear what she was saying.

"I was just saying..." said Kristen, knowing he had floated to the same world she too was inhabiting. For the last two hours, she had thrown out the building blocks of relationships. Of the roads she had driven down and the towns she had visited. The easy luggage of life that is passed across the table, handed to another to carry by his side. And Kristen felt it. She could feel the blood of their veins mingling. This was so much more than too many drinks and a beautiful body and a fast car and a fat wallet. This was laughter and listening and dots connecting to make a circle out of blank spaces. In two years she hadn't shared any of these stories with Ken. He had never asked. Had never cared. It was always another call on his cell phone. Always business away from home. Always his car that needed attending. Always going to the garage to check on this. Always the computer to check on that. And always twice a month, his magnificent body lying on top of hers for the two minutes it took for him to finish, not nearly enough time to be classified as intimacy. People would never believe her if she told them about Ken, but would wonder instead, what was wrong with Kristen and somehow hope that they could take her place and show Ken what a real woman was capable of.

"Ooh. I'm not sure what you were saying," admitted James wincing. "I hate it that I kinda floated off. That's the truth."

"Don't ever hate the truth," smiled Kristen, as she put her glass of wine on the table. She reached across the table and squeezed his hand. And then left her hand on top of his.

James was as lost as Mr. Magoo in a maze. Her hand had squeezed his and now was lying on top of the fingers that hadn't been touched by anything but an acetylene torch for the last two weeks. "Oh my god, I could fall in love with you right now," he wanted to say. "I want to kiss you and hold you and squeeze you right through me." His feelings were making words difficult to utter. "OK. I kinda spaced there for a few seconds. My mind took a quick vacation. What were you saying?" James admitted.

She patted his hand a couple of times. "It was just something stupid about dollar menus and dollar stores." Kristen slid her hand away from his and raised her glass of water to her lips, finishing what was left. "I should probably get going."

"Are you sure you're okay to drive?"

"I can't spend the night here with you, even if... Yeah, I'm fine. I only had two glasses of wine," said Kristen, feeling James' words of protection hugging her safely.

"I'll walk you to your car," he offered, trying to come up with what to say next.

Kristen walked toward the front door of Scully's a step in front of James, until he maneuvered around her and pushed the door open. She waited a split second for him to join her, and as he did, he grabbed for her hand. The slight tug of her fingers on his was a crescendo of enchantment. The softness, the warmth, the connection their fingers made was electric. They walked in the direction of the parking lot, her shoulder brushing his, her hair swaying ever so slightly. At his side was a treasure. A treasure filled with gold, the gold that is worth nothing monetarily but is worth everything a person could want.

She stopped at a metallic BMW and reached in her purse. "James. I don't know what is going to happen. I know we didn't talk at all about, you know. I do know I want you to have my number."

As James entered her number in his phone, he felt her arm around his waist, her fingers clutching his side. As he settled the phone on the roof of the car, his right hand slid from her shoulder slowly to the small of her back. His eyes were blind to the world around him, only the blue of Kristen's eyes entranced him. His left hand gracefully grazed her cheek and swept her brown hair behind her ear and then gently coaxed the nape of her neck toward his lips. The moon above was ambivalent, as he tasted the softness of her lips, the seductiveness of her tongue, the sensuality of her mouth, the trembling of her body. This was more than a kiss. This was a promise of more kisses.

During this moment of eternity, Kristen was set free from Ken's disinterest, set free from time and commitments, set free from the wealth and the car and the doll that had suffocated her for the last two years, and became aware of lips that could love, aware of a man that cared, aware of what was possible in her future. She gave a longing smile as she unlocked the door and her hand lingeringly slipped away from James' touch as she entered the car.

"I'll call you," said James.

"Good," said Kristen, drenched in contentment.

James stood watching as Kristen's taillights disappeared down the street. The sign in front of Scully's beamed "Fine Dining." "Yes, indeed," thought James. "Fine" was an understatement. Exquisite…. Marvelous… Stupendous. There were no words that could describe such an evening. Despite meeting only twice at Scully's, James was doing somersaults of love off the high dive. Now he needed to figure out when the best time would be for him to call. To be with James, Kristen would have to call off her marriage, and James knew that would be difficult, knew that would be a difficult hurdle to jump over, knew that would cause an avalanche of boulders that Kristen would have to dodge. But this girl was special. They could overcome anything. They would bulldoze the problems away. They would take shovels and pick axes and power saws to clear the debris, and soon their hands would be welded together as one.

Chapter 5

If James had been under oath and asked to describe what had happened on his ten- minute drive from Scully's to Sarducci's, he would have been hard-pressed to give any details. After Kristen left, he knew he had started his truck and then ten minutes later found he was in front of Sarducci's, the restaurant that still had sawdust on its concrete slab. During the drive, his mind had replayed his night with Kristen, the touch of her hand on his, the kiss that made the earth stand still, the recognition that the beautiful woman at the bar wasn't with anyone, and then the gaze from her eyes and the realization it was Kristen. He would have testified that his truck was clairvoyant and knew exactly where to go, without being steered.

As he made his way inside, he saw Noe's troubled Honda Civic parked aslant in the lot. When James walked through the door, Noe was eye level with the pool table. He straightened his stance and walked to the far end of the table, checking the angles and the possible combinations and what the best chance was to make the balls behave properly. He chalked his cue and walked to the other end, as his mind sifted through the possibilities and the outcomes of one stroke of his stick. He decided to bank the thirteen toward the middle pocket and bent over, readying the cue. The contact was good but the proper angle was miscalculated, leaving the white ball in the middle of the table, perfectly positioned for his opponent to find success.

"Hey, how'd it go?" asked Noe, as he backed away from the table and noticed James walking toward him. "Shouldn't you still be with her? Did she even show?"

James couldn't think of how to start, but the smile on his face alerted Noe that the evening had gone well.

"Dude. What happened? You're grinning like you just robbed a bank and your pockets are stuffed with money."

"You know how I told you I didn't even know if I would recognize her. So I get there and I'm checking everything out. And she's not there."

"What time'd ya get there?" said Noe, as the sounds of the pool table continued behind them.

"Ten. Like you said. And there's this chick who is smokin,' and I mean smokin' hot, sitting at the end of the bar with her boyfriend. Well the seat is open, so I think it is her boyfriend." The smile on James' face was unmistakable.

"Oh shit. Don't tell me. It's her. No way."

"She's so hot, I expect the fire department to show up any minute. She has on this blue dress that makes me want to jump off my bar stool and scream and I'm hopin' no one with a fire extinguisher tries to cool me off. I mean, Christ, from a sweatshirt and baseball hat to Miss Universe in one week."

"So what happened? Is she gonna marry the guy or what?"

"Get this. She loves *Harold and Maude.*"

"Hotter'n a volcano and loves *Harold and Maude.* Man, you might have hit the fuckin' lottery," smiled Noe, placing his pool cue against the wall and waving the white flag of surrender

56

to his opponent. Noe was done thinking of balls rolling across green felt.

The black eye of the week before was a distant memory to James. His troubles with Molly not even a blip on the radar screen. The atmosphere he now inhabited was rarefied air. Not many breathed the elixir of the gods that had permeated his being for the last two hours. If there is a heaven, he was floating in it.

"So we keep talking and she's telling me who knows what. I mean I am just lost in her beauty, when she reaches across and takes my hand. Shit. The electricity in that touch. Oh, man. Smoke was coming out of my fingers."

"D'you get her number?" asked Noe, leaning on the edge of his seat.

"Yeah. Kristen Taylor. In my phone. She said to call her. Shit. The guy she's supposed to marry must be some dumb shit because she is, I don't even know how to say it," said James, shaking his head at the mysteries of life. "One week a text message is the cause of a fist hitting an eye. And the next week, the black eye has taken me on a journey where I discover a treasure that I never knew existed."

"So when are you calling her?"

"Probably not for a couple of days. I'm definitely not going to text her."

"With your track record, probably a good idea. Fuckin' A. Does she have a sister?" Noe asked, realizing maybe there was a chance for him in the future.

"But the best part is when we leave. Remember how I told you about kissing Samantha Carnegie in the third grade behind the portables?"

"Everyone was talking about that for days."

"Forget Samantha Carnegie. I'm doing a disservice to Kristen's lips by even talking about it."

"That good, huh?"

"Better."

"First time since the third grade you have even talked about kissing. Guys don't talk about that stuff."

"I'll take another twenty-year break before I mention it again. Wow!" The emphasis in James' voice, the delight in his eyes, the aura of his physicality, spoke volumes of the state of euphoria that he currently resided in. "I'm happy you were here, strokin' the white ball."

"I need to be strokin' something else. My time will come," added Noe, gazing around Sarducci's, hoping a dream of his own would become reality, that some beautiful woman that he could touch all over would step forward, that someone sizzlin' could throw him into the frying pan of love and melt him in seconds.

Chapter 6

Kristen's fingers touched the garage door opener, and the mouth of the garage opened its empty throat as Kristen parked. Inside, she removed the cork from one of the expensive labels at the unoccupied bar and poured a glass to remember her night. Behind the bar the mirror reflected the contentment that she felt. Reflected the beauty that she possessed that had remained hidden in plain sight to Ken. She turned to the side to make sure the curve of her hips hadn't disappeared in the last two years. It hadn't. For two years she had gone without compliments. Nothing about her eyes. Never a mention of her hair or what she was wearing. Ken was devoid of language. He had a mouth that was used to command, to bark orders to be followed, to state the mundane, to declare the obvious. On the other hand, the mouth of James had tasted like nectar, had devoured her senses, had stirred her to row on a silky lake of ecstasy. The thought of an oar parting the silky waters of the lake made her tingle with anticipation. God. To make love. To be touched and caressed and held and excited and to scream hallelujah so all the world could listen to her ecstasy made her look in the mirror with a smile of want and desire. God, how I deserve that she thought, lifting her glass of wine to her reflection, toasting herself and her future.

She knew James would be the one to stand across from her, slipping the ring on her finger, saying, "in sickness and in health, til death do us part," knew he was the one who would carry their crying child to her breast to be fed, the one to wrap his arm around her shoulder as they slept, the one to pitch a softball to their little girl, and to play catch in the backyard with their boy, the one to set up a tent as they camped at the beach, the whole family telling stories, wrapped in blankets around a campfire. A family of love and togetherness. Of goals and dreams. Of course there would be the difficulties every family faced, but when every player in the family is on the same team, what difficulty can't be solved? A Porsche in the garage and a few million dollars in the bank and a ring the size of Texas were nice, but money, jewelry, and cars don't bleed or laugh or love. Now it was just a matter of how to call off the wedding. She knew James would call. And when he did she would tell him. Would tell him to get ready for a waterfall of garbage, an avalanche of blame, to get ready to catch her when she would be thrown overboard for calling off the wedding.

Kristen finished her triumphant glass of wine and walked with the luxury of being a person who mattered into the bedroom. She kicked off her shoes and pulled the navy blue dress, her thirty-nine-ninety-nine special, over her head. She unsnapped her bra that made her breasts even more wonderful, although they were pretty special by themselves. Her panties were the next to depart, and then she danced au naturale to the rhythm of her heart and the silence of the night. After a toothbrush and a toilet, the sheets welcomed this naked spirit, wrapping her in the comfort of her thoughts. Her transformation stopped quickly, as did the comfort of her thoughts, when she realized that tomorrow she was having lunch with her sister Kathy, and their mother at the Castaway. She would attempt, if she only knew how, to calm the excitement that the wedding was stirring in everyone but herself.

60

Chapter 7

When James awoke Saturday morning, the first thing he did, before the mandatory emptying of the bladder, before the brushing of the teeth to destroy the foreign tastes that inhabit mouths through the night, before, he checked his rainbow eye, the eye that for a week had exhibited so many colors, and somehow had led him directly to a pot of gold, Kristen Taylor. The yellow had almost disappeared, and within a day the eye would be fully healed. No longer did he wonder what he had done so wrong that made Molly treat him like a punching bag, instead he grinned that the sabotaging trash that had rained upon him had turned into a mouth and a kiss he could treasure forever.

Seven forty-five in the morning on a Saturday was early for anyone under thirty to be up and moving about, especially without a welding job to go to, without chores that needed to be done, without a breakfast date that needed to be attended. Besides who would have breakfast that early on a Saturday? He wondered if it was too early to call Kristen, to make a list of children's names, to pick a location where they would like to live, to start researching what would be the best colleges for their children to attend, where the family should take their vacations. The future was endless, and James knew that a soul mate was hard to find, almost impossible, yet Kristen Taylor, he felt, was the one. He grinned thinking of Sir Isaac Newton's third law of motion, for every action there is an equal and opposite reaction. A punch had sent him down for the count, and now he was up in the heavens, flying with an angel.

James was obsessed with the thoughts of Kristen as much as he had been with the thoughts of his high school crush, Myra Brighton, but Myra had been a rookie mistake, someone who didn't know how to play the game at all, someone who wanted to open the can of love but didn't know how to use a can opener. James wasn't a veteran of romance, but the kiss he received from Kristen and the kiss he gave her last night were of major-league proportions. A grand slam of affection. His hand on her face and hair, her eyes closed, his arm around her back just under her shoulders, his hand pressing her toward him. James had seen *Anchorman* five times and had memorized too many of the meaningless lines, but kissing Kristen he knew he would replay at least a thousand meaningful times. Wearing Scooby Doo boxers, which he realized would soon be in the trash heap, and a plain black tee shirt, maybe a year or two before it also would be ready for a burial ground, he went in search of his phone, forgetting the idea of waiting two days before calling Kristen. He found the phone next to last night's leftovers, checked for messages, and then touched the raised exalted numbers of Kristen. The first ring of the phone was comforting, but even more comforting, he thought, would be her voice and not her recorded message. He hoped he wasn't calling too early in the morning or too soon after he had just seen her, but what can a person do when he's in love?

When Kristen heard the ring, she didn't think it was James, not this early on a Saturday morning, probably her mother

62

or Kathy with a slight change in plans. She never had a boyfriend that called her the next day, especially when they had just met. It couldn't be James, even though the slight chance it was him raised goosebumps over her skin. When she didn't recognize the number she answered with an unsure, "Hello."

"Hey. It's James," said a smiling young man, dressed for the city dump.

Kristen's naked body stirred in the sheets. "I can't believe you are calling so early," said Kristen, realizing immediately the negative tone her words might convey. She quickly recovered. "I can't believe you didn't call even earlier," and her voice was evidence of the happiness she felt.

"Last night was pretty special. How is it that I can talk to you only twice but I feel like I have known you my whole life." James was pacing as he held the phone, around the kitchen table, past the bathroom, into the bedroom to his bookshelf and then returning to the starting line for another lap. His hair still hadn't found the proper wave, and although his stomach rumbled with the absence of food, his heart was overflowing with emotion.

"I can't believe you like *Harold and Maude*. And you're drinking wine," added Kristen.

"Look, I know there is a bunch of stuff going on in your life right now, but I don't think I can wait a whole week to see you at Scully's again. I couldn't wait to call you. Obviously," James said, looking in the mirror at a spaghetti sauce stain he hadn't seen on his black tee shirt, scratching it with a fingernail to make it disappear.

"I can't do anything today. I have to run a bunch of errands with my mom and sister. Tomorrow, Ken's coming home in the morning," said Kristen, with an immediate pang of guilt, "and Monday isn't good because we're supposed to have lunch, but Tuesday…Tuesday would be great."

James had fallen from the heightened atmosphere he had been floating in and started plummeting toward the earth when Kristen's schedule wouldn't fit, but when she said that Tuesday

63

would work, that Tuesday would fit into her schedule, that James would fit into her schedule, for the chance of another kiss to fit into her schedule, his jets blasted him above the clouds once again. "Tuesday it is. How does a trip into Los Angeles sound? Just walk around, check out the city."

"I haven't been to Downtown L.A. for years. Sounds great. I love L.A. Why don't we meet in Scully's parking lot and take off from there?" prompted Kristen, with knees bent, prone on her bed, her free hand hugging herself.

"Is nine too early? Shouldn't be too much traffic," said an elated James.

"Nine it is. I'll see you then."

"And if it gets cold that day, I can always buy you a new sweatshirt."

"And if you don't open the door for me like a gentleman, I just might pop you in your good eye. Bye James," cooed Kristen with the largest grin the bed had seen in two years, as she hugged her knees to her chest.

"See ya on Tuesday," swooned James, as he continued pacing, his boxers and shirt oblivious, his right fist pumping the air victoriously.

Kristen's feet felt the carpet next to her bed, the soles and her body as naked as a newborn baby. The garden of James had been planted in her mind and the temptation to throw away the rotten apple of Ken was overwhelming. As she slipped a red silk morning gown over her head she thought of the perfection that downtown Los Angeles would hold. Of holding James' hand and telling him that she wouldn't, couldn't, marry Ken, that she didn't love him. And then she would kiss James. Would kiss him and say they were free to find out if the world was ready for the truth of their love. Los Angeles would be their first exploration together, while the rest of the world awaited their love to bloom and flower.

Chapter 8

James was organizing the garage when Noe pulled up in his car. James was a changed man, a forgotten memory of his youth, when dirty Levis wandered his room, when hangers didn't exist for shirts already worn, when books couldn't find shelves, when a "Game Boy" was a constant companion, when whatever was in his pocket was emptied on the top of his dresser, and loose paper was plastered to the floor as modern art. Cleanliness was as close to James as a stalk of celery is to a filet mignon.

Now everything had a place. The two fire extinguishers, spray bottle of water, even a five-gallon bucket always filled, were within easy reach of his portable bench. Three welding blankets were neatly folded, and recently James had installed a circular fan that offered a soft hum, while sparks flew below. James nodded toward Noe, folded the last hand towel neatly, punched the garage door opener and then with the nimbleness of a cat, slipped under the closing garage door and into the front seat of the Honda. Saturdays were spent at Trevor's. College football played on the four televisions in the living room, while three to five of the "we haven't reached the shore of wife and children and job and mortgage" friends threw the plastic poker chips around Trevor's dining room table, a blue table cloth shielding the table's oak from destruction.

"You look like you just had sex with yourself," Noe joked half-heartedly, noticing the bounce in James' step and the clearness of his eyes, no black at all to be seen.

"I look that good?" James kidded.

"Even your hands are grinning," continued Noe with the same idiocy of friendship.

James understood that there were times when sexual innuendo wasn't brought into the conversation, but at the moment he couldn't think of one of those times.

"You're bouncing like a Superball. What gives?" asked Noe, throwing an Usher CD into the car's system.

"What happened to your iPod?"

"Don't you remember? I left it in my backpack when I went to work out. I'll have to stick to the CD's a little longer."

"What will they think of next?"

"What's with the bounce? I hope you didn't call her. Man you called her. You shouldn't have called her. Did'ya call her?"

"Yeah, this morning."

"Man, you never listen to what I tell you," replied Noe, his head keeping beat with the music.

"And with good reason. I want to know why *you* listen to what you say. Why you don't know any better than taking your own advice."

"Nobody else tells me anything. Who should I listen to?" continued the beat of Noe's head.

"I told you you should get rid of your CD's and put your music on your iPod," answered James, as the Honda made a U-turn and parked in front of Trevor's house. The house had been owned by Trevor's grandmother before she passed away, and Trevor's parents felt it was in his best interest to live there rent free. Now he was twenty-eight and the horizon was nowhere in

66

sight. Yesterday was as good as tomorrow and today ain't so bad either was his general feeling.

Five years ago, they had met Trevor through a mutual friend, when they had attended the University of California at Santa Barbara. Trevor had majored in English and History, dismissing each as the ultimate in boredom, and then sociology and communications, rejecting those as too limiting, and finally, after four years and a hundred and ten credits called the college scene quits. Trevor, though, wasn't filled with the stories of his life, wasn't filled with the stories of his athletic accomplishments, wasn't filled with stories of parties, wasn't filled with stories of vacations or even of great rock concerts. Trevor was filled with the stories of sex that happened to him in the same amount of time as it takes a woman to bear a child, nine months.

Trevor loved to reminisce about these escapades that occurred during his senior year in high school. As many times as James had heard these stories, his interest was usually piqued as new kernels of distant memory became dislodged from Trevor's marijuana-infected mind.

Trevor's father had been an accountant for the Dole Factory in Hawaii, and Trevor had grown up in Mililani, right in the middle of Oahu, about a half hour from Waikiki, and a half hour from the North Shore of the Island, home of the famous surf spots, the Banzai Pipeline and Waimea Bay. Trevor went to the beach three or four times a year, but, as he would say, he was allergic to the sand and felt much more comfortable on concrete. Trevor was nondescript through the eleventh grade. He would study for tests most of the time, but homework wasn't necessary for a healthy outlook on life. Geometry was a complete mystery. Where lines intersected or why angles were congruent, and why anyone would want to prove that two triangles were alike were beyond his comprehension.

Devastation hit Trevor his senior year of high school when his father was named managing partner of a granite company in Victorville, California. He didn't mind moving to

California, but to Victorville? Santa Monica he would have welcomed. San Diego or San Francisco would have been more than a treat. The OC and their beaches would have been truly a blessing. But Victorville? Bob Dole was much more like John F. Kennedy than Victorville was like Beverly Hills. Victorville was famous for nothing, surrounded by sand and blistering heat and occasional high winds that would have been perfect for sailing if water was within a million miles. But Victorville it was.

In September when Trevor was in his first class and he casually mentioned that he had just moved from Hawaii, he didn't expect that bit of information to make the news, to make the bold headlines of that day's gossip. The news traveled faster than Superman's speeding bullet. Trevor became the hottest ticket at the school, and the truth of his past life in Hawaii became as flexible as a gymnast, and twisted and turned and spun out of control. During his sophomore year in high school in Hawaii, he had unhooked Maria Tibbet's bra with the usual difficulty of inexperienced hands and touched the holy grail of her breast and nipple, a great accomplishment, he thought, no matter the size of her breasts. That had been a milestone, but in his one year in Victorville, as the "vaunted Hawaiian," a mountain of pussy was fondled and squeezed and kissed and licked and entered as if his was the only cock in Victorville worth having between one's thighs. When cheerleader Holly Minton and Winter Formal Queen Staci Barnes, his date to the dance, fought after lunch in the halls outside the library over him (Staci thought she had seen him holding hands with Holly the day before though he had actually done much more than just hold her hand) he climbed to the mountaintop of importance. Now, ten years later, he still had the stories to tell, but the action in his pants since that year had become a Victorville drought of large proportions. Who would have ever known that moving from Hawaii to a small town out in the middle of nowhere could be just what the doctor ordered?

James and Noe knew better than to knock, and as they entered the haze-filled room with Trevor bent over an eighteen-inch bong, filling his lungs with the "best bud" in town, they each placed a ten in his hand as he exhaled in their face.

"A little early isn't it?" asked James, nodding toward the clear glass goddess held like royalty in Trevor's hand.

"Never too early," answered Trevor, flicking his lighter for another round, a loaf of weed in a plastic bag, its Ziploc seal sealed for the moment, resting on the table.

Five years ago, James and Noe had become members of this Saturday church, as they liked to call it, of football and poker and weed and beer and profanity and, of course, the stories of sex, imagined or real. James had shied away from the beer, but he was a firm believer in the other four. From September to January, attendance at the pews in front of the television was almost mandatory, and even Molly, James' girlfriend until her knockout punch had knocked out their relationship, had understood that Saturdays were reserved until five in the afternoon for James to partake in friends, male friends, that brought him home, not in the shape that he had left, unable to boil water if he needed to on some days. Saturdays became Molly's day to have lunch or shop or try on dresses for three hours, and especially to reach the profound depths of relationships in long conversations with her best friend Denise, two amateur psychologists attempting to analyze the world. "He didn't open the door for me" and what that meant. "He bought a dozen pink roses for me", and what the pink symbolized. "He yelled because a big fork was in with the small forks." "He never pays attention to what I am wearing," or, "He pays too much attention to what I am wearing." Sometimes James would stumble into the house before Molly had solved the problems of society. At five o'clock they would take a three-hour halftime of napping and nibbling, of regaining wits and composure, of relighting their fires, and then at eight they would have a night of their own. Saturdays worked for James and Molly until texting and punching tossed them out of the ring.

Two hours after they had entered Trevor's, the room had readjusted, the Biagio's pizza box on the kitchen table had only a streak of cheese left on the empty cardboard, six crushed Sierra Nevada Beer cans tilted like the tower of Pisa, and nine empty Heineken bottles were scattered in different parts of the room. The glass bong had rested for half an hour and the six heads around the kitchen table were oblivious to the sounds of football surrounding them. Only when the shrill of the announcer's voice reached their ears did they look up to watch the replay that had caused the sudden inflection to change so dramatically. Otherwise the sounds of cards shuffling, of chips being pushed into the middle of the table, and the occasional slamming of a hand on the table when the river card, the last card to be turned up, led to destruction for one and redemption for the other. A half an hour was enough time for the haze of marijuana smoke to have dispersed in the room, and Trevor fetched the bong to add a new cloud to the atmosphere. Around the table drug paraphernalia was passed and tasted, and as the cannabis settled into James, he understood what he wanted from the world, understood that this woman he had first met in a sweatshirt and ratty jeans and then saw in a dress and a smile and a kiss, oh that kiss, was everything he wanted. Understood that sitting around a table on Saturdays with a bunch of his friends, playing poker, watching football, smoking a little bit of the forbidden plant was good, really good. But he wanted more than fun. He wanted Kristen. God how he wanted her. To put both of his arms around her and hold her. To kiss her more than once, more like a thousand times. To kiss her neck and her ears and her cheeks, her stomach and back, and every other inch of her skin. He was lost in the world of Kristen when he heard Noe's voice.

"C'mon, man. Man, where did you go? It's up to you," said a disturbed Noe.

James pushed away from the table, awkwardly pushed his chair back and reached for his cell phone. "I gotta make a call. Only be a sec," he said, as he walked toward the door. He had to call Kristen, had to tell her he loved her, had to let her know that the few moments that they had been together were more

70

wonderful than anything he had ever experienced. That being in her presence was an honor, a delight, a treasure of riches he could never have imagined.

James' fingers fumbled across the raised numbers on his flip phone, when Noe's hand grabbed it forcefully. "Man, what the fuck are you doing?"

James stood there stupidly, unable to articulate the depth of his feelings and what he was trying to accomplish. "I was." he started.

"You're trying to call Kristen. Man, you're like a shooting star, right now. You don't want to burn this thing out. You could make a mess of this, and maybe even end up with two black eyes. You gotta know what you're liable to say." Noe placed a hand on James' shoulder and herded him back toward the table.

James knew he was right. "Ya always know, Noe. Jesus, Noe. Always there to save me," and as James spoke he was overcome with the friendship of Noe. It was almost an "I love you, man" moment.

When James was escorted back, he reclaimed his seat at the table, while Trevor was in the midst of one of his Victorville Tales of Tail.

"I didn't even know this girl." Trevor continued, "I had never seen her before, but she passes me in the hall right after fourth period and hands me something, and they are her panties. I had never seen her. I go to the restroom during fifth, Mrs. Duggles' class, boring as shit. Went to the restroom every day during fifth. Who walks into the restroom. No panties on chick..."

James didn't even care to hear the rest of the story. Trevor's Victorville Tales of Tail were one of the hallmarks of Saturday afternoons, but James realized the end was in sight. Life contained a finite amount of time, and these Saturdays had been his erector set for the last five years, but now it was time to make a new foundation, so he could erect a building that would last for the rest of his life. The haze in his mind was sharpening the vision of his future. Waking up to Kristen on the pillow next to him. Placing a dish of chicken cacciatore that he had cooked in front of her at the dining room table. Trying on a paisley shirt that she had bought for him, in front of a mirror and seeing her smile of consent as he spun without embarrassment, like an Abercrombie and Fitch model. Watching her eyes dance as she unwrapped a small box, and then opening the lid, revealing a pair of diamond studded earrings, and leaping from her seat, throwing her arms around his neck, and renewing their first kiss, always renewing their first kiss. A couple of days or nights throughout the year he would want the shuffling of cards and hearing a tale or two of Victorville, a connection to his past, to the years of fun and games, to the years when his friends were number one in his life, before he drove down the boulevard of life with his arm around the gem he had been so lucky to discover. Everything about Kristen mesmerized him.

"Deal 'em," said James, as Trevor's tale was coming to an end. James would enjoy these next two hours, two hours of laughter and the rattling of poker chips, two hours of smoke floating through the room, two hours of touchdowns and replays and money changing hands when the chips were cashed in at the end of the day. This would be his last season of Saturdays at Trevor's. Like leaving elementary school, where he had learned to read and write and add and subtract, to enter junior high where he noticed hair growing in new places on his body, and then high school, where he almost became a person with responsibilities and drama and choices that mattered, to college and jobs where the accumulation of knowledge and cash were goals. And now it was time to take the next step. To put Trevor's house in his rear view mirror. James could look through the windshield and see a future with Kristen, a winning hand, a touchdown, a high from which he would never come down.

Chapter 9

As she slid into the backseat of her mother's Lexus, Kristen regretted immediately not meeting her Mother and Kathy in town. She had always felt that her sister had been her mother's favorite and that no matter how hard Kristen tried, she would always be riding in the trunk or backseat or caboose. It didn't matter that she scored higher on the SAT than Kathy, didn't matter that she received an "A" from Dr. Fitzgerald in AP European History, deemed impossible by almost every student, didn't matter that Kathy didn't get a job for three years after graduating from college, didn't matter that Kathy married Frank, who was more interested in golf clubs and couches. It just didn't matter what happened, she felt like a second fiddle. What made the feeling even more bothersome was how in the last three years, she had finally made it to the top, had finally been elevated to the heights of a goddess, a celestial being, a portrait on the ceiling of the Sistine Chapel. Not for anything she had done, except for her engagement to Ken the Great, the doll of perfection, man of the universe, the catch of the day.

As she pulled away from the curb, Kristen's mother started glowing in the brilliance of Ken's family light, especially his father, Kenneth Sr. "I can't believe Kenneth has given us carte blanche on the florist. He called this morning to make sure that every bouquet had a bird of paradise." Her head shook assuredly as she checked the rear view mirror to see Kristen's response.

This is going to be a long day, Kristen thought, as she pulled her own mirror out of her purse, trying to convince herself that she could lay down the tracks for her mother and sister to see that this marriage train that she was supposed to be hopping on in two weeks was better left at the station. And when Kathy started to tie her husband Frank to the tracks as the train whistle approached, Kristen jumped at the chance, not to free Frank or unlace his hands, but to tie Ken right beside him.

"Frank couldn't have left the house any quicker this morning," started Kathy, with rope in hand. "Saturday. No reason to rush. But he's playing golf, so he's out in fifteen minutes. He left at quarter to seven and won't be back until three. I can't even get him off the couch to pick up a letter that I need ten feet from him."

"He's really changed a lot?" Kristen asked, already knowing the answer. In high school Frank had been a defensive lineman at a hundred and seventy pounds. He was usually fifty pounds lighter than the offensive tackle that he faced, but he was an overachiever, a machine that ran and ran and ran and led his team in tackles and quarterback sacks. During the off season he exercised without stopping. When he went to college at San Luis Obispo, he was ambitious, walked on, with the coach even saying, "Are you sure you want to do this?" and then proved everyone wrong by making the team and even starting the last two games when two outside linebackers went down with injuries. The last two games he led the team in tackles for a loss, but fifteen years later, the machine had broken down, and Kathy would see him "sacked out" on the couch, a remnant of the man who commanded

74

the altar of their wedding, handsome and charming and strong, so many years before.

"I don't know what's happened. I guess it's just marriage," said Kathy, opening the door wider than Kristen expected and leaving a little rope in Kristen's hand.

"Ken doesn't even open the door for me now. He'll probably be slamming it in my face in a couple of years."

"Oh, Kris," started her mother. "You hooked the biggest, most drop-dead gorgeous fish in the ocean."

"Mom, come on. He's not as cute as you might think. He practically doesn't say a word. And he never cleans up after himself. I think he sees me as a wife in a French maid's costume, rather than as a partner. A dirty dish is infected with rabies to him," said Kristen, tying one of Ken's wrists to the tracks.

"Well, he's got the right person to clean up after him," smiled Kathy, as she turned toward Kristen. Kristen could only shake her head in disgust, knowing what was coming next. Kristen had watched Disney's Cinderella for the first time when she was six. Who didn't love Cinderella? The week after she watched Cinderella, Mom gave the order for her and Kathy to clean their room "or else". My Little Jewel Ponies and a few Barbies with fashions askew, littered their room, one sock hung from the lampshade, a half eaten cookie hid under a backpack, and a week old piece of string cheese that even a mouse wouldn't eat, rested on the alarm clock. When her sister asked if she wanted to play Cinderella, Kristen agreed to play only if she was Cinderella. Kristen remembered shaking her head in disbelief when Kathy agreed to be the ugly stepsister. For the next four years, every time they had to clean, Cinderella polished and scrubbed and carted out the trash, while Drizella, the ugly step sister, sat on her bed and read. Who could see the ramifications of such a decision, to be Cinderella, when you are six?

"Maybe if you had cleaned a little, the karma of Frank wouldn't have come back and bit you in the butt, big time. What goes around, comes around." A little mean, but Kristen couldn't resist the shot.

"Well, Prince Charming is about to put your foot in the slipper," said her mother, smiling and shaking her head. "I probably should have stopped the whole cleaning thing, but you were so adamant about being Cinderella."

"That's just it, Mom. Sometimes you don't know when to stop something. I don't blame either of you for Cinderella. I was lost in the character. I just loved her. I still do. It wasn't even like I was cleaning. But cleaning up after Ken, it feels like every crumb he leaves on a plate is a boulder."

"It can't be that bad. Istanbul. Paris. New York. I'd trade a few crumbs to go to those places. I'd happily swap Frank for a round trip ticket to Paris," sighed Kathy, untying Ken's hands from the train tracks.

"Did I miss the florist?" asked Kristen's mom, her head twisting as she drove down the street.

"Two more blocks," said Kristen. "It'll be on the left. I'm just saying that I sure hope I'm not trying to yank Ken off the couch in ten more years."

"A body like his. That would be a sin. If he looks like Frank in ten years, I'll come help you. I'll come over and we'll Fargo him," remarked Kathy, referring to a gruesome scene of a murderer disposing of a body with the help of a wood chipper.

Kathy opened the door to Flo's Flowers and breathed in the sweet aroma permeating the room. They walked to the counter where Jane, the florist, with shears in her hand, was bent over a bouquet. Kristen felt there was now a spot of tarnish on Ken's perfection, a dose of doubt about the future, a smudge in the corner of the polished screen. She needed to feed the doubt, to soil the smudge, to let the shine fade. The flowers in the shop were vibrant and colorful and alive. But what would happen to their beauty in a week? Their rich colors will have faded, never to be seen again. What would happen to Kristen, married to Ken in a year, a decade, a lifetime? The flowers didn't have the earth to replenish their

76

spirit. Ken could never replenish Kristen's beauty, but she knew that James was that earth, that soil, that gardener that would help her grow and bloom and stretch to heights above the heavens.

For twenty minutes, Kristen's mother was a conductor of an orchestra of flowers to be blended together to make a symphony of beauty on every one of the thirty-one tables at the reception. Tulips and roses and birds of paradise and lilacs and daisies and sunflowers and violets and snap dragons all became team members in the pursuit of a centerpiece. Jane, with shears still in her hand, and her glasses resting comfortably on her forehead, grabbed and clipped stalks for the arrangement. Kristen noticed how the different colors, vibrant by themselves, found opposition when placed next to colors that refused to complement, but with the sorcery of a wizard, Jane was able to wrap each separate identity of flower into a wholeness whose fragrance was a perfume of delight.

The tip of the bird of paradise was aimed directly at Kristen, as Jane raised the bouquet and handed it to her. "The way you handle the flowers. You are like a magician. These are beautiful," said Kristen, absorbed by Jane's skill. Even as she spoke, she was wondering how to put Ken back on the train tracks with the engine approaching. The smiles on the faces of her sister and mother reminded her of the difficulty of calling off a wedding. But she had to. The thought of thirty more years of being a piece of furniture in a house was impossible. She knew she couldn't do it. Why hadn't she spoken up before? Why hadn't she called the engagement off after a month? Why did she say yes in the first place? The ring was so damn big, but since when did the size of a diamond or the size of a bank account or the value of a car mean anything to her? Why, she wondered, couldn't she just say she didn't want to marry Ken and make them believe her and rush to her side and comfort her for all she must have gone through? What was it that was leading her down this path of destruction, knowing she could take a detour at any time, and that James now offered her the possible yellow brick road to the wonderful land of her future?

Kristen held the bouquet in front of her heart as she opened the back door of the car. Her mother slid behind the wheel and asked where they wanted to go for lunch. Her sister sent a text to Frank that she knew would go unanswered. Kristen's mind was a thousand-piece jigsaw puzzle of possibilities of breaking the news, of announcing the bulletin, of dispatching the story, that the pending marriage of Kristen Taylor and Ken Anderson was officially crossed off the calendar. An imaginary story of Ken's possible infidelities on his business trips, finding a note in his pocket, discovering sensationalized text messages on his phone, even lipstick on his collar, the old, really old standby of yesteryear, were possibilities, but she knew she couldn't lie, couldn't leave open the door of doubt and then have it slammed in her own face if she couldn't deliver the proof. An imaginary story of how he hit her she knew was beyond the realm of possibility. The truth was boring. He just didn't know how to love her. He didn't know how a woman felt or didn't care what made a woman tick.

Kristen was brave. "Mom, Kathy," and from the sound of her voice, they knew it was important.

"What is it, Honey?" buttered her mother.

"I am getting really cold feet. Really cold. I don't think I can..."

"Oh, Honey. You're twenty-seven. Guys like Ken come around once in a lifetime."

"But I'm not sure I love him. And I'm not sure he loves me," said Kristen. A weight, a boulder, a sack of cement, that she had been carrying for the last six months, dropped from her neck and shoulders.

Kathy wasn't as generous to pick up the fallen weight and hold the heavy burden that Kristen had been carrying and understand the pain she had been in. "Are you kidding me? A guy like Ken doesn't ever come around. He is the prince every girl waits for and you just happen to be the damn Cinderella that actually gets the guy. Shit. I'd have cleaned the room all those years myself if I would've ended up with him."

"Kathy, when did your mouth become so nasty?" gasped her mother.

"About the time we had the couch delivered with a permanent stain on it. Damn I hate that couch." Kathy was in fine form today.

"I just don't want to end up like Kathy. All nasty all the time," said Kristen, feeling good about turning the tables on Kathy but knowing she was only two weeks away from suffering a similar fate. She hoped the clues were enough for the future to unfold how she wanted. "Well, if I call off the wedding, you two will be the first to know."

"And you better be ready for World War III," offered her mother. "Uncle Cecil is flying in from New York. You don't want to tick off Uncle Cecil. He's been talking about finally making it to California, and after forty years of shoveling all that snow, especially this year, he is foaming at the mouth. You'll have to deal with him. I'd rather deal with Godzilla. Wanna go to Shakey's?" she kidded, switching gears, as they headed down the street.

A smile settled over Kristen's lips. She would be more than happy to deal with Uncle Cecil and Godzilla. Now all she had to do was call off the wedding. By Tuesday night she would know for sure about the future. She went through her checklist of what makes the right guy and realized that where love was concerned, the ability to communicate and laugh and respect were boxes to check five times the size of the others. These were the things that really mattered. Sure the chemistry was needed to fire up the engines, but without the gasoline, the fuel, nothing could start. James had plenty in the tank, his lips and tongue had revved Kristen's motor. Ken had the Porsche and the money and the body, but he didn't know how to turn the key, how to make a spark, how to step on Kristen's pedals and make her go. For

Kristen it was simple. James was the one. She would know for sure on Tuesday.

Chapter 10.

The right-hand punch that Molly had thrown two weeks before had set in motion events James could never have foreseen. Two weeks ago he was a twenty-nine year-old employed welder, with a girlfriend, with Saturdays with the guys, quite content and happy. And then the punch had hit, turning his world to a shade of black he hadn't seen for over twenty years, since his father caromed off lawn chairs, along the sidelines of soccer games, too drunk to walk a straight line, yelling obscenities at the referees, making a son cower in his skin. But this blackness had found the light, had found a woman sitting in Scully's dressed to the one's, in her sweatshirt and flats, who he found to be charming and open, found her eyes able to see into his soul, found her words inflate the air that had been knocked out of him by Molly. And then the next week he found the woman, who had been dressed worse than a thrift store, had changed her wardrobe, and soared to heights of beauty he could never have expected. If she wasn't a ten, she was a nine point five, and when quibbling about beauty, who cares about a differential of five tenths?

Woodrow's Welding had reassigned him to the Western Hills Homes, a hundred and forty new homes being built in the Simi Valley. From Burbank he would always be driving the opposite direction of the traffic, away from Los Angeles. The Ford 150 drove quicker than usual down the five, as Ice Cube's, "It's a Good Day," shook the interior, and James was all too happy to rock along. "Today I didn't have to use my AK." James wasn't sure how that could be a good day, but it didn't stop him from rapping like he was on the street. The mood shifted quickly as the next song, Train's "Drops of Jupiter," softened the sounds of the speakers, sending his thoughts in orbit. Even though he had just been reassigned by Woodrow Welding, tomorrow he would be taking the day off. He had already taken care of that with his foreman Mr. Mark, who remembered working with James' father when he had just been hired, twenty-five years before. Besides, the company knew he was dependable, only missing one day in the last six months, the Monday after the punch, when he was too embarrassed to show his face, even if it would be covered most of the day by his welding mask.

He was passing Hollywood Way and made a mental note to make sure he showed Kristen Grauman's Chinese Theater on Hollywood Boulevard. He was pretty sure she had been there, had tried to place her feet in the concrete shoe prints of Judy Garland, placed her hands next to Meryl Streep's, or found that her shoe was larger than John Travolta's. James remembered taking Molly to Grauman's and her commenting on how small Shirley Temple's hands were, a child mega star by the time she was five, the adoring favorite of a nation, who Molly had never heard of except when ordering a drink once when she was twelve. Grauman's was a sure thing, but only for someone who had never found the historic theater. The crowds could be claustrophobic and the clamoring of the street hustlers impersonating Elvis or Chewbaca, the big Wookie from Star Wars or Batman or Superwoman could be insulting and disgusting. They could manipulate a twenty-dollar bill out of the hands of an unaware tourist hoping to touch the fame of Hollywood for a few seconds.

James knew his first stop in Los Angeles was going to be Grand Central Market off of Third and Broadway, right across from the Bradbury Building. They would walk through the market and grab a couple of carnitas tacos, even if it was nine-thirty in the morning. James knew he would throw out the textbook of propriety and launch random darts at the wall that he knew would stick, knew would be bullseyes of flavor or sight or touch. Maybe a fresh raspberry juice, maybe a Mexican pastry, maybe a pound of cherries or a basket of strawberries before they left the market and walked across the street to Angels Flight where James would show his chivalry by buying a ticket for Kristen on the funicular, even if a round trip cost less than a dollar. They would ride the car up to the top of Bunker Hill where James would wrap his arms around her as their eyes gazed over the sprawling city of Los Angeles.

After the ride back down James would drive over to Caesar Chavez Avenue, just above Olvera Street. He knew parking places were at a premium in most of Los Angeles, but on this street there was always room, and it was perfectly situated between Olvera Street and Chinatown and Philippe's Restaurant. James kicked ideas around of what to see. He knew he would have to play this one as it came. No making plans here. Philippe's is usually a must, a stop along the way for those traveling to Dodger games at Chavez Ravine or Clipper or Laker games at Staples Center, but he and Kristen would have just eaten at Grand Central Market, so he might have to let go of the sawdust on the floor, let go of the French beef double dip sandwich and let go of the best baked apples this side of the Rocky Mountains. Olvera Street was a little too touristy for James' taste, but it wasn't his taste buds he was concerned with. Whatever Kristen wanted to sink her teeth and luscious lips into was what James wanted, and he wanted her to sink her lips into his before the day was over. A carnitas taco was one thing. Kristen's lips were in another galaxy.

Maybe a picture on the cart with the donkey, one they could place on the front of the refrigerator, a memory of youth and first meeting. A reminder of that first real date when the skies had opened and they could see their names written in the atmosphere. Chinatown would also be held in reserve, a few streets of tastes and smells, that you just couldn't find in the middle class enclave of Burbank. Chinatown and Olvera Street and Grand Central Market were only twenty-five minutes away, but how many of the hundred thousand people living in the city, the home of Warner Brothers and NBC, had ever ventured to these tastes, seemingly in foreign countries?

James' phone was ringing with Noe's recognizable number, but James was too deep in his thoughts of tomorrow to be disturbed. In a couple of minutes, the phone rang again, but James was only fifteen minutes from work, and he wasn't about to chance another ticket for talking on his phone while driving. He drifted into tomorrow once again. He went to the climax of where they would go, the Getty Museum. He knew that even if she had been there before, the magnitude of the buildings, the view of the ocean and Los Angeles and the gardens would overwhelm even the most jaded person, and Kristen was as far from jaded as the Mona Lisa is from a stick figure. He would take her into his favorite room of the museum, the room with Van Gogh's *Irises*. A room full of magic, of masters, who created timeless work. Paul Cezanne and Augusté Renoir and Claude Monet and Mary Cassat and Edgar Degas, their creations, a testament of humanity and creativity to inspire eyes and hearts to reach for immortality.

James' mind wrestled with other possibilities: Pink's Hot Dogs, but the line was always long; the Museum of Tolerance, which he would save for another day, a stop everyone should have to make, to understand what it means to be a scapegoat; Tito's Tacos, more famous than necessarily good; Farmer's Market, a sure stop twenty years ago, before the Grove was built; and the Santa Monica Pier, maybe the last stop after the Getty, a stroll along the sands letting the tide tickle their feet, or a ride on the

Ferris wheel. He wondered if anyone became engaged on the Ferris wheel while going in circles above the ocean. James' mind was dancing with ideas.

James exited the Ronald Reagan freeway to his job site, his home away from home for at least the next six months, hoping for the stability of two years at one place, at one job site. Although he wondered what his world of welding would be in the future, Kristen still dominated his thoughts of the present. James walked past the chain link fence as his phone dinged with a text from Noe to call him, but seeing as he was ready to punch the clock, he couldn't imagine anything that important that couldn't wait for lunch.

Mr. Mark, his supervisor, met him enthusiastically. "Damn! Do you look like your old man. If you ha' half the arm that golden arm had, you'll do him fine up here. You let me know if there's anything you gonna need. I been sober fer ten years, so don't let me catch you with your hands on aluminum and not steel rod."

"Appreciate it."

"Be workin' with Hank. You'll like 'em. Everybody does," said Mr. Mark, as he shuffled off toward the work shed, stopping next to a man with a beard, about six foot four, and then pointing back toward James.

The beard approached James, with his hand, the size of a catcher's mitt, extended toward him. "Boss says yer James. We gonna be Lewis and Martin. No bad fits here. Ya hear me? We'll keep the popcorn in them boxes at the movies."

James wasn't sure what Hank was talking about, as he sounded exactly like Mark, and wondered if he would sound that way in a few years. He knew he was good at "frying bacon," of fitting pipes together, and was determined to make a good impression. For the next four hours, the work was strenuous, and Hank kept reminding James that he was hired from the neck down. "Don't you do no thinkin'. Man, they don't pay you to do no imaginin'. Jus' fry that bacon. Do the cookin' now, we'll do the

85

eatin' later." Working with a character like Hank had made it easy to stop thinking, and James hadn't thought of his trip into Los Angeles. That was the beauty of work, of focusing one's attention, of a goal to be reached, of expectations to be met, of details to take care of. The weld around the pipes, to seal them together. A leak in a pipe could weaken a foundation, and with the base wobbling on solid ground, imagined solid ground, the structure would be in danger of collapse.

"You got plans fer lunch?" asked Hank.

"Not really," answered James, his body breathing relief, his shirt sticky with sweat.

"I bin restin and nibblin' over by that tree and stack a wood," offered Hank, motioning with his hand toward the shade.

"Sounds good," said James, comfortable in his new position, not the job one would expect a biology major from UCLA to be dirtying his hands with. James grabbed his cooler and started maneuvering toward the stack of wood, when he felt his pocket vibrate. He immediately remembered he needed to call Noe and discover what made his phone so popular. He figured it was probably Noe, which it was.

"Hey, what's going on? First day on the job in Simi. Pretty cool," started James.

Noe didn't know what to say. He was relieved to have finally gotten ahold of James, but now that he had him, he couldn't find the words. For a few seconds, there was only silence.

"Noe, is anybody home? Dude, why'd you call?" asked James shaking his head in wonderment.

"She's dead," was all that leaked out of Noe's mouth.

"Who's dead?" asked James, finding irritation in the conversation.

"She's dead, James. She's dead. She was hit by a car."

"Who?"

"Kristen. Kristen Taylor."

The words turned James to stone, a statue of disbelief. "What the fuck are you talking about? She's dead?"

86

"My mom was reading the Times this morning. She comes in and tells me some girl was killed in Burbank. Hit by a car. I don't even think anything of it, but I can't go back to sleep, so I get up and see the headline and start reading and there it is, Kristen Taylor pronounced dead at the scene.

"Kristen Taylor? Oh God!! It can't be."

"Kristen Taylor. Twenty-seven years old."

James was welded to the ground, unable to move. He didn't know what to do. It couldn't be possible. His hands trembled as he tried to type Kristen's name into Google News. On the third try, he was ready, not ready at all, to touch the search key. News of the world was at his fingertips. James wondered how many people had died during the Civil War because they hadn't received the news that the South had surrendered, and the fighting had continued as if the war was still on. He wondered how his mind could waver and think so tangentially even though the most important woman in the world to him, the woman he saw holding his hand forever, might be gone. He hit the search key.

A Los Angeles Times article from fourteen minutes ago popped up on the screen.

"Pedestrian killed, two injured, driver released." Patrick Rhone, 25, of Sun Valley was released by authorities. Rhone was the driver of the Cadillac SUV that killed pedestrian, Kristen Taylor, 27, of Burbank, and injured two unidentified bystanders."

A bullet shot through James' heart. He left his cooler next to the stack of wood on the ground. He didn't hear Hank's voice asking him what happened. He didn't see Mr. Mark with his hand raised, trying to stop him. He walked to his truck, in a fog so thick it would make pea soup think it was water. He was driving but he didn't know where. A 7-Eleven at the corner lured the Ford 150 into the parking lot, as James, a zombie, walked toward the newspaper racks in front of the store. "Governor Schwarzenegger Dips Into Education" was the headline of the paper James placed on the counter gingerly, afraid of what was inside, afraid to face the words printed on the page. After the perfunctory exchanging of money with the clerk and the automatic "have a nice day," James returned to the front seat of his truck. For once he had no interest in the sports section. On page two of the LATEXTRA section was the story that would change his life forever.

"Woman Killed, Two Injured" was all the headline said.

Twenty-seven-year old Kristen Taylor of Burbank was hit and killed yesterday, as she walked along the sidewalk on Magnolia Boulevard, just north of Hollywood Way. A Cadillac SUV, driven by Patrick Rhone, 25, of Sun Valley, jumped the curb, striking Ms. Taylor. Ms. Taylor was pronounced dead at the scene. Two bystanders suffered minor injuries in the accident.

Witnesses said the SUV came out of nowhere. No one in the SUV suffered any injuries.

Miles Harrison, a witness, was unsettled by the accident. Harrison, walking with his wife and two children, Jason, 4, and Ben, 2, had walked past Ms. Taylor moments before the accident. Said a distraught Mr. Harrison, "She had just patted Jason on the head and said I hope I have kids this cute someday. They are adorable."

James placed his forehead on the steering wheel and sobbed. He could picture Kristen walking down the street, filled with love, the love they were going to share. He could hear her voice. He could feel her touch. He could see her tenderness. In less than two weeks, he had found the richest gem in the world, a woman who would have made his life worth living, and now, in an instant, she was taken from him forever. His body heaved with sadness. Through his tears he kept reading.

"Three seconds later she was gone. We didn't see the car hit her. She was beautiful. Her smile was beautiful. One moment.

One moment. It could have been my whole family. One moment.
I can't believe so much life left so quickly."

Two bystanders were slightly injured by debris. One was
released at the scene. The second was transported to St. Joseph's
Hospital and released. Neither was identified.

Ms. Taylor is survived by her mother, father, and sister.

Through his tears, James started driving toward Magnolia
Boulevard. He thought of walking into Scully's that Friday night,
having hidden in his room for a couple of days, until finally
finding the courage to face humanity, and then discovering that
humanity could be pretty accepting, especially that disheveled
sweatshirt and baseball cap that had poured goodness through
him, had pumped helpings of strength and self confidence through
his veins and rebuilt the walls of laughter that he was used to
bouncing off of. She couldn't be gone. She was too filled with
the beauty of life. James wondered where on Magnolia Boulevard
she had been hit. The article said just north of Hollywood Way.
He exited the freeway at Burbank Boulevard and maneuvered over
to Magnolia. He drove slowly and sadly down Magnolia
Boulevard. He couldn't see anything out of place as he passed
Lima Street and then Avon Street, and even Cordova Street, but
as he approached Hollywood Way, a store, "Newly Vintage" had
plywood covering most of the store front. James found a parking
spot after turning the corner and checked the rear view mirror to
see what kind of mess his face portrayed. He breathed slowly and
deeply three times and opened the door and slowly walked toward
the plywood.

Three lighted memorial candles, one with a picture of
Jesus, one with Mary Magdalene holding Baby Jesus, and one of
Jesus on the cross, were alongside a bouquet of yellow roses,
surrounded by green foil, and a store-bought bouquet of Easter
lilies. One message was stuck between the candles, written on a
lined paper ripped from a spiral notebook. 'Kristen. You were

the beauty of the world. Now you are the beauty of heaven. RIP We love you.'

James noticed the door to the antique shop was open. As he entered, the wreckage that remained inside the store was voluminous.

"We're closed buddy," said the voice of the shop owner as he straightened from under an aisle in the middle. "Be open in a coupla' days."

"What happened?" asked James, walking toward him. "Can I give you a hand?"

"Cops are here for five hours yesterday. Measurin' this. Askin' that. First voice I heard offerin' to help. Ya really wanna help, 'cause I can use it?"

James was more than ready to do something physical. To help. To find out what took place. To imagine what Kristen must have felt.

"Girl was killed here yesterday. I coulda been a goner too. Big ol' Cadillac comes busting into the store goin' bout forty. Shit, I went to Nam, never been so God damned scared in my life," he started. "Just put anything ain't broke on that table over there."

James bent among the rubble, pieces of glass, red and green, probably over a hundred years old, maybe even two hundred years, antiques that had survived two world wars, earthquakes and tornadoes, only to find their end through an out of control vehicle. James found three small dessert plates that had survived, and even two wine glasses, as fragile as a house of cards, had remained whole, despite the upheaval. He twirled one of the glasses in his hand, amazed at its beauty and delicacy, amazed that the faint light blue line encircling the glass had been in existence since Teddy Roosevelt had been president, amazed at how fragile life is, amazed that on the ground he was now stooped over, Kristen must have taken her last breath. "I'd like to buy this wine glass, if you don't mind," said James, choked with the emotion of his thoughts. James wondered why the tears weren't flowing like the Nile River, why he was willing to help this man, why his body wasn't convulsing in sobs.

"You help me son, and you just take that. I was standin' over there," said the man, pointing in front of him about ten feet, where a wooden bookcase had two splintered shelves and a back that had disappeared, "I didn't know about the girl yet. She was decapitated you know."

"What?"

"Poor thing was pushed through the window, and I don't know what happened. Just horrible. But I dint even know til a half hour after the accident. This lady, she was about sixty, was looking at a lamp over by that bookshelve. Asked me for help and I tell her I'll help her in a minute. I have this mannequin in front a' the store. The car must a hit it just right, 'cause it come flying through the store like one of them missiles and grazes the lady, destroyin' the lamp and crashes through the bookcase. I coulda been standin' there helpin' that lady. Coulda been in Nam for a year, survived, and then shot down by a flyin' mannequin. Kid in the store got hit by some flying glass, give him a slice in the ear and scalp. Had to go to the hospital.

"She was decapitated?"

"Yeah, some guy run in, place his jacket over the lady's head. Horrible. Happy I dint see the head. Guy was pretty shook-up. Could hardly talk to the police. Guy in the car. He goes and sits in that chair over there, just holding his head in his hands, cryin' like a baby. Can't believe what he done."

"I read the article in the Times. You know who that family was that had just talked to her?"

"Nah. They musta been outside 'cause I never saw em. I don't know what was happenin' out there. Did you know her?" asked the man.

"Yeah. She was the one. I only knew her a little while, but I knew." said a strangely composed James. "It wasn't love at first sight because the first sight wasn't the best," James continued, a slight smile on his lips contrasting the emptiness in

91

his heart. "But when I saw her again, she was magic. She was..."
and the smile had turned to tears.

"I know what ya mean. Got back from Nam in '71. Three
weeks later I walk into Baskin Robbins for a scoop a chocolate,
and the prettiest little thing behind the counter with the prettiest
little smile, and the prettiest voice. And when she hand me the
cone, her hand touch mine and I just want to scoop her up right
then. A month later we get married by a judge and here it is over
forty years later and best thing I ever did. Not even close. Man,
I'm so sorry. You take whatever you want from this store young
man. You lose somethin' so precious, aint nothin' in this store
worth nothin'."

James let go. His body heaved with sadness, shook with
grief, convulsed with the anguish of losing a living jewel. The
man put his arm around James' despair. "Come on son. You
don't need to be here helpin' me out. You helped me more 'n you
know. Now, you stop on by anytime you want. Ain't nothin you
can do about the injustice of life sometime. Just don't make no
sense." He looked James in the eye, picked up the wine glass and
placed it in his numb hand and led him to the front of the store.
"You take care now."

James squatted by the memorial candles and tried to
compose himself. He covered his eyes with his sunglasses, took
three slow, deep breaths, unwrapped the green foil. He slipped
one of the yellow roses from the bouquet, brought the yellow
petals to his nose, and breathed in the sweet aroma, a scent of the
gods, sweetness unmatched by any other flower, the floral jewel
of beauty. He stood and made his way to his truck. In one hand
dangled the antique and fragile wine glass and in the other hand a
long stem with a yellow rose swung by his side.

As James climbed in the front seat, he placed the rose and
wine glass on the seat next to him, but he couldn't start driving.
His body was empty. Kristen was gone. Gone. Without hope.
Without a chance. Without a chance to kiss her lips that had
electrified his being. Without a chance to hold her hand and look

into her eyes and feel her smile radiating through his body. Without a chance for tomorrow in Los Angeles, a first step in a journey that would pave a trail of infinite footsteps. Without a chance to wear a tuxedo next to her white dress and say "I do." James had been taught there was always hope. There was always another chance. Didn't the Beast get another chance to show his true beauty? Didn't Shrek, that big ugly green monster, get another chance to show he was lovable? Didn't Ford get another chance to show they could make a decent car? Didn't the Red Sox take the slimmest of chances in 2004, down three games to zero, with two outs in the ninth, and turn that seeming impossibility into their first World Series win in eighty-six years? But this was different. There was no more hope to be with Kristen. No chance to be a fool in a delivery room as Kristen would be drenched in sweat, pushing a new life through her womb, into her husband's hands, a welder, who knows how to hold life together. Without a chance.

James wondered where Kristen lived. He didn't even know what her address was. They had met each time at Scully's, and that was where they were supposed to meet tomorrow. Did she live by the high school right next to IKEA above Glenoaks Boulevard? Did she live by McCambridge Park? Did she live in the hills, parallel to Debell Golf Course, the fancy part of town, or did she live just around the corner from where she was killed, somewhere between NBC and Disney and the Burbank Airport? He didn't even know the last name of her fiancé, Ken. James knew he was a lawyer who had money and a Porsche and didn't treat Kristen the way she deserved to be treated. Someone who didn't believe in the golden rule of treating others the way they wanted to be treated. Someone who had a jewel in the palm of his hand and threw it in the trash. James hated Ken and didn't even know him. James was sure that Ken would create a play of emotion at the funeral, an act with tears and cries, that would quickly disappear after he left the stage.

Turning the key in the ignition, the motor fired, like it always did, and the Ford 150 inched backwards before swinging to the left and into traffic. The morning had started with James comfortably behind the wheel, driving toward a new beginning of work, a day away from a new beginning of love. How life can change so quickly! Twenty-four hours before he had been sitting in front of the television, watching Tiger Woods trying to pull off a miracle shot through a slight opening in a tree, over water, and fading the golf ball onto the green. Down by a stroke with two holes to go, he had no choice but to go for it. The ball responded to its master, found the left side of the green and rolled toward the pin where it stopped, fifteen feet away. The crowd went wild. The announcers were in disbelief. The replay was shown over and over again. When Woods made the putt to tie for the lead, everyone believed the momentum would drive him to victory, like he had done so often, but on the last hole, when he had a three-foot putt to make to force a playoff, a putt he could make in his sleep, a putt he practiced until he made one hundred in a row, he inexplicably missed, the ball circling the edge, halfway around the cup, and not dropping, a horseshoe, an unlucky horseshoe. James shook his head at the absurdity of life. The miracle followed by the mishap. Life had a way of evening things out. Yesterday, James was shaking his head, with his notepad in his lap, planning his journey with Kristen to Los Angeles, watching Tiger Woods on television, while, at the same time, police were questioning witnesses to an accident. While the coroner was picking up the lifeless body of Kristen Taylor. While those who were there at the scene of the accident on Magnolia Boulevard, who narrowly escaped serious injury of their own, were understanding a definition of the meaning of life that can't be found in any book, that can't be explained by any professor, that can't be understood through any sermon. A personal meaning so profound, so life affirming in the face of death.

Last night he and Noe had driven by Scully's on the way to P.F.Changs. They were listening to Noe's mixed tape, and

James Brown was belting out the classic, "I Feel Good," and all James could think about was Kristen and the effect she had on his existence. And at the time, Kristen was dead. When they arrived at P.F. Changs and were seated, close to the kitchen, an energetic five-foot-two blonde walked past them on a mission, direct strides, arms churning, mouth foaming, not noticing Noe or James. When she reached the kitchen, her words, angry words, echoed to James and Noe. "Stick these fucking chopsticks up your ass," and then, thirty seconds later, as composed as a president, she found the front of their table and took their order as sweetly as "a summer day in June." James and Noe couldn't control their laughter. Their sides started to hurt from their mimicking her command of the chopsticks becoming invisible and when, much later, some of James' sticky rice was accidentally spit from his mouth onto Noe's shirt, they were almost a scene by themselves. And at that time, Kristen was dead. James conjectured how he could have known about what had happened sooner, conjectured how he could have been there to protect her from the car, conjectured how he would have been happy to have been in her place, been the one to have been hit by the car so that one as beautiful as she could have made the world a better place.

The Ford 150, carrying wounded cargo, wandered aimlessly down Hollywood Way toward the airport, when James finally became aware that he was driving, and driving in the wrong direction, as if there was a right direction. As the truck made a U-turn at Victory, James was lost, lost in the knowledge that the impossible was possible. Kristen couldn't possibly be dead. He wanted to draw curtains around the truck and fall asleep and awaken to Kristen sitting next to him. He wanted to hide under a blanket and come out to the sounds of her voice whispering "I love you" in his ear. He wanted what was impossible to have. He wanted to talk to her and hear her voice. James quickly pulled the truck into a parking space in front of the Sizzler on Vanowen. He wanted to hear her voice. James' hand inched toward his phone. Would someone answer if he called her number? Would Ken answer? Is her phone with the police, the undertaker? His hand shook. The steady hand that could weld anything together shook. His fingers tap danced across the raised numbers on his phone until Kristen's number lit the screen, lit the screen like she was still alive, lit the screen unaware of Magnollia Boulevard, lit the screen, an unfeeling piece of technology that doesn't need a heart to breathe. James hit the send button. The phone rang. And rang again. And rang a third time. And then the voice of Kristen spoke, the angelic voice of Kristen, "Hi, I'd love to talk. Please leave a message." And with her voice, James' protective shell was shattered. He became a mumbling mess of inconsolable heartbreak. All he managed to say into the phone, a speaker without a pulse, without a sense of humor, without a heart, was, "I am so..., so..., sorry."

Chapter 11

In her walk-in closet, Kristen turned, trying to decide what she would wear tomorrow, that perfect something that would be both classy and seductive. Her fingers swept along her blouses like the keys of a piano. She stopped at a white lace blouse, wondering if this would hit the right note that could tune James' heart. The wedding was less than two weeks away and Kristen knew that she was playing with fire to call off the wedding this late, but the fire could be put out. With enough time and enough water, the flames of anger and the scars of embarrassment would vanish and in place of the barren and vacant land of where Ken once stood, would be a new field of James, of flowering growth that has blossomed. Time can hide the pain of the past. History has a short attention span. Even the most momentous moments fade in color, lose their taste, as the days and years progress. And besides, the world is filled with women who would gladly take her spot in the line-up and be on Ken's team of wealth and body.

The play was reaching the climax: the twist in the story where Kristen would surprise everyone, everyone that was licking the syrup of her and Ken's romance, the rising action of meeting and falling in love, the engagement, the white wedding dress with the ten-foot train, the lace veil, the sounds of the wedding reception set to permeate the air with righteousness and exhilaration, and the congregation of families wedded together in bliss. The twist would leave a bitter taste, mouths agape, angry arms raised in defiance, blasphemous monologues uttered without an audience. Ken would be the hero. Kristen knew that was bound to happen. All fingers would be pointed at her. She didn't love him enough, too fickle to know what she wants, too crazy to understand that you don't throw away a shining star for a cloudy sky, too immature to know how to hold a family together, too selfish to share a piece of toast, too lazy to get off her ass and see that the glass wasn't half empty, that the pouring of Ken's heart into her was overflowing the glass with love and life and family, that she, stupidly, refused to take that final drink, that final drink of wedlock, that final drink of trust and loyalty. She knew no one would lower a finger to listen to the real story, to watch the real play, to see that Ken was never the protagonist, but always the antagonist, a character that no one could love. But she also knew that over time, the pointing fingers of blame would lower.

She hung the white blouse on the back of the chair and changed into her running gear, the Nikes, which hadn't been touched in a month, the sports bra and Athleta tangerine tank top, and her iPod and earbuds. But no, today she would leave the music at home, no iPod, much too much to think about. The galvanizing of thought during the monotonous motion of running would be a blessing. Normally she would relish the music, the rhythm of the beat, of the guitar solos, of the soothing sound of a saxophone, the energy of rap, pulse of techno, but today she would listen to the silence of her thoughts, of James and Ken and Los Angeles and the downfall of a wedding. Running down Country Club Drive until she reached Sixth Street would be easy, her legs moving without effort, but the return trip would be all uphill, legs burning to reach the door that when opened would change the pain to comfort. Her hand glided over the banister as she skipped down the stairs to the kitchen. Ken was a monument of nothingness, a meaningless mass, seated in front of his computer. His head didn't move as she tested her decision to leave him, running her fingers across his back.

"I'm gonna go for a run," she said and watched as nothing in the room moved, not even a hand to signify he had heard her. Her decision was cement. She wouldn't marry him. That was all. This wasn't Truman having to decide whether to drop the atomic bomb on Nagasaki and Hiroshima. This wasn't Kennedy deciding to blockade the Russian boats from continuing to Cuba. This wasn't Bush deciding to invade Iraq over weapons of mass destruction. Those were decisions of life and death. It wasn't even Atticus Finch deciding to defend Tom Robinson in *To Kill a Mockingbird*, an act of courage, or Hamlet deciding to avenge his father's murder, and then letting his conscience make a coward of his oath. This was only one person deciding to exit the road, to choose another avenue while there was still time to change direction. Kristen entered the kitchen and opened the refrigerator and poured herself a glass of water. She leaned against the counter and felt the cool liquid slide down her throat. Her phone lay on the tile. She checked for messages, and smiled when she saw that James had called. She listened to the message. "I'm so…, so…, sorry!"

What? Are you kidding? Like an atomic bomb being dropped. Like an invasion of her life. A blockade of her future. Kristen was a volcano ready to erupt. How could she be so wrong? How could she have been swept off her feet by the phony broom of James? How could she have let someone she had only known for a couple of weeks make such an indelible impression on her? How could she have been so wrong? This pathetic sad voice on the phone. What was he so sorry about? What was he crying about that he couldn't have at least stood like a man and said what was on his mind? What a wimp. What a coward. How could she be so off the charts on James' character? Two evenings. That was all and she was ready to hand over the keys to her life. Two evenings and she was ready to have his children. Two evenings and she was ready to sail the world with him. One kiss. One entanglement of tongues and she had felt he was the one. She had hinted to her sister and mother that there was someone else. She had a white blouse hanging on a chair that was going to be a lure of love. Tomorrow she was to have walked the streets of Los Angeles hand in hand with this chameleon of a man. God, her taste in men was worse than the dollar menu at Wendy's. Her heart wasn't broken, it was shattered. Her feelings for James had been coated with the sugar of two meetings, of the perfect blend of ingredients that created a tasty icing. The recipe for the cake, though, was never mixed, and Kristen twisted in the kitchen knowing she was the chef who had failed the most basic lessons of any recipe or blueprint for love. How could she be so foolish, so trusting, so ready to love a phantom that she couldn't possibly have known. Kristen stared through the kitchen to where Ken was sitting at the computer. Staring at the monument of nothingness. Staring at the meaningless mass in the chair. The molten lava erupted from her soul. She threw her phone with the force of a hurricane toward the meaningless mass of Ken. Ken felt the tip of the phone graze his ungreased hairline before the phone exploded into pieces against the mirror over the fireplace, splintering the reflection into a hundred likenesses.

"You fucking asshole!" Kristen roared, her face a demented portrait of rage. Her hands gripped the empty air, unsuccessfully, for something else to throw as she strode toward Ken.

Ken backed out of his chair, a mass of bewildered nothingness, unprepared for this surprise attack. "Kristen…"

It was the first time Ken had said her name in a long time, but she wasn't even cognizant of it, didn't even hear his voice, didn't even know he was there. She flowed over to his computer, burning with anger, burning with the embarrassment of mistaking James for one she could love and trust, burning with her choice in

100

men, burning with the knowledge that she had known Ken wasn't the right man for her and yet had let the charade continue, burning with the fuel of being terribly, terribly wrong, and her flames were forty feet high leaping toward Ken. He was helpless to stop the fire's onslaught. She ripped the computer screen off the table and swung the screen like a ball and chain, grunting as she released the cord, as Ken watched the screen hit the already splintered mirror into a thousand more images. Her flaming hands wrapped around the keyboard next and her flames screamed, "I hate this fucking computer," and started beating the keyboard against the desk like John Henry driving a spike into a rail. "Why don't you ever talk to me?" she screamed. "Why don't you give a fuck about anything but yourself? You fucking piece of shit!" Most of the lava was out of the volcano. She bent to pick up the computer tower off the floor but only had a few bursts of steam left in her. She hugged the unit to her chest and sank to the floor, exhausted, and the steam turned to water that flowed from her eyes.

Ken surprisingly wasn't mad, just confused. "What happened just now?" he said, putting a hand on Kristen's shoulder, a look of real concern in his eyes.

"Don't touch me. Don't you ever touch me," she said, with the remaining steam in her tank.

Ken walked away into the kitchen. He pushed a glass against the refrigerator door and walked toward Kristen with some water. "Why don't you drink this and then throw the glass at me if you want," said Ken, still trying to decipher the surprise attack.

A surprised hand reached for the glass. "Thanks," she said, puzzled by his kindness, replacing some of the lost water.

"You know I'm not very good at talking," said Ken. "Not very good at all. I'm just as scared as you are that we're getting married."

With one arm still wrapped around the computer tower, her other hand hanging limply over the top of the unit with the glass of water wobbling between her fingers, Kristen was unable to speak. She watched Ken walk over to the computer screen resting face down on the carpet, the cord and plug hidden under its face, apparently unharmed by the violent attack. Ken lifted the screen to the arm of the couch for support, ambled to the mirror and carefully lifted the shattered reflection of a thousand images that it now possessed, from the wall, and carried it into the garage. When he returned he found the keyboard under a chair and the letters S and Q that had been dislodged during the beating, and unexpectedly gave two final violent whacks of the keyboard against the floor, causing the keys, B and R and T to be severed from their home. Ken picked up all the pieces and returned to the garage. Kristen released her arm from the tower, found a home on the carpet for the empty glass, and laid back staring at the blank ceiling. How could she have been so wrong? How could she have thought that James was the one? And who is this person cleaning up my destruction, trying to comfort me? This is not the Ken doll I have known for the last two years.

From the garage came the sound of the Porsche's engine coming to life, backing out of the garage and heading down the street. She was too drained to lift herself from her carpeted bed and instead turned on her side and made a pillow of her arm. Kristen replayed the barbarity of her actions. She shook her head in disbelief. She remembered when she was seven and Natalie Crumplic had taken her Baby Rollerblade doll and was trying to drown it in the blow up swimming pool in her backyard. She was so angry she had tried to grab Natalie's hair and pull it out of her head, before her mother stopped her and sent her to her room, grounded for a week. Her anger had been dormant for two decades, and Kristen couldn't believe that she had just acted so insanely. Who was that person? Again she shook her head in disbelief. She walked into the garage and bent to where the mirror rested against the wall; her reflection was a jagged ruin of a face. A tear escaped from her eye. James' kiss seemed so sweet, so genuine. How could she be so wrong?

She went to her room and noticed her face wasn't in ruins, wasn't in a thousand pieces that didn't fit together. James didn't want her. How could that be? All the laughter and all the stories they had shared. Thank God she hadn't called off the wedding. That would have been too much. She brushed her hair back into place and refreshed her mouth after the bitterness and filth that had exploded from it. She smiled at the thought of Ken hammering the keyboard against the floor, a sane mimicking of her insanity. The wand of her lip gloss returned the sensuality to her lips that had disappeared in the last half hour. She listened as the sound of the Porsche arrived back in the garage. She walked downstairs, embarrassed and ashamed.

"I don't know if it is too early for a glass of wine, but I think we should talk," said Ken, holding a brown paper bag, the end of a wine bottle sticking out the top. Any one of a hundred bottles of expensive wine, Ken could have retrieved in seconds from his Wine Guardian, but he had chosen to leave the scene of the battlefield and give the casualty a chance to take care of her wounds.

"Yeah, we should," said Kristen. A chance to talk. Did she hear Ken correctly, she wondered? The man who says nothing, thinks we should talk. She walked into the kitchen, through the combat zone, and grabbed two glasses and the wine opener, which she handed to Ken. "Let's go outside."

They walked in silence to the patio, and Kristen gazed at the city sprawled before her. A million lives that she knew nothing about, encompassed in one sweep of her eyes. "I'm really sorry, Ken. It's me. I don't know how to communicate with you. And then I go all psycho on you. I'm really sorry."

"I'm not very good at talking, Kristen."

"Everyone thinks we are this great couple, and you don't even talk to me," said Kristen, as she felt a lump starting in her throat.

"Remember that first night? I came outside at that party, and my dad wanted me to meet one of his partner's daughters, who I didn't want to meet, and you were standing there. You were beautiful. So beautiful. And I asked if you wanted to get out of there. And you said yes. Then we got in my Porsche, and the whole time I'm driving, I can't think of anything to say, so I keep switching the channels to different music, thinking maybe you'll think I'm cool, but feeling so stupid because I have no idea what to say, but you're not really saying anything, so I just keep quiet. I'm good at keeping quiet."

"I know. I know. I should have said something. But you were like... I don't know... A Porsche. And you know you're handsome. I was scared to say anything."

"I had a girlfriend every year of school and I barely ever spoke. I mean, I've needed someone to throw a computer at me for a long time, but no one ever did until today."

"That was really stupid of me."

"No. That was really good," continued Ken. "Every year a friend would tell me, hey, so and so really likes you. And we'd meet at the movies and then we were officially together, but I never knew how to say anything, and if I did have to speak, I was scared to death I would say the wrong thing. I could say yes and no and that was about it."

Ken had mesmerized Kristen the first time she had seen him, and now for the first time, she was aware of moving parts inside. For two years she had seen a face found on the cover of a book, handsome and intoxicating, but was never aware of the softness of some of his interior pages, was never aware that there were really pages inside his cover. Ken sat across from her, his eyes full of ache and compassion. This monument of nothingness, this meaningless mass was beginning to change the scales, was beginning to give weight to his words, was beginning to be more than a vacuum of ideas. Kristen felt something stir in her. Ken had spoken more to her in the last five minutes than it seemed he had in the last two years.

"You know I have a sister that is five years older than I am. She lives in New York. I always ask myself why I can't be more like her."

"You have a sister?" asked a surprised Kristen. "And she lives in New York?"

"She won't have anything to do with our dad. He's not a bad guy, but she never liked the way he wanted her to run her life. He didn't like her boyfriends or the fact she wanted to be a designer; Andersons aren't designers. She wasn't scared of him. She actually told him to go fuck himself and lived through it. I've been afraid of talking back to him my whole life. So, anyway, she left. She said it, right to his face. She's never coming back."

"You should have said something. Is she a designer?" asked Kristen, relishing every moment of a glass of wine and a conversation that never should have aged this long.

"No. I haven't talked to her for about a year. I sent her an invitation to the wedding of course. I never even told you about her. I should have. I haven't heard a thing from her."

"It's all right. You didn't talk to me. I didn't talk to you," said Kristen, sipping from her glass.

"We're supposed to be married, but you know, I don't blame you for exploding. I wouldn't want to marry me. I mean, all that two souls becoming one. I haven't said enough to you for you to even know if I have a soul."

"I honestly don't know if we should get married. I haven't been very good at being a partner. I'm more like part of the help."

"That's my fault," said Ken.

"Yeah it is. But it is also mine. Partners talk and don't send planes loaded with bombs. It's as much my fault as yours."

Ken leaned forward in his overstuffed patio chair. "None of your bombs, as you call them, hit me. So far there are no casualties. And I'm really happy to be sitting here with you. I'm thirty-three years old, and I feel like a kindergartener who has just been taught to tie his shoes, one who has just been taught how to speak," said Ken. "I remember in high school we were reading *Cyrano de Bergerac*, and I wasn't paying too much attention to the play. I knew I could study and ace the test. The teacher showed us the Steve Martin movie, *Roxanne,* and there was this scene where this guy, Christian, I'll never forget this scene, goes to Roxanne's door to speak to her and he's wearing a hat, and underneath the hat are earphones and Steve Martin is speaking into a microphone and is telling him exactly what to say. At one point Christian has to take the hat off and his ear pieces and now Steve Martin can't tell him what to say. Roxanne is there and wants Christian to say the right thing and he is helpless. A deer caught in the headlights. And everyone in the class was laughing so hard except for me. I was terrified. Christian was me. I was Christian. Scared to death to talk to a girl. Scared to death I would say the wrong thing. It still is me." Ken gazed into Kristen's eyes. "But today has been pretty good."

"I don't get it, Ken; you're a lawyer. All you do is talk."

"That's the weird thing. In court I have no problem talking. Give me a client, and I am locked in to their case. The outside world doesn't exist. I know if I am ready for everything the prosecution can throw at me, that I have a very good chance at winning. No one can blame me for anything if I do my job. I can hide all my fears. The whole truth and nothing but the truth, so help me God. The most comforting words I know. And when I win the case the look of love in the eyes of my client, the look that now my life can continue the way it should, the look that says I am a savior is the love I have banked on for many years. It's what I know best. Kristen, I can't promise you I'll be a good husband or a good father. Love and fatherhood scare the shit out of me. But I can promise that I'll try my best, which might not be very good. I don't want you ever to have to resort to tossing computers again."

"Right now I need you to hold me, Ken," remarked Kristen, as she left her chair and crawled in next to Ken. She leaned her head back on his shoulder, and his arms awkwardly encircled her body. She squirmed a little, trying to eradicate his discomfort. Only two hours earlier she had been in her closet, touching the clothes of her future, anticipating a trip to Downtown

Los Angeles, desiring to spend the rest of her life with this phantom of two meetings, James, who had hinted at a life of passion and understanding during two glorious nights at Scully's. Only two nights, less than eight hours, only to discover that the golden ring was made of plastic, only to discover that the chandelier had no electricity, only to discover that the ocean of love was only a mirage. Kristen took Ken's hand that limply lay on her lap and squeezed it tightly to her body. She felt secure but unsure nonetheless of what to do.

How could Kristen have known that less than five miles away James was in mourning? That James was grieving with his thoughts that Kristen's body had flown through a plate glass window, shattering the glass into a thousand pieces, shattering his dreams into a thousand pieces, shattering their future together into a thousand pieces. How could Kristen have known that James thought she was dead?

Chapter 12

Tuesday was one of the longest days of James' life. From the moment he awoke at a quarter to six in the morning, he was in a perpetual daze. Today was supposed to be a day of fulfillment, a day where memories would be sculpted in marble, a day of adventure and love, a day of passion entwined in hands, moving to and fro like the tide, as Kristen and he touched the skin of Los Angeles. How does one depart from the top floor of a skyscraper of happiness and take the elevator to the basement of misery? James was in the basement and didn't know what to do.

James drove to Starbucks and stood in line, but decided that he wasn't ready to associate with people and all the small meaningless dialogues of life. "I can't believe she dyes her hair." "The Lakers were world champs and now the Detroit Pistons swept them like sawdust from the floor." "My boyfriend never called me back." "Bush lied the whole time about the weapons of mass destruction." He couldn't take the small talk and catapulted out of line, away from the smell of coffee and back to the safety and quiet of the cab of his truck. A news rack beckoned him from the truck and soon he returned with the L.A. Times in his hand. Maybe there would be a follow-up article about the accident.

When he returned home and opened the paper to the same section that had reported Kristen's accident, he found only the usual suspects. Two died when a wrong-way, speeding driver on the 5, crashed into a minivan just entering the freeway at Tuxford. A man, 18, was slain, stabbed by two assailants, in the early morning hours in Pacoima. A Northridge city councilman was being investigated for using taxpayers' money for an unauthorized vacation in Hawaii with his wife and children. For James the stories had no meaning, just names and places, but he realized that some families were facing the devastation of this news, just as he, only twenty-four hours before, had been destroyed by the news of Kristen's death.

He found himself lying on the hardwood floor, trying to make sense of the ceiling. As he stared at the dismal design, he brought his knees to his chest and hugged them. James was flexible for someone his age, his nose on his knee. He repeated this exercise eight more times, each time his eyes never wandering from a fixed spot on the ceiling, a white map of a thousand lakes. He turned on his stomach and began slowly pushing his chest from the floor, staring at the grain of the wood in the slats directly below him. Effortlessly, his body rose from the ground, hovered, and then returned, his nose within an inch of the mahogany grain, only to rise again. Unaware of the motion of his arms, James listened to his breath, strong puffs of wind, until his arms gave way and the wind calmed to a gentle breath. He lay there, his left cheek on the ground, as his eyes scanned the floor's point of view. The legs of the chairs, the legs of the coffee table, the white molding outlining the wood floor, the top of a vitamin wrapper hiding under a Time magazine leaning against the bottom of the couch, the frayed edge of the brown and white throw rug aslant on the floor. James eased himself from the ground. Kristen, he thought, will never get back up.

109

Golf, he decided, would be a good way to pass some time. Alone on the fairways. One with nature. A chance to think. A chance to contemplate. He threw his clubs into the back of his truck and started the trek to Debell Golf Course in the hills of the city. His truck wandered through the streets of Burbank, wandered like James' mind, a jigsaw puzzle path of streets that James knew would finally result in the arrival at the course. He wandered up Alameda on the outskirts of the city toward the mountains, turning left on Sunset Canyon. At Country Club Drive, thinking about Kristen, he put his forehead to the steering wheel, a moment's reflection while stopped at the red demanding stop sign. Then, after fifteen seconds, he slowly continued on toward the course. This would have been another fluke of fate that could have changed the course of James' life, for Kristen had just backed her BMW out of the garage and would be at that same stop sign in one minute. The same silver BMW that James had watched disappear, as Kristen had driven away from Scully's. The same silver BMW that he had stood next to, as his lips and Kristen's lips had met in love and passion. James would have recognized her car immediately, but the fickle finger of fate, after its pause, pointed his truck past the stop sign to the golf course.

The tee box was empty and the course looked deserted, as James made his way into the clubhouse. Three minutes later, how powerful a minute can be, he was pressing a white wooden tee into the ground. It didn't seem fair that the first hole was the most difficult hole on the course. It didn't seem fair. James tapped his driver behind the ball again and again. Didn't seem fair. His swing was out of control, a twisting tornado of motion. The ball flew like a plane veering from its straight course toward the rocks and gully that beckoned on the right. For the next five holes, James was a natural disaster. A tornado of anger, a hurricane of indignity, an earthquake of exasperation. The white golf ball's innocence was disregarded, as James slashed and smashed and hammered with a vengeance. Finally, on the green of the fifth hole, he had a four-foot putt for par, with a slight break to the right.

110

He crouched behind the ball and studied the contour of the green. As he stood quietly over the putt, he thought, "What does it matter? What does it matter if I make this or I miss this? Will anything in the world change one way or the other? Kristen is gone and nothing is going to bring her back." In his disgust with the world, he walked off the green, leaving his ball still awaiting a tap, a touch of success or failure. He grabbed his clubs from the apron of the green, and walked to his truck, leaving the last thirteen holes to wonder what they did wrong to be treated so unfairly.

Meeting at Biagio's in an hour was the message he found on his phone as he climbed into the cab of his Ford. Noe had sent it forty minutes before. James listlessly turned the key in the ignition and headed to Biagio's. His timing was perfect, as Noe's dilapidated Honda rattled in right behind James' truck. Noe and Trevor ambled toward James.

"Sorry I couldn't come over yesterday. My bad. Shoulda been there," said Noe apologetically, as they made their way to the door. "You see the article?"

"Yes."

"Noe said you met her at Scully's," said Trevor opening the door.

The casualness of the conversation made James cringe. How could anyone understand the devastation that he felt? No one else he knew had ever met Kristen, had ever shared the comfort of her conversation or the charge of electricity she could generate with just a touch. Words kept flying over the table, but James remained lost in space until he came back to earth, holding the last couple of bites of his meatball sandwich that he couldn't even remember ordering.

Trevor was either starting or continuing a story. James wasn't sure.

"The second girl I made it with in Victorville. She died. She had a brain anarchy, I think," said Trevor, despite a mouthful of vermicelli.

"Probably an aneurysm," corrected Noe, putting the finishing touches on his sandwich.

"Yeah yeah. You shoulda' seen it. She brings me to her house. She's wearing this short skirt that's almost up to her ass. Wants some help with her Spanish, but she was part French. Her mom was from France. She asks me what all the cuss words are in Spanish. So I go through them. You know hell and damn and bitch and bastard and shit, but when I get to fuck, chinga, she says, "So chinga means fuck," and I can see it in her eyes. Man she had the whole thing planned and I took the bait, hook, line, and sinker. Damn best bait I ever tasted, and then she died like six months later. You gonna finish that last meatball?"

The meatball was forked and placed in Trevor's mouth, before James could even say go ahead. James decided there was very little in life that had meaning, just a bunch of actions driven down the freeway of life until one got to the end of the road. But Kristen was worth so much more than a meatball or a piece of ass or a story you could tell that made everyone laugh. James looked at Trevor chewing on the best of Biagio's, understanding that Trevor's stories were the only triumphs, that made him feel he was floating on top of the water instead of struggling to breathe six feet under. Trevor still hadn't grown up and still hadn't left the past where it needed to lie.

"I gotta go," said James.

"Whatcha gonna do?" asked Noe.

"I don't know. Hey thanks for lunch," replied James.

"Hey. Were you guys doin' it?" asked Trevor.

"Do you ever talk about anything else?" replied James, seething at Trevor's insensitivity.

"Is anything else important?" responded Trevor, wiping the edge of his mouth.

Noe cut in before James had a chance to boil over. "Are you going to go to the funeral?"

"I hadn't even thought of that," said James.

"I'll go with you if you want," supported Noe.

112

"Dead pussy. Man what a waste," chimed in the out-of-tune Trevor.

James just shook his head, wanting to kick the shit out of Trevor, and walked to the door, not even looking toward the kitchen or back at Noe and Trevor, awaiting his first step into the blinding sun outside.

Where would Kristen's funeral be held, he wondered, as he returned to the confines of home. He googled Burbank Mortuaries and found O'Connor and Pierce Brothers and Burbank Funeral Home and Valley Funeral and even Forest Lawn, the resting destination of many of the rich and famous in Hollywood. James wasn't even sure there would be a funeral, but he was determined to be there if there was. He dialed the number for Forest Lawn and was pleased to learn that his first try was all that was needed. The funeral was scheduled for three in the afternoon on Friday at the Wee Kirk O' the Heather in Forest Lawn with limited seating. James was informed to be there early if he wanted a seat as many people were expected to attend the service. With Forest Lawn being no more than fifteen minutes away, James knew being there on time would not be a problem. He allowed himself his first sigh since realizing Kristen was gone.

He went into the kitchen and found yesterday's paper still open to the story that would change his life. The story that Noe's mother had read. The story that Noe had then read. The phone calls Noe placed to James to make him aware of Kristen's death. The phone call at lunch where James finally connected with Noe. James leaving work to stop at the 7-Eleven and buy a paper and then read the story himself. James' trip to the scene of the accident on Magnolia Boulevard. And then his sad, sad, call to Kristen's phone, hoping to hear her voice. One step after another down the road of destiny. A chain of events that can change the course of the future. If Noe's mother had never mentioned the death, if Noe had let the comments fly in one ear and out the other. If James had waited at the stop sign only a little longer. If, if, if. If James only knew that the woman that died wasn't the Kristen Taylor he

113

had met at Scully's, wasn't the beauty he had seen at the end of the bar, wasn't the same young lady whose kiss had melted his heart, wasn't the woman he wanted to hold hands with for eternity. She was a different Kristen Taylor. A cruel coincidence, the death of a young lady with the same name, the same age, living in the same city. It was providence, javelining an arrow of mistaken identity through his heart.

Another deep sigh emanated unconsciously from him as he started reading the article again. His eyes didn't rush over the sentences, instead slowly digesting each difficult word. What the witness said was the most difficult part of life and death to comprehend.

Miles Harrison, a witness, was unsettled by the accident. Harrison, walking with his wife and two children, Jason, 4, and Ben, 2, had walked past Ms. Taylor, moments before the accident. Said a distraught Mr. Harrison, "She had just patted Jason on the head and said I hope I have kids this cute some day. They are adorable."

"Three seconds later she was gone. We didn't see the car hit her. She was beautiful. Her smile was beautiful. One moment. One moment. It could have been my whole family. One moment. I can't believe so much life left so quickly."

"I hope I have kids this cute some day."

Kristen's last words were enough to create an earthquake of silent sobs in James. She could have had James' children. They could have walked their child to the first day of kindergarten. They could have felt their children's little arms around their necks, squeezing the purity of innocent love through them. They could have. They would have. The emptiness in his eyes mirrored the emptiness in his heart.

The last thing that the witness, Miles Harrison, said was crushing. "I can't believe so much life left so quickly." So much life. Kristen was the epitome of life as far as James was concerned, the quintessential element of a meaningful existence. Ken didn't appreciate the treasure he had in Kristen, but James knew a woman like this was one in fifty million. For James she was perfect. He read the sentence again, "I can't believe so much life left so quickly." James backed his chair away from the table and went looking for scissors. He knew he had a pair; he just couldn't remember ever using them. He opened the junk drawer in the kitchen, the most likely place, he thought, for a pair of scissors to be, but among the throwaway realtor pads, loose pens and pencils, scotch tape, and faded Biagio menus, two Taylor Made golf balls, three tees, and a remote control to a television long since disappeared, the scissors didn't exist. Four other drawers were opened with the missing pair of scissors still remaining hidden. He finally found them in his night stand under a copy of Fitzgerald's *Great Gatsby*. He wasn't sure why he still had that book or what made him look underneath it for the pair of scissors, but there they were, just waiting to be found. He walked to the newspaper and carefully clipped the article of Kristen's death. He trimmed the excess off the right edge of the article and then folded the article neatly, removed his wallet from his back pocket, and meticulously placed the story inside one of the flaps. James patted the wallet, almost caressed the wallet, as he returned it to his back pocket, walked to the window and contemplated the wind rustling the leaves, contemplated the shadow of the lamppost, contemplated the crushed beer can on the sidewalk, contemplated the wilted rose on the bush. "I can't believe so much life left so quickly." James nodded to himself and knew Kristen would be with him forever. He knew that he would never take life for granted. He knew that life would never be fair. How could it? But he knew no matter how dark the skies might be, he would always be ready for the first ray of sun. He would always be prepared to protect so much life from leaving so suddenly ever again. Posthumously, Kristen would always be with him.

115

Chapter 13

With only her panties and bra on, Kristen danced around the bedroom to Christina Aguilera's "You're Beautiful" in her head. She pirouetted three times at the corner of the bed, and then ran like a ballerina and leaped through the air, not a very elegant leap, with an exhilaration unknown to these bedroom walls for the last two years. An adjustment in attitude can do more for the soul than twenty years of exercise can do for the body. The resentment she had felt toward Ken, his money, his demands, his lack of affection, his inability to have a meaningful conversation, his love of a car that could be tuned to perfection without his having to lift a finger, had been washed away. The molten lava from her meltdown had cooled to form a new surface of life, one that had enabled a seed of conversation to grow into a relationship that with enough watering and care and gardening could possibly spur a continuous ripening of her life. Of course, there remained in her an unanswered question that gnawed through the lining of her stomach: What had made James change so dramatically?

What had she done wrong? What had made him cry his sorrow into the phone? The feeling lingered. Was it something she had said or done? She did miss the way he spoke, the way he made her laugh, the way he touched her. This morning when she awoke and found an arm holding her tightly, she first imagined it must be James, only to find, only to happily find, it was Ken's arm, the one that usually just hung by his side, that was for a change wrapped around her.

Last night they had gone to the Castaway for dinner, a clear evening, with the lights of their future shining in the distance. Ken was actually talking about the absurdity of the case he was working on, a lawsuit against one of his clients, Zingy's, a line of women's apparel. Mrs. Jerome Jinstur was suing the company for their responsibility in not procuring a job she interviewed for and, Mrs. Jinstur knew, she was, without question, the best candidate for the position. She claimed a thread on the side of her dress was found dangling, taking the focus off of her responses. She said she saw the eyes of Mr. Jessup, head of Human Resources, drifting to the side of her body where the thread dangled. She had bought the dress the day before specifically for the interview. A dangling thread. Ken laughed every time he said "a dangling thread." The smile on Ken's face was unmistakable. Kristen had reached across the table and squeezed his hand. "I think we are going to be okay," was all she said. He nodded his head toward her and affirmed her thoughts. She was marrying a person, not a machine, and she would make this work. In a little more than a week, she would be Mrs. Ken Anderson.

What a difference an epiphany can make. The idea she held dear to her heart, seemingly cemented there forever, is suddenly thrown out the window, and run over by a steamroller, flattened, unable to rise, replaced, repaved by a different understanding. The attitude of yesterday resurfaced by the fresh perspective of today. Kristen rock and rolled into her closest and twirled a yellow sun dress from the hanger and shimmied it over her shoulders and body. She half turned in the mirror and made sure the bra straps fashionably showed under the spaghetti straps of the gown. How the times of fashion change. Bra straps showing. An absurdity ten years ago. An act of embarrassment or class level or even sleaziness, now as mainstream as Led Zeppelin, that rebellious band of the past, that band that broke the walls of decency, that is now accepted as classical.

"Money is the root of all evil" had been cemented to every vein in Kristen's body, but a jackhammer of attitude had broken the foundation of that belief into pieces. Why did money have to be so bad? Kristen was ready to embrace Ken's wealth, to enjoy what very few ever have the opportunity to experience. How can you worry about the other ninety-eight percent of the population, almost seven billion people? Not everyone can afford to take lessons from the best teachers, not everyone has the opportunity to surf the best waves or climb the highest mountains, not everyone can afford tickets to the Super Bowl, to the Final Four, to the Masters, to shows on Broadway, to shows in London, to shows in Paris, not everyone can taste the delicacies of the finest chefs in the world, not everyone has the money to treat himself to the very best life has to offer. Not everyone can fly first class. Kristen was, beyond a doubt, fortunate and she would appreciate her good fortune. Today she would love herself and shower herself in the luxuries of life that she had fought so hard against. Money wouldn't change the goodness of her heart. After shopping today, the hangers in her closet would be shouldered by famous names, and the tubes and jars of cosmetics would be worth an ounce of gold. She remembered Julia Roberts in *Pretty Woman*, shopping on Rodeo Drive and thought they'd better not make the same mistake they made with her. And the first person she would share her good fortune with would be her sister, Kathy. Today would be a feast of pampering to bite into.

When she arrived at Kathy's, Kristen had barely opened the front door of her car when Kathy flew over the front lawn and eased excitedly into the front seat.

"I am ready for the Jungle Cruise. I love Adventureland," said an animated Kathy, as happy as Kristen had seen her in years, or since she had said "I do" to Frank.

"You're in a good mood!" exclaimed Kristen.

"Just start the car and let's go. One last fling, just the two of us, before the big day."

"We have to start doing more."

"Yeah, we do," added Kathy securing her seat belt.

Kathy floated above the clouds as they soared over Barham Boulevard into Hollywood and down Highland Avenue until a valet opened their doors and welcomed them to Ivy's, rumored to be one of the best spa experiences in Southern California. Kathy couldn't wait for the revenge of a five-hour pampering at the hands and fingers of the staff at Ivy's. How many times had she boiled over with an eight-hour round of golf that brought Frank through the door at three on a Saturday afternoon, only to fall asleep like a sad sack of potatoes on the couch.

For the next five hours, the two sisters luxuriated in steam, with cucumbers over eyes, with hot rocks on the body, with fingers caressing and digging delightfully into tissue. Five hours of stretching the skin and wearing masks, pumpkin spice or cinnamon candy or celery clay, and feeling that breathing lavender or peppermint or vanilla was a delight. As Kristen's masseuse kneaded her shoulders, Kristen could feel whatever tension remained from the last two years being expelled from her body, an exorcism of the anxiety she had felt. Whatever had bedeviled her was now wafting in the vanilla atmosphere of the room. The two sisters sat in chairs never seen at a dining room table, waiting for their nails to be treated like royalty, each finger as worthy as an amendment to the constitution, each palm as important as roots to a tree. Waiting for their toenails to become a blank canvas, for an artist with a small, very small brush to paint a scene ready for them to hang, to exhibit, in the museum of an opened toe shoe. When Kristen and Kathy left Ivy's, they wondered what drug they

119

had been slipped. They were intoxicated with life well above the legal limit.

Rodeo Drive was their last stop before their return to normal. As they entered Roberto Cavalli, a young man, dressed impeccably in a Ralph Lauren charcoal suit, asked to help, and then backed out of the way. Kristen couldn't keep a straight face at the nineteen-hundred-dollar price of a beige and chartreuse cape, obviously made from the finest materials. When they left the store, he didn't even look in their direction, knowing they were not people he would consider clients. At Celine's, Kristen purchased a pair of calf skin and python shoes for six hundred dollars. She took a deep breath when she went to the counter, trying not to give away the extreme fear swelling in her breast that a judge would slam a gavel on the polished marble counter and scream guilty of one count of materialism. Even though Ken drank ridiculously expensive alcohol, six hundred dollars for a pair of shoes was still out of Kristen's comfort zone. But today Kristen would try to enjoy her good fortune.

"Will that be all?" said the young lady behind the counter.

Kristen nodded, as she handed her plastic across the counter and opened her wallet to her driver's license.

The girl behind the counter paused for a second and searched for the right words. "My friend … was also named Kristen Taylor."

Kristen was still trying to justify six hundred dollars for a pair of shoes. Her epiphany on value and the cards she had been dealt wasn't as easy as she thought. She was holding four aces of financial security with Ken, but she still imagined it was a losing hand. "Yeah, I imagine there are a lot of Kristen Taylors in the world," she replied, still shuffling the cards in the deck of opportunity.

Exhausted and happy and a little guilty, as Kristen felt the pangs of conscience, the two sisters headed home.

"Once you're married, we need to make a point of getting together. Maybe Ken can take up golf," said Kathy. "I know I'll have to if this marriage is ever going to work."

"I'm not sure golf is up Ken's alley."

"I guess the cold feet aren't so cold anymore."

"They were almost frozen there for a while. I don't know. Sometimes you think you know something and then the next minute you don't know why you felt that way. I blew up the other day."

"At Ken?"

"Yeah. He looks better than he tastes," said a laughing Kristen, proud of the wittiness of her comment.

"He looks perfect."

"My point exactly."

"What happened?"

"I was just stupid. Thought the grass was greener on the other side of the pasture. I thought there must be someone out there who was better for me than Ken was. I thought Cinderella had found the wrong Prince Charming."

"So?"

"So when I blew up, Ken actually turned out to be much more of a prince than I had ever given him credit. I found out the king of the castle he was raised by wasn't so benevolent. His dad sounds like a jerk behind all his money and power. Ken's not perfect, but he'll do."

"Well, I think Frank must have fallen in the moat in front of the castle. That's about as close to the palace as we will ever get."

The taillights of Kristen's car dimmed as she drove toward Kathy's house. The dusk was settling over the valley and the trees along the side of the road stood silent and straight, silhouettes in the windless sky.

121

Chapter 14

Ten minutes to three. How difficult could it possibly be to drive three miles in fifteen minutes? James had left his house at twenty after two to arrive early and without any problem to Forest Lawn. He had the option, which he took, of saving three minutes by way of the freeway, or choosing instead the extra lights and distance and little chance of accidents that the surface streets used as a lure. The stretch of the freeway from Hollywood Way to Forest Lawn Drive, less than three miles, was never crowded, not even during rush hour. So why, today of all days, was a lady with a brown scarf out of her car, smoking a cigarette? Why was a man in plaid shorts and a striped shirt and an oversized belly walking a Scottish terrier between the fast lane and the shoulder? Because a cement truck lost its balance and spilled its guts onto the freeway, when cut off by an angry motorist. James had already sat for half an hour, without moving. He was only a hundred yards past the Buena Vista off-ramp.

James knew that the system of freeways flowing through and around Los Angeles was an enigma, a puzzle where the pieces seldom fit. He knew to stay away from downtown Los Angeles between six and nine in the morning and between three and seven in the evening. He knew that the Five from the interchange, where the Ten and Thirty and the 101 all meet is usually a disaster and that the 405 is extremely dangerous through Santa Monica. But those are small border pieces of the entire traffic puzzle that James always faced living where he did. But this piece of the freeway, from Hollywood Way to Forest Lawn. This should have been a piece of cake.

When James saw the jiggling striped shirt of a man with a gray poodle on a leash jogging slowly past his truck, he checked his rear view mirror. He noticed the police had made a break in the traffic behind him. Cars were turning around and taking the Buena Vista Street off ramp. Maybe, he thought, checking his watch, he could still make it to the church in time for some of the ceremony. He could almost touch Forest Lawn across the flood channel, but knew he had to take a circuitous route to finally reach his destination. Why hadn't he just taken the side streets to begin with? How could a seemingly innocuous decision stop him from something that was so important, being on time to Kristen's funeral? Why had an innocent stroll down the sidewalk of a city street ended in such tragedy? James' anxiety and anger faded, as thoughts of Kristen's last fateful day crept through his consciousness.

At twenty minutes after three, James finally arrived at the church. No one was outside in the overflow area, and James straightened his tie and shrugged his shoulders, as he opened the large door a couple of feet. A sea of black coats and black dresses with an occasional buoy of color drifted in front of him. Three other men besides James stood in the back, behind the filled pews. A dark casket surrounded by flowers was propped in front, and a large picture of Kristen rested on an easel, although, from where James stood, he could barely see her features.

The absurdity of life. James was late to the funeral, despite his best effort to be early. If he had been on time, a seat

123

close to the front would have shown him that the picture of the deceased was not the Kristen of his dreams, was not the person he thought had died, was not the tragic victim that he had assumed, was not the person in the article in his back pocket. But today a cement truck had overturned, and his heart was still a broken stone. And now he was in the middle of an ocean of grief, of eighty people crushed by the loss of their Kristen Taylor, dumbfounded that their lovely girl of twenty-seven had her life pulled from her as quickly as a cork from a bottle of wine, never having the opportunity to age.

A tearful young lady continued speaking from the microphone on the stage. "…in the night. She was my sister. When she was thirteen she wondered what she could eat that would make her breasts grow, and being the older sister, of course I told her…liver. And that night she asked Mom to make liver. She never forgave me… I don't know why. I don't know. In high school she was so proud when she was the president of Uganda in her United Model Nations class and thought she was Nelson Mandela, the president of Uganda. Oh, Kristen…

The tears around the chapel flowed like the tide, and James' eyes were as awash in tears as everyone else's. The sound of tissue and noses resonated through the room.

"I will never get to hold your children. I will never get to hear you say 'I do'. I will never get to grow old with my sister, my best friend, my spirit, my confidante, my… Thank you so much for coming. Kristen would be so happy to see how much she was loved." James' eyes flooded with water. He turned away from the man standing on his left, a stoic jerk, who had just checked his phone for messages.

As Kristen's sister sat down, the pastor started sermonizing about God's will and Kristen's place in heaven and how a belief in Jesus Christ would give everlasting salvation, and many heads nodded like seals in agreement. James surveyed the church for a sign of Kristen's parents and for Ken, the one she was trying to escape from, the one who had a treasure in his hands and

124

had no idea of the value. Finally, the priest added, "Kristen's family would like all of you to stop by her sister's house for a chance to remember and rekindle Kristen's life and to thank you for all you have done for her. Please ask an usher for the directions. Thank you."

As the congregants arose from their seats and headed for the exits, hugging many around them, James, an island of sadness, reached for directions from an usher and pushed through the door to the sunshine outside. The directions showed that her sister lived in North Hollywood on Chandler Boulevard, not very far from the church, and James wondered if he should go. Who was he anyway? A guy Kristen had met in a bar and talked to and kissed. He would leave that out. James felt he owed it to Kristen. He knew there was no one else like her. She was his perfection. She was his diamond. She was the woman of more than his dreams; she was to have been his future of brilliant colors and sounds and tastes.

As James drove towards North Hollywood, he stopped at Scully's. He wanted the others who had assembled for the funeral to arrive before he did. He paused after entering the foyer and scanned the pictures hanging on the wall, the wall of fame from the glossy fresh to the faded portraits of the past. The newest was from Jimmy Fallon who had just finished his six- year stint with *Saturday Night Live* and Jay Leno, the host of the *Tonight Show*. Tom Brokaw, long-time anchor of the nightly news wrote an inscription on his picture: "Scully's is the news." There was the cast of *Friends*, with Jennifer Aniston and Courtney Cox, lying on a couch with their feet in the air, pointing at each other, while the rest of the cast points at them. Another picture read only, *Cheer*s and the autographs of Sam and Diane, and a ton of other names and pictures that James hadn't heard of or just forgot who they were. A picture of someone named Jack Paar and someone named Johnny Carson. Of someone named Goldie Hawn and Rowan and Martin and something called *Laugh In*. Scully's had seen enough fame walk through the front door for a hundred restaurants, but for James the best memory was walking though the door the week after meeting Kristen and realizing the goddess sitting at the bar was actually her.

At four fifteen on a Friday evening, there were other suits and ties, some loosened, around the bar, enjoying a libation of their choice before fighting the rush hour traffic of the evening. A group of five women sat on the edge of their stools, leaning toward the left and then toward the right and then throwing their heads back in laughter. One old man sat in the last seat around the corner of the bar, and James speculated he was waiting for an unsuspecting young lady to swim into his pool of degradation. James recalled a setting not too different from this less than a month ago when he had seen that goddess, Kristen.

He grabbed a stool next to the old man and found he misjudged the gray hair and spectacles on the edge of his nose. "Let me buy ya a drink. You look like you could use one."

"Thanks. But just a Sprite," said James.

"My grandson is crazy about Sprite. Thinks it is the best thing ever made. The kid is only seven, but he keeps me laughing. My daughter should be here with him any minute," said the now respectable old man.

The man was gone within a minute, meeting his daughter at the entrance with a hug, and picking up his grandson, seemingly weighing him with his hands, and then returning him to the earth. James was alone with his Sprite. No black eye or woman wearing flats. Just a heavy heart. He was surprisingly calm, nursing sips of sweet soda from a straw. He glanced at a meaningless puck being whistled around an ice rink in New York as the Rangers and Blackhawks were engaged. He was estranged from the outcome of their game. He could care less who won or lost, but his eyes still followed the movement of the puck.

Halfway through the period, after a slap shot trickled under the pads and behind the Blackhawk goalie and the red light lit excitedly, James removed himself from the stool, pushed the empty glass of Sprite to the edge of the bar, checked his watch, and readied himself to face Kristen's family.

James watched as a lady in a gray dress, balanced a pink pastry box in her hand while walking up a driveway. She was the clue James was waiting to see as he drove past the appointed house on Chandler. After finding a parking spot around the corner, he felt naked approaching the house with nothing to offer. He had only known Kristen less than two weeks and knew none of the people that would be mourning inside, yet the overwhelming desire to know her, propelled him past the junipers lining the driveway, past the camellias flowering under the windows, through the screen door, and inside the house. A few men in their fifties populated the front room, the walls sparse with pictures, with an indistinguishable sofa and easy chair and forty-inch television above the fireplace and a lamp with a faded red shade. James walked through the kitchen, a gas stove, a sixty-inch Amana refrigerator and little counter space, updated recently with granite that matched nothing in the house. He passed through twenty to thirty people, and went through the back door, where he found a guy his own age bending over a cooler, pulling a Heineken from the ice. James grabbed the top of the cooler before it could close and extracted a bottle of water.

"How'd you know Kristen?" James asked the man who had pulled the beer from the cooler. James was pleased to be away from the crowd inside.

The man, about twenty-eight James assumed, paused as he twisted the cap from the Heineken. His tie loosened into a loop on his collar. His dirty-blonde hair, a couple inches in length, ran wild and untrained on his head. "We'd been friends forever. We grew up together. And then I moved away and started my family in Boise, Idaho. I can't believe she's gone. We went to the senior prom together in high school. I always thought that we would get married some day. You know how those thoughts are when you're young. So strong."

127

"You're still living in Boise? You just came down for the funeral?" asked James.

"My dad still lives down here. He called me when it happened. My dad always said she would be perfect for me. Even in the ninth grade ... man ya never know. I always think about cars coming up on sidewalks when I'm just minding my own business."

"She was pretty special."

"You an old boyfriend?"

"I guess you could say that."

"Did she ever sing for you?" I always thought she could make it as a singer. That's all she ever talked about. They let her sing at the senior prom. What a voice."

James realized that there was just so much he didn't know about her. How he would have loved to hear her sing. Although she had never mentioned a love for music or singing, James understood that the time he knew her was only a fraction of her life, and that fraction had been enough for him to multiply into a whole number of love. James knew that whatever had happened in her past had made her who she was, and she was the diamond James had always hoped to discover. Now she was singing with the angels.

"Were you coming down for the wedding?" asked James.

The eyes of the wild hair squinted questioningly at James and then turned to the approaching figure behind him.

"There you are. Fanny and Franklin are in the living room. They wondered if you had come down. I told 'em I'd find you," said a man dressed in a black suit, as he neared them.

The wild hair nodded with his Heineken in hand and left James alone with the cooler. James assumed Kristen's senior prom date would have been invited to the wedding and would have been in attendance. James returned to the house, dodged three young children holding chocolate chip cookies, stepped around a group of four whispering quietly and shaking their heads sadly, then found himself inching along the perimeter of the room, checking the walls for clues to Kristen's past, but the walls were devoid of evidence.

"You look a little lost. I haven't seen you before," said a woman, well past fifty, her graying hair covering the back of a lavender scarf.

James considered her for a second, knew it was time to leave, and glanced around the room, before speaking. "Yeah. I am a little lost." He walked past the luncheon meats and cheeses spread on the white linen cloth over the dining room table, past a bouquet of red zinnias and pink carnations and white roses, past a young lady stooped over a book of memories, past her sister, the one speaking at the funeral when he arrived, wearing a picture of Kristen on her lapel that he didn't look at, past the three plates hung above the front door, each plate a different word, faith and hope and love, and then out the front door and past a man carrying the funeral picture of Kristen into the house, the picture facing away from James.

When James reached his truck and climbed in the cab, he took his wallet out of his back pocket and fished his fingers into the flap and pulled out the article. He sat quietly as he unfolded the story and stared at the words. "So much life could leave so quickly."

Chapter 15

Ken was statuesque in his black tuxedo as he smiled at the approaching Kristen, her white gloved hand through the crook of her father's arm. All of the wedding guests were on their feet, their eyes glued to the radiant bride as she made her way toward Ken as Mendelssohn's Wedding March guided her steps. Kristen was at peace with her decision to marry Ken, at peace with the vow that each of them would remain faithful. That despite the circumstances, whether rich or poor, whether sick or healthy, whether the times are good or whether they are bad, that from now until death would part them, she and Ken would be there for each other.

Only three weeks before, Kristen had been as stable as an earthquake, but now, as she was only feet away from her husband-to-be, she knew the Cinderella story of romance was only a fairy tale for the big screen and not the flesh and blood of real life. James had been an imaginary minor character thrown into the plot to prove that there is no perfection in people. Just when she thought the ending was going to say "happily ever after", she turned the page to find a bus running over the ending that she had desired. Kristen wrapped her arms around her father's neck when she was inches from Ken and then clasped Ken's hand as the priest welcomed them.

Looking into Ken's eyes, Kristen saw a lifetime of challenges. For two years she had hidden her resentment toward Ken until it had come out in a torrent of angry passion, and although her eruption had helped heal some of her wounds, as well as Ken's, there was still much to do. The last few days had been some of their best: a two-hour dinner at Joe's in Venice, where more conversation was consumed than food; a drive from Malibu to Oxnard on Highway 1, where they listened and laughed hysterically to Jeff Foxworthy explain how you know if someone is a redneck. They even played a game of tennis at McCambridge Park, even though Kristen hadn't played in years and it was obvious Ken hadn't either. Kristen knew she was lucky to be in such a position, knew she was lucky to be marrying Ken, knew that Kenny Rogers was right, "You've gotta know when to hold em, know when to fold em." She knew it was time to hold on to Ken. A few weeks ago, she was ready to throw in her cards, to toss Ken into the muck, to fold this hand that on the outside looked like it couldn't lose, desiring the hand that James offered, that didn't appear to be that strong, but that she knew, that she felt would give her an unmatched future, but those cards of James' turned out to be worse than she had supposed. Fools gold. A bluff. She would be thirty in three years and how many more chances were going to walk down a city street and bend at the knee and propose to her? A bird in the hand is worth two in the bush, and she had Ken in her hand, and Kristen didn't imagine there would be two birds taking up residence in the shrubbery any time soon. Better to stick out her ring finger and see a large diamond sparkling in the sunlight than to take the chance of a finger with only a worn and wrinkled knuckle to look at.

"Do you have the rings? Repeat after me," said the priest nodding toward the best man, who teasingly searched his pocket like so many others had, and then miraculously found the gem. "I, Ken Anderson…"

Kristen smiled as the ring slid onto her finger. Minutes later they turned to the crowd as the priest introduced them for the first time, Mr. and Mrs. Ken Anderson.

The awakening sun lightened the French doors in the wedding suite of the Wellsley Resort in Fiji. With silk sheets caressing her naked body, Kristen rolled onto her side and sighed and closed her eyes again in the comfort of her memories. Last night, Ken had swept her off her feet and carried her over the threshold and onto the bed. The atmosphere of Fiji worked wonders. Away from the office, away from his father, away from his Porsche, Ken was a different person as he explored her body with a passion he had never shown. A honeymoon in Fiji would be the first step of the rest of their lives, and Kristen was sure that Ken would remain a changed man. Kristen's hand sought for the reassurance of Ken's chest, or his stomach, or his arm, or any part of his body, but her fingers only found the coolness of the silk sheets.

Kristen eased out of bed and stretched her body. The body that had been explored with passion eight hours earlier was now seen only by the rays of the morning sun. Ken's head was bent over a computer and hadn't turned to witness Kristen's rising. "Go back to bed. I just have to tie up a few loose ends."

"Last night was wonderful," Kristen cooed.

"I'm almost done. A half hour at the most."

"Ken. We're on our honeymoon," said Kristen without any cooing.

"A half hour. That's all I need."

"I'll get us some coffee and bagels."

Ken's head didn't move nor did his eyes. Kristen could have walked naked to the coffee shack and Ken wouldn't have known, but she slipped on a skirt and blouse and flip flops and quietly closed the door. When she returned ten minutes later, she

132

placed a cup of coffee next to the computer, stroked his neck without a response, and found the toaster in the kitchenette.

When the bagels, burnt to a crisp, popped from the toaster, Kristen was embarrassed and thought it was not a very good introduction to her skill as a chef. Boiling water, she had down, but number two, toasting bread, needed a little work. She was pretty sure that after another twenty years of marriage she would have perfected toast. She covered the burned surface with a layer of walnut cream cheese and placed the bagel a foot away from Ken's left hand. Mechanically he took a bite.

"Oh my god! What is this?"

"I burned the bagel."

"You burned the bagel? How can you burn a bagel?"

"It wasn't easy," said Kristen, taken aback by the seriousness of Ken's tone.

"And then you gave me the burned bagel like I wouldn't taste it. Why would you do that?"

"I'll go get another bagel."

"I don't want another fucking bagel. You shouldn't have burned this one. What, you don't know how to use a toaster?"

"Give me the bagel, Ken. You're being a baby." An irritated Kristen snatched the bagel from Ken and left. She returned a few minutes later with another bagel, properly toasted, and gently laid the peace offering next to Ken's hand and gently brushed the back of his neck. She knew she had been rejected by the shrug of his shoulder to the touch of her hand.

"I hope you didn't get me another bagel," Ken said, his voice calm, his eyes never leaving the computer screen. "But if you did, just don't burn this one."

Kristen couldn't help but think about James and the softness of his voice and the calmness of his character, but there was obviously something about him that she didn't know and would never, she felt, ever find out. What had made him turn so quickly, she couldn't help but wonder? What was it that had made James 'so sorry?' But she had made her wedding vows with Ken, and in good times and in bad she would be there for him, whether it was bagels burning or computers consuming. The first morning of their honeymoon hadn't been the best beginning of "until death do us part," but Rome wasn't built in a day.

After a long shower, a very long shower, Kristen was prepared for the day. Her turquoise bikini exhibited just enough skin to excite, and her flat toned stomach was more than enough to add even more excitement. She entered the room of the burnt bagel and noticed the chair in front of the computer was vacant. Ken was sitting in front of the television, something he rarely did at home, since he was always working. He was immersed in a Discovery Channel documentary on the Space Shuttle Columbia that had disintegrated when it reentered the atmosphere killing all seven astronauts on board.

"They said at the front desk that the snorkeling is great. Right in front of us," offered Kristen, with the conviction that the history of the bagel was long forgotten. "Do you want to go?"

"This is almost over. Go ahead and go. I'll meet you out there."

"Why don't I just wait for you? I can start reading Auster's new book."

"Did you know that when a spaceship returns to earth, the temperature can reach over two thousand degrees Fahrenheit?" retorted Ken, still enchanted by the images on the screen.

Kristen didn't even bother to respond. She didn't want to reach a boiling point of her own in their honeymoon suite, so she calmly closed the front door on her way out. Her sheer white linen summer dress left little to the imagination, and as she made her way to pick up her snorkeling gear, two middle-aged men made little effort to camouflage the lust in their eyes as she passed their turning heads.

Floating on top of the ocean with her face and mask gazing through the water, Kristen was soon lost in the underwater world of her own. Fish were everywhere. The city of Manhattan on a summer day. Kristen didn't know their names, just an

134

underwater population going about their business, immune to the plastic face mask watching them dart about. Some had vertical stripes of blue and yellow and white, some wider vertical stripes of blue and white and a flippant gray tail. Some had even wider vertical separations of white and black with a solid yellow tail, and many smaller fish light purple, some orange, some blue. Even a sea turtle slowly swam by, its little legs paddling ahead.

Kristen felt exhilarated. She wanted to jump out of the water, yank Ken off the couch, and introduce him to this hidden spectacular world of color and commerce. Her fins continued to move her through the current to different locations, each a part of the underwater city she was examining. As she moved a little further out, a hundred yards at the most, two manta rays, at least ten feet in width, oblivious to her presence, swam underneath her, stopped for a couple of seconds and then continued toward the shore, veered to the right, and then swam underneath her a second time and then disappeared into deeper waters. If the sea turtle had caused exhilaration, the manta rays had broken the sound barrier of emotion. Kristen wanted to scream orgasmically, but the snorkel in her mouth stopped any sound from emanating underwater. She knew she had to yank Ken off the honeymoon suite couch and drag him down to the water. This was too amazing to miss. Her arms and fins became a whirlwind of movement as she headed toward the shore.

Her white linen dress clung to her even more seductively, turning even more eyes, as she hurried toward the room. Ken's bare back was once again hunched over the computer screen.

"Ken. We are turning off the computer and you are coming with me." she said excitedly. "You wouldn't believe it. Two manta rays! Oh my god! Two manta rays swam right underneath me. And then swam underneath me again. It was the most amazing thing I have ever seen. You have got to see this! There are so many fish and so many colors." She was almost too excited to talk.

"I'm almost done."

135

"No. You're done or I'm going Mount Vesuvius on you," Kristen said, pulling Ken from the chair as he was hitting "sleep" on the computer.

It took Ken five minutes to properly dress for the water, fins and snorkel and mask, as he listened to Kristen ramble about the underwater world she had just populated. He wasn't excited.

For two minutes they swam on the upper lanes of the ocean watching the city unfold underneath them when Kristen spotted a sea turtle ahead of her. She grabbed Ken's ankle to redirect him toward the turtle, when his leg flinched spasmodically, and he surfaced quickly.

"What are you doing?" he said agitatedly.

Kristen rose from the water, unsure of what Ken was saying. "What happened? Did you see that sea turtle?"

"I don't need this. You grabbed my leg. I thought it was a shark. Scared the shit out of me."

"A shark?"

"Shit! I'm going in. You might like this, but I don't." Ken's hair glistened in the sun. The muscles in his shoulders and arms were taut and strong. His jaw was the epitome of strength. Kristen wondered why he was being so weak.

"I thought you were a god damn shark," Ken snarled for the last time and swam toward shore. Kristen tried removing the stinger of Ken's words and put her mask back in the water. She was delighted to return to the peaceful city of gills and fins and little mouths puckering without speaking.

When she left the ocean, she didn't even bother returning to the room to find Ken. She located an empty lounge by the pool and prepared to catch her breath in the warmth of the sun, before returning to her suddenly less than idyllic honeymoon. The sun felt good on her body, as the salt water of the ocean sparkled on her skin. Soon she walked to the edge of the pool and jumped in, cooling her warm skin and just as quickly climbed back out and onto her lounge.

"Are you here by yourself?" she heard a voice ask her.

136

She turned to see a middle aged man, maybe fifty, with a daiquiri in his hand.

"No. I'm on my honeymoon. We just got married on Saturday."

"Where's your husband?"

"He's inside. He had a little last minute business call to take care of."

"Last minute business on a honeymoon?"

'He's a lawyer."

"I hope he knows if he leaves you alone too long, you'll be hiring a lawyer of your own."

"That's not very nice."

"I don't wish anything bad for anyone. It's just that he shouldn't be leaving a pretty lady like yourself alone, especially on her honeymoon. Best of luck to you," he said, somewhat embarrassed as he sauntered off to find a lounge chair of his own.

"I wish me the best of luck, too. Thanks," whispered Kristen to herself. With that Kristen headed toward the room. Not even forty-eight hours since the wedding had ended and already Ken was from a different planet, an alien she didn't know. When she had exploded and thrown Ken's computer against the mirror, he changed. That Ken had started talking and listening and seemingly cared about what Kristen said and thought and wanted. Even the Ken last night had made love to her like he had never done before, but this morning and afternoon had yielded the sun and a beautiful underwater city, and her husband, Ken. Her husband, who couldn't handle the grabbing of an ankle or the burning of a bagel. Kristen didn't know what to expect when she arrived at their honeymoon suite door.

Chapter 16

The pool cue was steady in James' hand as he pointed to the corner pocket with the tip of the stick. He bent over the rail of the pool table, his eyes shifting between the eight ball and the white ball, and then drained the eight ball right where he expected.

"Damn, James, you are hotter than a college freshman without panties," said Trevor, as he leaned his cue against the back wall of Scully's.

"I'm hoping you are talking about a freshman chick," said Noe, gathering the pool balls from the different pockets and preparing them to be broken apart from their solid triangular position into the chaos of a new game. Noe slid the white ball down the green felt of the table where James waited to see which balls would be his in this new game.

With a solid strike from the cue, the balls scattered in all directions, with the four ball disappearing into the side pocket. "Solid," said James, as Noe chalked his stick and awaited his turn. As James walked around the table, planning his next sequence of shots, Noe's eyes had a heightened sense of awareness as two young ladies inhabited the pool table adjacent to theirs. One was sipping the head of the beer that had just been poured, then wiped her hand across her mouth to erase the slight foam mustache that had been there a moment before. Her long hair was pulled back in a ponytail that hung just below her shoulders; her short skirt and lace blouse said more night club than it did pool table. Her opponent was dressed just as provocatively, short white skirt with calf length boots and a red and black blouse that was happily unbuttoned enough for ample cleavage to be seen. Noe nodded to James in their direction as he circled the table. When his eyes left the balls on his table and saw the white skirt bending over, preparing to break the racked balls on the adjacent table, his glance quickly became a stare. He tried to regain his composure and focus on his next shot.

"It's been a few months?" questioned Noe.

"Time never stops, does it?"

"Hey, the one with the dark hair kind of reminds me of Maria, the chick I would meet up with after track meets in Victorville," said Trevor, forever bringing up his one and only glorious year of female success.

"Ya know, she might not have been all that you imagined she was. Have you ever thought of that?" said Noe, oblivious to Trevor's tangent.

James caromed the five ball off the far rail with little success. "No, she was all that and even more. Sometimes you just know. And Kristen. I knew."

"All I'm saying is maybe that," and Noe nodded toward the adjoining table, "is even better than Kristen. Ya never know."

"That is Sahara Desert hot," said Trevor, making no effort to be casual about examining the merchandise at the next table.

"Kristen was amazing," said James, watching Noe's shot push the twelve ball on the rail next to the corner pocket.

"Maybe it's time for you to get back out there. Maybe you'll find I'm right for a change. Maybe there is someone out there even better for you than Kristen would have been."

139

"I doubt that."

"You carry that thing in your wallet. You know. About so much life. Don't you think it's time to start living again?"

Noe and James watched as Trevor wormed his way over to the short white skirt and revealing red and black blouse and soon returned, defeated. As Trevor slumped in failure, an encouraging smile was directed toward James who nodded with appreciation toward the luscious lips.

"Time to start living, James," said Trevor, still stuck in the same rut for the last twelve years and unable to steer his life back on course. "Remember what Red said in "Shawshank," 'Get busy living or get busy dying,' or something like that."

James knew they were right. He backed away from the table and racked his cue and reached for his wallet and just stared at the worn black leather. "Get busy living or get busy dying." Kristen didn't have a chance to live. Her life was taken from her like a carton of milk is taken from a refrigerator. The spout is open and the milk's life is poured out. Life is just not fair. "I guess it's time for me to get busy."

James sauntered over to the young lady in the white skirt, the last remnants of her beer disappearing from the glass. Noe and Trevor watched as James started talking, his eyes on her eyes, as she tossed her long black hair to the side in laughter and then placed her hand on his shoulder. They watched as James retrieved his phone from his pocket and copied her number.

"What the hell," said Trevor, less than amused that his efforts had failed so miserably and that James had been so successful.

James gave a small wave of farewell as he left their table and returned to Trevor and Noe. "I'm gonna take off. Thanks. 'Get busy living or get busy dying.' I am forever in debt to *The Shawshank Redemption.* Stephen King, right?"

Noe nodded. "That's right, brother."

Rebecca Warner lived in a two-bedroom house on Willis Avenue in Van Nuys. When James began his approach to the front door, she bounced through the door before he could take two steps up her driveway. Her long black hair glistened in the sun, and her A-line red skirt, three inches above the knee, and her black spaghetti strap tank top left everything to be desired. Becca bounced toward James, both her feet and her breasts, as he breathed excitedly inwards. She smiled broadly and even pecked him on the cheek as he opened the door to his front seat.

"I've never been to the Promenade. I can't wait," Becca said, as she latched the seat belt across her ample bosom.

James knew she was much younger than he was, probably twenty-two or twenty-three, but what she lacked in maturity her physical attributes would more than make up for. He had just lost Kristen, whose physical beauty and compassionate heart would be almost impossible to compete with, but there was no reason for him to live his life bent over a pool table, wondering if he had the proper angle for green felt success.

Noe had been right. Time is fleeting. Make the most of it. And Becca was filled with positive energy. When they arrived at the Third Street Promenade in Santa Monica and found a parking spot on the third level of a parking structure, and as he opened the door for her exit from the truck she took his hand immediately. Her hand felt good in his, and the slight squeeze she gave his fingers was evidence she liked him. They walked the streets and entered the businesses that lured them inside. Urban Outfitters found Becca plastered to James' side, as they laughed at the ridiculous books they offered for sale, like *Understanding Rap* and *Little Book of Drinking Games* or *What the F___ Should I Drink*. Not every author is a Hemingway or a Fitzgerald.

They walked hand in hand to the Santa Monica Pier, as Becca revealed her future plans of soon becoming a dental assistant. She wanted to practice in Brentwood or Bel Air or possibly Beverly Hills, a lofty goal for one so young, James thought. But lofty goals are better than no goals. When they

141

arrived at the end of the pier and white clouds littered the sky, Becca positioned herself directly in front of James, and he reciprocated the gesture by placing his hands on her shoulders. For ten seconds they stood and stared over the ocean to the horizon until Becca turned, gazed into James' eyes, paused with a tantalizing taste on her lips, and kissed James, whose lips were just as eager to join the celebration. Her mouth and tongue were passionate. He knew it was time to start living, and Becca's mouth was a delicacy to savor. That was pretty good, James thought to himself. A few steps below Kristen for sure, but the apex of Mount Everest is difficult to reach. Becca's kiss was well up the side of the mountain.

As they drove home, James replayed his time with Becca, pleased with his first step into the batter's box of life since Kristen had unexpectedly been killed. Becca was exuberant, frisky, enthusiastic and encouraging, and sexy as hell. Worldly she wasn't. She knew Bush was the president, but thought he was from California. She was stumped by the idea that *Schindler's List* was about the saving of lives during World War II. She had often made a shopping list, but couldn't grasp why you would make a list for people. A list for people didn't make any sense especially during a war when things needed to be bombed. And when it came to the world of sports she was as lost as a penguin in a desert. Kobe Bryant. Who? Shaquille O'Neal. Doesn't he make shoes? Peyton Manning. Never heard of him. The Super Bowl. It's a football game I think. But her body was her 'get out of jail free' card that she could play any time she wanted. And as James' truck hummed down the freeway and Becca's hand rested on his thigh, it was a card he hoped she would play frequently.

As they pulled up to her house, the front door opened and an older gentleman wearing a pair of brown Dockers and a long-sleeved light blue shirt and reading glasses dangling from his hand, walked toward James' truck. Rebecca's expression quickly shifted gears from happiness to dread.

"Who's that?" asked James.

"My dad."

The Ford 150 limped away from Rebecca Warner's house. A high school senior, she had just turned eighteen. James couldn't believe she was still in high school. She was drinking a beer in Scully's only a few nights ago, and she held herself with such confidence, besides her obvious other charms. It's just not fair. James knew all about life not being fair. His first step toward living had been more than he expected: a great kiss, an animated, spirited young lady, and then way more than he expected, with her father's revelation that she was about to graduate from the twelfth grade.

His next few dates went better than his first, and he didn't have to worry about a fake ID with Eileen Jackman, who looked twenty-five but was actually thirty-two. He had met Eileen in Ralph's on the condiment aisle, in front of French's mustard. He had noticed her two aisles earlier, reaching for a box of matzoh on the top shelf for an older woman driving a three-wheeled cart through the store. Her face spoke kindness, and her stretched body spoke a different language of geography. With a deep breath, with the lesson of Kristen as motivation, he approached Eileen by the mustard, as she was studying the label on a box of croutons.

"Do you have any rules about talking to strangers, especially in a supermarket?" asked James, his cart, mostly empty except for celery, a package of Franciscan coffee, a dozen eggs, AA large, a half gallon of orange juice, a rectangle of Philadelphia Cream Cheese, and two cans of white albacore tuna fish.

Eileen never lowered the box of croutons. She eyed James for seconds. "Of course, I have rules. Who would possibly set foot into a supermarket and not know the rules of the game she might be playing? I don't know if you have enough time to hear all the rules."

"I have all the time in the world."

"That's a lot of time," Eileen said, returning the croutons to their building block-like position on the shelf.

143

"The Ten Commandments of the supermarket?" wondered James.

"Oh, there are much more than ten. I lost count after twenty-five."

"That's a lot of rules."

"First rule is never to trust anyone who weighs his produce more than once, especially broccoli or cauliflower or asparagus," offered Eileen.

"Yeah. If you can't trust the scale the first time, you must have issues," agreed James, maneuvering his cart to the side of the aisle, as another pusher searched for catsup. "But I'm not sure the asparagus weigher should be in the same category as the broccoli and the cauliflower.'

"That's the rule. I didn't make up the rule."

"What about kale?"

"Doesn't say anything about leafy green vegetables. The second rule is..."

"Ya know," interrupted James, "maybe I don't have enough time to hear all the rules right now, but maybe we could have dinner, probably a really long dinner, and then I could listen to the rest then."

"A really long dinner. I think I can do that," said Eileen Jackman.

After exchanging details James went to register seven to check-out. He removed his wallet and thought again of Kristen and the article he still carried. He marveled how the aisle of a supermarket could be the stage for living life. He could never imagine replicating the two meetings with Kristen in Scully's, and although Eileen didn't possess the knockout beauty that had enhanced Kristen, she was as charming as any princess is expected to be. James had known, with more assurance than the Ten Commandments, that Kristen would be the one, and now that she could never be the one, the new search was difficult. Rebecca Warner had been a disaster, but the first taste of Eileen Jackman's

144

charm, next to the French's mustard, had burst with a tantalizing flavor of laughter.

When James and Eileen had dinner two nights later at The Park Bar and Grill (Eileen's suggestion), James couldn't have asked for a better atmosphere. A woman who suggests dinner in a sports bar moves way up the draft board for many a man. When they entered, the Monday night football game between the Tennessee Titans and Kansas City Chiefs had just entered halftime, and a few Chiefs' fans, dressed in their team's red, went in search of the water closet.

"I hope Chris Johnson has a big night tonight," said Eileen, as they settled into their table surrounded by sports maniacs. James sat beaming; a woman who lived in Los Angeles and knew the starting tailback for the Titans. Eileen mentioned hockey and the NFL draft and A-Rod's performance-enhancing drug saga and how sad she was when the Red Sox finally ended the curse of the Bambino after eighty-six years. She said the Lakers would bounce back after their dismal showing against the Pistons. She was a guy's dream, an encyclopedia of sports, a woman who appreciated one more letter than the initials of ESP. She was even in a fantasy baseball league. James couldn't believe his good fortune and even rolled the dice on his first date with her, living on the edge, with two beers, two Blue Moons invading his system, while Elaine wasn't worried about any invasion, wasn't worried about any edge in a world that is a sphere, throwing caution to the wind with five Heinekens. As the Chiefs game came to a close, down by three with under two minutes to play, they scored twice, with Eileen running with excitement toward red jerseys exchanging victory salutes. James was still floating in heaven. From the moment he had picked her up until the moment she closed the door to her apartment, it had been "game time," and she could play. James thought she had every characteristic of being an all-star.

He could tell she wanted to see him again after that first date, her tongue had been far down his throat as he was parked in

145

front of her place. As he walked her to the door, she said she'd invite him in if her place wasn't such a mess. When she kissed him again, he could feel her breasts breathing against his chest. Her groin pushed anxiously against his, and James wanted more, wanted to be on the other side of the door, forgetting the memories of Kristen and making new memories with Eileen.

When their next date ended without an invitation inside, James wondered why? They had just glued their bodies together as one against the wall of the garage, each mouth attacking the other's lips like dessert. Her hands cupped his buttocks, pressing him into her, while his hand wandered through her blouse to her breast's nipple. They were a slow dance of lust, never leaving their spot on the dance floor, their arms and a leg entwined. After ten minutes Eileen had released her hold and backed away with a whew and a shake of her hair and a repositioning of her breasts. They were on the same wavelength of desire, no crisscrossed wires between them. James could wait. Good things come to those who have patience. Eileen was a fireball of fervor.

After he left Eileen, his heart still beating heatedly, Noe called and asked James if he wanted two tickets that he couldn't use for tomorrow to the Laugh Factory on Sunset. James phoned Eileen to see if she could make it the next night. At first she wasn't able to hear what James was asking because the television in the background was so loud, but once she returned to the phone and heard about the tickets, she almost jumped from cell tower to cell tower in her excitement.

The next night, the Laugh Factory was anything but funny. The first two comedians were bad, and the sparse crowd on a Tuesday night was in no mood for mediocrity, and this was two steps below that. The silence in the room was deafening, but Eileen's hand on James' shoulder and thigh brought applause to James' heart. They almost wondered if the comedians were purposely trying to be serious. When the third comedian grabbed the microphone, the audience anticipated a change in the atmosphere, welcoming him, greedy for laughter, but he was the

146

worst of the three. So bad, in fact, that when he reached every dud of a punch line, James and Eileen couldn't help but laugh hysterically at how bad he was. A few others in the audience joined the laughter of horrible humor, and when the comic's set ended, many gave a standing ovation to the end of the evening. The whole way home they laughed at the preposterous show and tried to imagine the ramifications of what happened that night. What profession would these comics seek after this line of work failed them so miserably? Would the person who booked the comics be fired? Who thought they were funny? Did they all try new material written by the same person? How can a comic go onstage and not be funny? Like a chef not being able to cook? An author who can't write? A surfer who can't swim?

"Do you want to come in tonight?" asked Eileen, squeezing his hand and kissing him on the cheek, and letting her tongue slide from the side of his face toward the tip of his ear, as James' truck pulled to a stop in front of her place.

"Yeah. I'd like that."

Inside, a navy blue blanket hung over the arm of a worn, brown leather couch. A small round kitchen table with two folding chairs was dimly lit by a ceiling light that Eileen turned on.

"I'm just gonna have some water and some Ecstasy if you want some." Eileen opened a cabinet over the refrigerator and offered a pill to James.

Though James had just turned thirty, had heard about the meth heads and known about the coke snorters and the E ticket riders, this was his first time being a witness. "Not tonight," he said trying to give as much room for interpretation as possible. Eileen popped the pill into her mouth and took a long swig of water, reached above the refrigerator and returned the pills to their hiding place.

"Take a look in here," she said, as she patted the refrigerator door and disappeared into the bedroom. The light of the refrigerator revealed on the top shelf a plate with a half eaten

147

chicken breast, a few green beans, and some zucchini. Below the shelf were a sour cream carton, cottage cheese carton, three yogurts, a pint of half and half, and two heads of iceberg lettuce; the sides of the refrigerator were lined with salad dressings and mayonnaise and hot sauces, maybe ten or twelve. Three beers, a Bud Light and two Coors Light lay on their sides in the vegetable drawer. He opened the fresh drawer and grabbed a Bud Light not expecting to drink more than half. Damn he was responsible.

Eileen's voice rang from the bedroom. "Hey, James, why don't you grab me a beer and help me make the bed in here?"

When James walked through the door, she was bent over the corner of the bed, tucking the bottom beige sheet under the mattress. Her breasts were on display, almost spilling out of her red negligee, when she stood erect and pulled James toward her. She took a drink from the beer he was holding and then put her mouth over his and started rolling in the ecstasy of the moment. Before long they were naked together on the bed, two hedonistic animals of heat, their steady flames growing into a furnace of lust. Finally, Eileen spread her legs, and James moved on top of her, ready to enter her dampened slit, when a torrent of words spewed from Eileen's mouth. She was speaking Spanish. James didn't recognize any of the words except "puta" and "polla", and the more her throes of Spanish passion escalated in anticipation of his manhood entering her, the more his English prick shrank from extra large, to large, to medium, to small, to extra small.

"What happened?" Eileen asked, as James rolled to the side next to her.

"I think the Spanish must have thrown him off," replied James, giving his penis an identity, more than a little embarrassed but equally puzzled by the events of the last ten minutes.

Ecstasy and Spanish class during sex wasn't what James had expected, and then a quizzical look came over Eileen's face, as an internal crisis seemed to be building.

"James, you know when you called and I told you the television was too loud?"

148

"Yeah. Yesterday."

"Well that was really my daughter in the background. Not the TV. She's only two. I have her three days a week."

"You have a daughter?"

"Legally I'm still married, but my divorce is almost final. I married such a jerk. James, I don't meet guys like you. I was really scared to tell you the truth."

If James was the Goodyear blimp, all the air was out now. He was a tire flattened to the ground. "Oh, Eileen. I really liked you, too. You should have told me," he began as he started getting dressed. "A lady I thought I was going to marry was killed not too long ago. I really enjoyed the time we spent together, but I'm not going to do that to your daughter. And you're popping ecstasy. And you have a daughter. Where's your daughter?" It was too much. James didn't say anymore. He didn't turn around, just walked through the door and out, once again, into the darkness.

James was at a crossroads of understanding, and he didn't know which way to turn. His last four attempts at love had all backfired. Molly and the cell phone from hell, Kristen and tragedy, Rebecca still in kindergarten, and now the Spanish speaking, pill popping, still-married Elaine, mother of a two-year old, the icing on the cake.

Relationships are hard. Relationships aren't like products where you have test groups to see if the flavor is exactly right, if the packaging has the proper allure, if the size and shape are appealing. A team of engineers huddles around this thing, this material object, this glob of goo, this box of blob, and won't release it to the public until they think it is perfect. A car goes through so many tests, the brakes, the steering, the closing of the door, the opening of the window, the recline of the seats, and even crash tests. Crash tests. There's a concept! Why can't relationships have crash tests? So many relationships could be saved with crash tests. Your spouse was just reassigned to wherever for a year, and you won't be able to see her. Your significant other decides alcohol or drugs are more important than you. Now what? Here's a child in your life. Are you ready? Why don't relationships have tests? The woman you know you are going to marry is hit and killed by a car. Now what?

The dew in the air had coated the windshield of his truck and the road was a blur in front of him as he sat behind the wheel. James paused before he turned the ignition and hit the wiper switch. What was ahead he couldn't see. He couldn't see his next date in a month, after the new year, with Rheanne Davine, who was a receptionist in a Body Shop. Fifteen minutes after they were seated in El Torito on First Street, Rheanne would excuse herself to the restroom and never return. James would wait ten minutes before asking his waitress if she could check on his date in the restroom, only for her to return and tell him it appeared he was dining solo for the night. James would never understand what he had done wrong.

Continuing to look through the windshield of his future, he couldn't see the date he would have with Marianne Treeloggin, a friend of Noe's sister, when he would be the one to contemplate going to the restroom and disappearing, if it weren't for Noe and the damage that would follow. For the whole four hours of the miserable date, he couldn't help but worry about some poor guy who could actually end up with someone so negative, with such little ambition, and the personality of a pillow. He started counting the "I don't cares" an hour into the date and turned the last hour into the best hour when he purposely asked Marianne as many questions as he could, already knowing what her response was going to be.

He couldn't see the phone call he would receive in five months from a phone number he didn't recognize. He would recognize the voice on the other end, though. The first thing the voice would ask him after he said hello was, "How's your eye?"

Now, sitting in his truck, peering through the blurred windshield, he couldn't see that he and Molly would get back together, that their relationship and their eyes would have healed

150

to see a lofty mountain of promise in front of them. He couldn't see that he would propose to Molly on the same date that he had first met Kristen at Scully's. He couldn't see that on that very same day of his engagement to Molly, less than a mile away, at St. Joseph's Hospital in Burbank, seven pound, seven ounce James Andrew Anderson would be born, would be born without a right hand and placed in the arms of his mother, Kristen, very much alive.

Part II   Ten Years Later - 2014

Chapter 17

Nine-year-old J.A. Anderson peered into the catcher's mitt; the ball twirled in his left hand, his mitt held by the stump of his right wrist. He straightened his body, rocked slightly, threw his right leg to the sky, and slung a fastball, knee high across the heart of the plate.

"Ball!" The umpire's voice echoed with drama across the field.

"Come on, ump. Your blind gramma coulda called that one," screamed Ken, the Little League nightmare, from the stands, his black Nike polo shirt with a noticeable scent of alcohol and a indistinguishable beer stain rising with his disgust.

"Don't make an issue..." started Kristen, her fingers lightly gripping the bottom of his shirt. Ken's eyes glared at her, and he raised his hand for silence, but Kristen had had enough. "We'll talk about this later," she continued. Kristen grabbed the hand of her seven-year-old daughter, Kimberly, and walked away from Ken, down the stands, ready to leave the Little League field at McCambridge Park. Kristen's four-year-old son, Jake, was standing behind home plate, watching his brother, his fingers entwined in the fence, until Kristen extracted them and took her children from the poisonous atmosphere of her inebriated husband. They walked to the middle of the park, where they were greeted by a peaceful scene: jungle gyms and swings and slides and enough sand to hypnotize a four-year old for an hour.

J.A. turned his back to the stands and to the voice that had been yelling throughout the game, the loud yelling voice of his father. He had learned to ignore the voice, knew that if he was going to be the player he wanted to be, that the outside distractions (there would always be outside distractions his mother had told him), had to be voices carried by the wind, of no value whatsoever. J.A. had learned early that his mother's words were golden and his father's twisted statements were of little meaning. One wouldn't expect wisdom in a nine-year-old's eighty-pound body, but J.A. wasn't your typical youngster.

He bent and looked at the catcher again, knowing full well that the only pitch he was throwing was a fastball, but he emulated the pitchers he watched on television, especially a pitcher for the Los Angeles Dodgers, Clayton Kershaw, who was considered the best pitcher in all of baseball. J.A. checked the batter, whose protective helmet was large enough to swim in, the bill almost covering his eyes. The batter's knees were bent, his front leg twitching, almost afraid to step into the pitch. J.A. knowing the batter was his, lost focus. He drifted to his father in the stands. He wondered how anyone in the stands could complain about a pitch. How anyone could yell at an umpire. An umpire making a few dollars a game, only a few dollars for an hour and a half of parental hell. How anyone could make a baseball pitch, one throw, so important. Particularly in this instance, when it would take an act of God for the slight young man at the plate to even make contact with one of J.A.'s pitches.

When the next pitch crossed the plate shoulder high, the hitter's bat, like a butterfly waffling in the air, feebly attempted to

153

contact the sphere but missed by more than a foot, mercifully ending the game.

"Ya got that one right ump. Bout time," yelled a voice scornfully. "See an optometrist next time. One blind mice." Ken gripped the railing as he made his way from the stands, without congratulations from any of his son's team's parents, who steered clear of Ken. When they reached the bottom of the steps an opposing father discovered Ken's inability to be gracious.

"Your kid's got an arm," said Noe, walking with his arm around his son Aaron's shoulder, the boy who had swung so delicately at the last pitch of the game. Noe was not amused by the level of arrogance that spewed from Ken.

"Fourteen strikeouts. Shoulda had eighteen," Ken pompously retorted.

"I don't think it matters," said Noe.

"I'm not asking what you think matters," Ken answered, as Noe walked away in disgust, his arm still around Aaron's shoulder.

"C'mon, dad," said J.A., pulling his father away from the meaningless discussion and toward the parking lot. Kimberly and Jake ran toward J.A., as they saw him walking with their father two steps behind, always a little bit of distance between them. Kristen watched her children. Her children had become her life. The reason the sun was always shining. The reason to jump out of bed in the morning. The reason why she was still married. They walked with the innocence of youth through the parking lot toward their car. The doors of their 2012 Dodge minivan opened as they approached and the kids found their seats, immediately anchored their earphones to their heads and were lost in games and music. When the doors were shut and the windows rolled up, the car began the tumultuous trip toward their house, the children immune to their parents' dysfunction.

"Don't you ever raise your hand to me again, you self-righteous bastard," began Kristen, her insides awash in anger.

"Every time we get in the car, it is the same shit," said Ken, with his usual agitation. "Why did you ever marry me? All you ever do is give me shit. The pitch was right over the heart of the plate. I'm supposed to let that pass? That's my son doin' the pitchin!"

"That's it exactly. That is your son doing the pitching. And you are supposed to be his father and act like a father, not some asshole who screams like a maniac," said Kristen, still bristling.

"I get in the car and there is always a problem."

"The only time I can talk to you is in the car. Otherwise you run in all directions. I thought you would change, especially after our big fight right before we got married. You actually listened to something I had to say then."

"That was then. You never have anything worth a shit to listen to now."

"Look at you. What in the hell has happened to you?"

"I didn't fuck up the law stuff. The law business fucked me," said Ken, and he was right. The law offices of Anderson and Anderson and McClure had laid golden eggs for over forty years, but one bad hire and one bad case and one badly timed bribe caught on an iPhone, had caused their entire empire to collapse. They weren't able to turn their tragedy into a windfall, like Donald Sterling of the Los Angeles Clippers had years later. Their mistake caused the obituary for Anderson and Anderson and McClure to be written, a little known excerpt, next to the larger, more publicized death of the financial mortgage giant Bears Stearns' in 2008.

"Our kids get in the car and the first thing they do is put on their headphones," remarked Kristen angrily.

"Because you don't know the meaning of relax," said a belligerent Ken.

"These are the times we should be talking with them, but they don't want to listen to us. Are you going to take J.A. to the Dodger game like you promised?"

155

"I never promised him that," said Ken, turning into the driveway of their home on Whitnal Highway, as auspicious transmission towers forty feet high and the never ending static of the electric lines that slumped from tower to tower welcomed the Andersons home. Ken escaped from the van a second after turning off the engine, before Kristen could respond, and marched angrily between the red geraniums toward the front door. Kimberly followed her dad, while Jake clung to J.A.'s stump as his four-year-old legs leaped the daunting geraniums once again. Kristen watched from the passenger seat, painfully and blissfully aware of how much life can change in ten short years.

The bliss of the ten years that had passed was her children, J.A, Kimberly, and Jake. The fulfillment of being a mother had no equal. And although she was at a "proceed with caution" sign in dealing with her husband, she also knew that without him, her three silver linings wouldn't be here. J.A. had been the first, and when he was born without a hand, Kristen had cried for days, felt guilty for delivering a child that wasn't in accord with nature's perfection, and worried that James, or Jimmy as he was first called, would suffer because of his imperfection. But from the beginning Jimmy was more capable than most every other child he was around, despite his missing hand. He could walk by eight months and was climbing out of his crib before he was a year old. Kristen had heard a thump from Jimmy's room only to open the door and find him hanging by one hand from the railing of his crib. When Jimmy was two, he could run as fast as four-year old Nathan, who lived two doors down, and when he was three, he could hit a golf ball sixty yards by swinging a cut down driver with one hand. Kristen and Ken had insisted he learn to use a prosthetic hand, at his doctor's orders, but Jimmy never liked the way the hand fit and felt, as it would pinch his wrist and become sweaty and uncomfortable. He removed it every chance he had, and his parents agreed to leave him alone until the first grade. When he was in kindergarten, the only difficulty arose on the second day of school when the teacher taught the children the

156

song, "When you're happy and you know it, clap your hands." When Ms. Colton, the teacher, saw a puzzled look on Jimmy's face and saw that he didn't have a right hand, she immediately realized her faux pas and explained to the class that for the song to be done correctly, she needed a volunteer for a very important assignment, to hit a drum right in the middle, every time they said "clap your hands." Jimmy, of course, was chosen for this special honor and carried it out to perfection.

In the first grade, Jimmy became J.A. After meeting with a prosthetic specialist before school started in August, Jimmy was unkindly urged by his parents to accept a new hand. On the first day of school, after carefully arriving at the lunch table with his lunch intact, his new hand knocked over his orange juice and Brian Bozeman, the third grade heavyweight, both in size and stature, had laughingly called him Captain Hook. His imitation of Jimmy had set off a chorus of laughter among the children. By the third day, a few others had joined in with the cruelty of children and castigated Jimmy and his plight. On the fourth day of school, the Friday after Labor Day, after an all-night battle with his parents that he victoriously won with his mother's support, to rid himself of the mechanical monster on his wrist, he walked through the hall without the burden of his mechanical hand toward room eight where Mrs. Dollop was writing the spelling words for next week on the board. As he walked he noticed a few boys approaching and then Brian Bozeman the third grade bully, pushed him in the chest, and said, "Hey Captain Hook where'd your hand go?" Brian Bozeman wasn't ready for what hit him next. Jimmy rushed him like a mad linebacker, rammed his head right in the gut of the third-grade giant and sent him crashing to the ground. Instantaneously he was on top of the stunned bully, who was powerless to move under the unexpected strength of one so small. "Don't you ever call me Hook again. I'm J.A. and don't you forget it," he said, glaring, his stump under the chin of Brian and his finger pointing menacingly an inch from his eye.

The news traveled quickly over the weekend, especially at the third grade pool party of Kandy Kline, where the news was whispered so Brian couldn't hear, and where everyone was a witness to this act of courage, by first grader, J.A. Anderson. Even fourth and fifth graders had heard the glamorized details of the truth, and when J.A. returned to school on Monday, he had earned the respect, the honor roll of courage, from most of his elementary school mates, an honor not normally associated with someone so young.

Now in the fourth grade, J.A. was already the best athlete in the school, and although he had only one hand, he was picked first for everything and was a friend to everyone. His sister, Kimberly, in the first grade, was proud and willing to follow in her brother's footsteps. His mother tried to make J.A. more worldly, wanted him to watch plays, to read poetry, to find passion in painting, but for J.A., running and jumping and throwing and catching were all he cared about. Math and English and reading and writing and history and projects and tests and quizzes and assignments were the necessary evils of school that had to be taken care of, especially if he was going to have the freedom that grades permitted. His "D" on a test in addition (he kept forgetting to carry over the number) in the second grade had resulted in a Saturday without the chance to watch USC play UCLA at the Rose Bowl. He never forgot the feeling of lying on his bed, his imagination working less than wonders with the wallpaper, of footballs and baseballs and basketballs on a light blue background, while a stadium rocked with intensity.

Although Ken and the children had left the car a couple of minutes before, Kristen was still recovering from another Little League game and another drive home gone awry. Slowly Kristen climbed out of the front seat, still pushing the mythical boulder of Ken, knowing she wouldn't be able to break free from this monolith of arrogance until her children were grown and out of the house, hoping it wouldn't crush her in the meantime. Their

158

three-bedroom house on Whitnall Highway was a far cry from their five bedroom and four-bathroom mansion on Country Club Drive, to say nothing of their three car garage that had housed Ken's always waxed Porsche and Kristen's BMW and their toy Cadillac SUV. They had overlooked parts of the San Fernando Valley and parts of Glendale and Los Angeles, the seemingly infinite city lights, a flashing reminder of grandeur and majesty. Now, from their bedroom window, they could see the bright yellow lights of the Shell station on the corner. At the beginning of the crushed rock path to the front door, Kristen hesitated before continuing. Before she had married Ken, there had been that moment of hesitation when she had imagined James was really the one she should marry. She often wondered what her life would have been like with James. That kiss. That kiss still lingered on her lips, even after ten years, even after the birth of her three children, even after the pain of that dreadful day when everything had fallen to pieces and James had never come to pick her up. The temporary glue that had wedded Ken and Kristen together had completely lost its strength within a year, and pieces had started falling from the picture of perfection. Now the only three pieces that mattered were J.A, Kimberly, and Jake, who would have to thank James for their existence if they could only meet him some-day. Even Kristen had to admit that her three children, her and Ken's three children, were a gift more precious than anything that could ever be found wrapped under a tree. Kristen, like most mothers, couldn't conceive of anything better than the six legs and six eyes and five hands that awaited her entry into the house.

Chapter 18

James never used measuring cups when he made the pancake batter for the kids. One egg, a little vegetable oil, a pouring of Aunt Jemima, better than Krusteaz, he felt, and then whole milk, and start stirring. Check to see if the batter was too thick and needed a little more milk, or too runny and pour a little more of Aunt Jemima in, until the batter was just smooth enough to make the best pancakes. He placed the griddle on the stove, and as the patter of little feet found the kitchen, he asked for the input of the shapes he was about to pour.

"All right. What is it today? Plants, animals, states, or Disneyland?"

Six-year-old Christian was the first to speak. "Can we have chocolate milk?"

"States, Daddy," said nine-year-old Amber. "Can you make Florida?" She pulled herself into her chair at the kitchen table, still wrapped in a blanket.

"I want Texas and Alaska," said Christian, as his dad was pouring geography on the griddle. "Can I have mine first?"

"I'll get the syrup," said Amber, letting her blanket slip to the floor as she opened the refrigerator.

James' spatula exercised over the batter and retrieved the states. "Oh my gosh, I think an earthquake must have hit Alaska," said James, as he placed the broken pancake in front of Christian.

"I don't want it if it's broken," said Christian, rejecting the split state.

James poured a spot of syrup on Christian's plate and swept broken Alaska over the syrup and into his mouth. "That is one good-tasting earthquake state. You shoulda had it." He poured new territories onto the griddle as Molly walked in, patted the kids on the head, and poured herself a cup of the waiting coffee.

"Make mom the Pacific Ocean," said Amber, as James sailed the finished pancakes onto their plates.

"Let's not rush your mom. She can choose anything she wants. Pacific, Atlantic, Indian, Cowboy."

"Cowboy is not an ocean, Dad," said a laughing Amber.

"You still feeling a little queasy?" James asked.

"I'll take the Atlantic, please. I don't know what it is," responded Molly.

"You should probably go to the doctor."

"I'll try to go this week. I haven't felt right since we were up so late after seeing *Fargo* last week. I thought it must have been something we ate, but I don't know. Are you finishing the ocean for *Finding Nemo*?"

"Yeah. A few hours and I should have it wrapped. I still can't believe you love Green Day now. From black eye to love fest. Amber, you are going to be the best Nemo ever. And if the part for Nemo ever opens up on Broadway, that will be your part. Feel like a little Iowa?"

"I'm full," said Amber, "Can I practice my lines?"

"All right. Let me put the spatula down for the full dramatic effect of my daughter starring as a clown fish," said James. He moved toward Amber and then spoke in his best fish

161

voice as Marlin, Nemo's father, "You know what? I was right. We'll start school in a year or two."

"No, Dad! Just because you're scared of the ocean..." responded Amber.

"Clearly, you're not ready, and you're not coming back until you are. You think you can do these things, but you just can't, Nemo!" said James, wincing with enunciation.

"I hate you," responded Amber.

"A bit more forcefully, I believe. You have to sell the hate to the audience."

"I hate you!" shrieked Amber.

"That was a little too believable," said James, wrapping his daughter in his arms.

"Are you sure the costume isn't too tight?" asked Molly.

"No. It really fits good," said Amber, dragging her blanket toward her room.

"Can you make me a walrus for Halloween?" asked Christian, disappearing down the hall, not even waiting for a response from his mom.

James' eyes never left his children as they evaporated from the kitchen. "Thanks, Molly. I have the two greatest kids in the universe, maybe even the galaxy if a galaxy is bigger than a universe."

"One black eye and two kids. I need to give you more."

"No. I think that was plenty."

"If she hadn't died, Amber never would have gotten to play Nemo," said Molly, reminding James of his loss ten years before. "But don't you think you can throw that article of her death away? That was a long time ago."

"It's not about her, Molly. It's about life. I don't ever want to forget. Besides, the kids are in their rooms and you could help me in the garage, like real quick, if you know what I mean."

"So much for the meaning of life," Molly grinned playfully. "A quickie in the garage and all will be right with the world. Maybe tomorrow. Go paint Nemo's ocean."

162

"We could do it underwater."

"Yeah and Nemo might be watching," and Molly left the open waters of the kitchen for dry land.

Chapter 19

The bedroom door was ajar, and J.A pushed the door until he could see his father asleep, his mouth wide open, wrapped in the blankets of his bed. He left the door open and went to the kitchen where he found the turkey sandwiches and sliced apples and sliced carrots his mother had left on the kitchen table. Jake's Spiderman lunch pail still had part of yesterday's carrots inside, J.A. noticed, as he cleared the trash and placed today's lunch inside. Kimberly's ageless Cinderella reusable lunch bag was then filled, as was his own Dodger Blue Bucket.

The refrigerator still had fresh milk, and the cupboard was down to only two choices in cereal, Fruit Loops, which was almost empty, and Corn Pops, which hadn't been opened. He tore the cardboard from the top of the new cereal and poured himself a bowl and then smothered it in milk. He ate the cereal silently and quickly, and then peeled a banana and woke Jake.

Jake stumbled into the bathroom and then returned to find the clothes J.A. had left for him to put on.

"You want Corn Pops or Fruit Loops this morning?" asked J.A.

"I want Poppers."

"We're out of Poppers."

"I want Poppers."

"I'll pour you a bowl of Corn Pops," said J.A, well aware of the rules of the breakfast game that he had been in charge of since his mom started teaching at his Aunt Kathy's school.

"No, I want a bowl of Fruit Loops."

J.A. knocked on his sister's door as his mother had taught him and then entered slowly. Kimberly was tying her shoes.

"Can I have an egg this morning?" asked Kimberly. "Mrs. Pratt says you should always have some protein in the morning."

"I don't see why not," answered J. A., as he made his way to the refrigerator. J.A. was the best one-handed chef in the family, even if he was the only one. Pancakes, waffles, eggs, bacon, even hash browns were in his repertoire, thanks to the tutelage of the head chef, his mother. He grabbed four eggs from the carton and cracked and beat them to a smooth yellow. He warmed the frying pan, as he found a bowl for his brother's cereal and readied the table for breakfast.

Jake climbed onto the kitchen chair and danced his spoon on the table before dipping into the cereal. Kimberly poured a small cupful of Corn Pops and covered them in milk, as J.A. brought the frying pan to the table and with a spatula gave half of the eggs to his sister and the other half to himself.

"You want some eggs?" he asked his brother who shook his head no. "I didn't think so."

"Is Dad awake?" asked Kimberly.

"Not yet. I'll try to get him up in a minute," said J.A., as he shoveled the eggs into his mouth. "Did you finish your homework last night?"

"Yeah, but the math was hard. I just don't get subtraction."

"Yeah, addition wasn't that much easier for me. Math is still hard."

J.A., again, walked into his father's room to find him still in the same position, his mouth wide open to the world. "Dad, you have to take us to school in five minutes." J.A. shook his dad's shoulder until his closed eyes made a grimaced opening to a new day. "You have to take us to school in five minutes. I'm taking Jake to Mrs. Kungel's. Get up."

Ken started to move, but J.A didn't wait for him to exit the bed. J.A. grabbed Jake's lunch box and grabbed Jake's hand and led him two houses down the street to Mrs. Kungel's front door. When he returned, his dad was standing over the kitchen sink with a cup of coffee in his hand. The backs of his slippers were under his feet, and the black baseball hat and black tee shirt attempted to hide his discomfort. "We'll be in the car," said J.A. "Dad, I can't be late again. If I am, I have to stay in during lunch and read some stupid story about a cat."

Kimberly and J.A. were in the car when Ken finally arrived five minutes later.

"Why can't you get up on time?" asked an agitated J.A. For as long as J.A. could remember, he couldn't count on his father to be on time. When J.A. was six, he was invited to Bethani Berlin's birthday party at Chuck E Cheese, and the talk during recess about the party had brought J.A.'s blood pumping with anticipation. He paced around the house, checking the plate glass window in the front for any sign of his father. Five o'clock passed and then five-thirty and then six and six-thirty and finally at six forty-five, his father showed up and J.A. threw a tantrum, screaming like the child that he was, breaking his Millennium Falcon Lego into a thousand pieces. When he was seven, it was more of the same. He made his first Burbank All-Star team but when he missed two team practices because his father failed to show, he didn't get to start in the game against the All Stars from Glendale. When he was nine, he begged his mother to always be the one to take him to his activities, but there was only so much

166

that she could do. He came to expect his father to not be there when he needed him. He learned he couldn't respect his father despite his mother's insistence. Wasn't a father supposed to make sure things were taken care of? J.A wished he could drive himself, but he still had many years to wait for a driver's license. He accepted his responsibility. His tantrum as a six-year old taught him that evil can create more evil, a notion that was always planted in the back of his mind. Every morning he understood the necessity of making breakfast and packing lunches and taking Jake to Mrs. Kungel and making sure all of Kimberly's i's were dotted and t's were crossed. He had come to accept that he was the left-hand man of the family. The times he had depended on his father underscored the saying that one should never count his chickens before they hatched. J.A. knew progress was never achieved by speaking with his father, but the zipper on his lips was opened too easily, and he knew trouble would soon follow. "Dad, I'm gonna be late. As if you care."

"Don't talk to your father like that, young man. I do the best I can. You should be a little more grateful. Now shut up, and I'll get you there as soon as I can," said Ken peevishly, as he jerked the car into gear and sped off for the school. The children were silent, lips sealed, in the back seat for the rest of the trip.

Chapter 20

A Ford 150 pulled to a stop in front of an open garage, where James was inside, drill in hand, scanning his workbench for a half-inch drill bit. Noe exited the front seat of the truck, while his son Aaron ran through the garage, without acknowledging James, and into the house to play with Amber.

"I can't believe it is still running," said James of the truck he sold to Noe six years before.

"I still think you shortchanged me," kidded Noe, understanding James' generosity. "The play is this Friday, right?"

"Yeah. She's gonna be a great Nemo. It should be hilarious."

"I never would have thought *Finding Nemo* would have been made into a Broadway play."

"And I never thought the Red Sox would win three World Series in ten years," said James.

"Thank God for that. Last year was bizarre. I thought they were going to finish in last place and they win the whole thing. Everyone had them picked for the city dump."

"Maybe it was the bombing at the Boston Marathon. Sort of galvanized the whole city and then the Red Sox won it all."

"Yeah. Big Papi put the whole city on his shoulders and drove them home," said Noe.

"I loved his speech. This is our fucking city. Classic," imitated James.

"What are you looking for?" asked Noe.

"Half-inch," said James, holding up his drill without the bit.

"Is this it?" said Noe, lifting the missing piece from the bench."

"You just can't see what is right in front of you," said James, as he drilled a hole for a piece of doweling, so the stage crew could twirl a starfish on the set. "How'd Aaron's team do on Saturday?"

"It was a nice day. Seventy-five degrees. Nine and ten year olds playing baseball. What could be better? Got a shake at Foster's Freeze after the game."

"So were they at least close?" asked James.

"Is 16-1 close?

"Closer than 16-0."

"Then it was close," said Noe, glowing in the sun of lasting friendship. "You should have seen this kid on the other team. James, this kid is a monster."

"That good, huh? Even at ten?"

"I think he's only nine. Not that big, but ridiculously athletic. Nine years old and he hammered one to the fence."

"Which field. One or two?"

"Two. The short one. But the kid's nine. And listen to this. He's only got one hand."

"No way!"

"And he pitched. Threw nothing but aces. One hand. Who was that guy long time ago? Campbell or something, pitched for the Dodger's, I think," said Noe.

169

"Oh, yeah. No, he pitched for the Angels. Something Abbott, wasn't it?"

"Yeah. Jim Abbott. This kid is the reincarnation of Jim Abbott."

"What's his name?" asked James.

"I never got that. Jay maybe. Not sure. Aaron made the last out of the game. I felt sorry for the kid. But at least he swung the bat. He missed the last pitch by a country mile. I don't even think he saw it."

"Ah, too bad for Aaron. I'll have to check this kid out someday, if he is that good," said James.

"I tried to congratulate his dad after the game, but talk about an asshole. The guy tried picking a fight with me. I tell him his son's got a great arm, and he goes ballistic. His son had to pull him away. A real tool."

"Kid must be cut from his mom's cloth. She must be the winner in the family," said James, drilling another hole through the expansive ocean.

"Didn't see her. But yeah, I bet you're right."

Chapter 21

"**Mom,** let's go," said J.A. standing at the door with his mitt and bat in his only hand.

"Kimmie, have you got your shoes?" shouted Kristen, grabbing a stack of history quizzes from the kitchen table.

The banana peel fell over Kimberly's fingers as she entered the kitchen with her pink dance bag, chewing on a bite. Indecipherable words mumbled out of her mouth, but her head shook affirmatively.

"What did you do to your hair?" asked her mom.

"Mom, you don't have time to fix it right now. I've got to get to practice," answered J.A., picking up Jake with his arm without a hand and carrying him to the car.

"Your dad didn't say what he was doing this afternoon?" asked Kristen on the way to the car.

"Does he ever?" responded J.A., securing Jake into his seat.

"Can we get Foster's after I'm done dancing?" asked Kimberly.

"It might ruin your dinner, but I think a cone dipped in chocolate might be just what doctor Mom would prescribe for her children," said Kristen, as J.A and Kimberly exchanged high fives and Jake threw his hands into the air. It wasn't often Mom would take the avenue of dessert before dinner, but she was just spontaneous enough to throw some unexpected twists into the daily routine. A few weeks ago, they had experimented with French fries dipped in a chocolate shake and before that, they had driven into Taco Bell, where mom had transformed into a Southern Belle speaking with a terrible Southern accent into the speaker, hoping to get a hot dog with extra taco sauce. Before that, a quick trip to Kuo's, the newest rage in Asian food, where they ordered the sweet and sour chicken sandwich. They found it to be quite good, except for Jake who couldn't handle anything that wasn't bread or fruit. There was no need for headphones when the kids traveled with their mother or on those few occasions, other than school drops, when they traveled with their father, but put the two parents together in the car at the same time and the kids had better have their headphones for protection.

As Kristen peeked into the rear view mirror, she marveled at her children. After a day of teaching high school United States History and facing one hundred and fifty students for five hours, she knew that when she arrived home, the afternoon was always a tag team of activity, a tag team of activity that she cherished. Baseball practice, dance lessons, and piano lessons for Kimberly, wall climbing at the gym and even yoga for kids. J.A. always joked about taking piano lessons, of playing at a recital, where he would walk on stage, and sit stoically on the piano bench, and then, right before he would start playing, he would raise his hands a little off the keys, that dramatic pause before the first note was struck, and then have his prosthetic hand fall from his arm and clang the piano keys, horrifying the audience.

"Mom, just pull in over there," said J. A., pointing to the same driveway Kristen always pulled into. J.A. was out of the car and dispatching his love for his mother almost before the car came to a stop.

"Is Daddy going to be home for dinner?" asked Kimberly on the way to the dance lessons.

"Yeah. Daddy'll be there," answered Kristen, not sure if her answer was filled with truth.

"Are we having spaghetti?" asked the girl who could finally enunciate her favorite food.

Kristen continued the innocuous dialogue until she had reached Kimberly's dance studio and followed the quick feet of her daughter through the front door and over the polished wood floor for an hour of tap dancing to "The Good Ship Lollipop."

In the front of the building, Kristen leaned against a pillar and reached for her phone. Ken's phone went to message. Kristen remained silent. She sat on the bench in front of the studio and reached for the bundle of papers in her purse and a red pen and started grading. She was amazed at how many students had no idea which was the Atlantic Ocean and which was the Pacific, had no idea that the Himalayas were not a part of the United States, had no idea that the Mississippi River wound through more states than just Mississippi, had no idea that World War I happened before World War II, had no idea that President Obama was the first black president. She was stunned by the mountain of things that people didn't know. Even when students did know the correct answer, Kristen thought, what did they really know? Answers marked correctly on tests. Franklin and Jefferson signed the Declaration of Independence. The Fourteenth Amendment gives every citizen the same rights under the Constitution. The Lewis and Clark Expedition was to explore the Pacific Northwest. But even with a red bold C marked next to the answer, what did the student really know? Who really knows, she thought, the story behind any events in history that are covered by a couple of paragraphs in a history book? Who knows the story of each person who signed the Declaration of Independence, of George Clymer from Pennsylvania who was once an orphan or Francis

173

Lewis from New York who was once taken as a prisoner and sent to France or Oliver Wolcott who didn't sign the document until after August 2? Everyone and everything has a story and there is just too much to know. Kristen thought of J.A., who at the age of ten, had already become a story at his elementary school and on the baseball field. Some parents probably used his story to try to motivate their own children to succeed and excel. And what about the stories of her own students, Kristen thought. A hundred and fifty different names and each with his or her own story. And all she knew were the red marks on their papers. She didn't know who had parents addicted to drugs, or who were once homeless, or who had witnessed tragedy, or who had been born with silver spoons in their mouths. And what did they know of her? That standing in front of them, teaching them the details of history was still a young woman, who should never be allowed to teach them how to pick a husband. She tried not to think about Ken. Her students were bad enough, but Ken was worse. How could she not think about him? When they were first married, Kristen really thought she could change Ken and make him a better person, but now she realized just how naive she had been. Soon after he slipped the ring on Kristen's finger, he reverted back into his obsession with work, and each new court case became his new girlfriend he could easily put his arms around, who would want nothing in return.

Kristen thought about her history with Ken. For the first seven years after they were married, Ken returned to the silence that he knew best, and Kristen surrounded her life with the love of her children. There are just so many times the volcano can erupt before one realizes even hot molten lava hardens after it cools. After Ken's disbarment and the destruction of the law firm, he wasn't any more available as a husband or as a father. The family still had enough money to buy a different house and have food and transportation. And now that Kristen was working as a teacher, a new stability had settled the earth below them. But Ken was still a mystery in the afternoon, a "Where's Waldo" in the landscape

174

of life and then, once dinner had been eaten and the house breathed rhythmically with sleep, Ken became a Netflix addict until the wee hours of the morning. Kristen called Ken again.

"Where's Waldo" was in the middle of the off-track betting parlor off Brand Avenue in Glendale. Once again Ken ignored the vibration in his pocket. He knew it was Kristen calling. When would she understand, he wondered, that he didn't want to talk to her? The horses were entering the gate for the fifth race at Santa Anita. The beer in his hand found his lips twice while his eyes were glued to the television screen. He placed the beer on the counter as the horses hit the top of the stretch. He raised his arm toward the horses as they raced the last eighth of a mile to the finish line. Ken was all words and antics. "Come on, Four, come on, Four, Four, Four..." Disappointment crept over Ken's face. "The Four should have won." He didn't answer his phone.

Chapter 22

Scully's looked different after ten years. The whole facade of the building had been changed to a pale stucco and the roof was switched dramatically from wooden shingles to Spanish tile that contradicted the history of the restaurant. New owners had made the renovations, though few of the clientele were pleased with the new wardrobe that was exhibited. But once seated at a table, or bending elbows at the bar, or rubbing blue chalk on the end of a cue, the familiarity made one forget the ensemble being worn, and once the vermicelli was forked and placed on the tongue, the atmosphere of nostalgia was swallowed once again.

Fresh photographs and autographs adorned the wall, of Bryan Cranston as Walter White from *Breaking Bad* and his signature, Heisenberg; an updated picture of newly named *Tonight Show* host, Jimmy Fallon; of Matthew McConnaughey, of Leonarado DiCaprio and Sandra Bullock, and even one of the band, One Direction. The pictures mingled with the fading pictures of Johnny Carson and Don Rickles and Eddie Murphy and Steve McQueen and Goldie Hawn and Barbara Streisand and Raquel Welch, a wall of Scully's fame, a pictured history of the studios, Warner Brothers and Disney and NBC, all within a mile of Scully's. Those entering Scully's for their first legal drink, born in 1993, had never heard of many of the faded pictures, of the names that once made headlines, of the faces that once graced magazine covers, of the bodies that once made a population gasp with excitement.

Kristen opened the front door and her eyes needed no adjustment to the dimming light. Immediately she found her sister sitting with four other teachers around a table a few feet from the bar. The last time she had been in Scully's was right before her wedding to Ken, and when she had left that night ten years ago, she thought she would never be married to Ken, that her knight in shining armor had ridden in on his white horse and saved her from a bleak future with Ken, only to find out her knight, James, was an impostor who fled the field of love before she was given a chance.

At the end of the bar, three bar stools stood like vacant soldiers, awaiting the first attack of a Friday night. Kristen remembered sitting there ten years before, tantalizing in her blue dress as James walked into Scully's and scanned the restaurant, not realizing that the woman in the blue dress was Kristen. A shiver went down Kristen's spine, a tingle of excitement, with the memory of that night and the kiss that followed.

Her memories and her eyes were redirected by Kathy's high-pitched laugh. Kristen walked toward the Friday afternoon group of teachers huddled over a table, with Kathy's hands and head in full animation. Kristen could tell they were exchanging the horror stories of teaching, and even though she hadn't been a part of education and the art of teaching until the last three years, she still felt like a seasoned veteran, as she secured a seat around the gossip column. Kathy was on a roll, releasing enough steam to have smoothed ten wrinkled blouses and enough laughter to have cured the worst depression.

"The mom was one hundred percent behind him. She insisted their printer was out of ink, insisted their email had a bug that couldn't be debugged. She actually said "debugged." The kid hasn't turned in an assignment over a "C" the whole year, and she still wants him in honors next year."

"Forget Ambien and Zoloft and Percoset. Parents need a reality...," added Kristen jumping into the fray, but then stopped mid sentence when a man her age ambled by and sat down on one of the vacant stools at the end of the bar. His brown hair combed to the side, his stride of confidence and character, his stature of broad, strong shoulders aroused the memory of ten years before, when James had swept her off her feet and spiraled her for a short stay in Heaven with that still-remembered kiss.

"What is it?" asked Kathy, as Kristen had momentarily risen from the table and was now walking toward the bar, unaware of her actions.

Kristen walked to the end of the bar and leaned against the wood a few feet from the stranger. "I'll have a Sprite," she called out to the bartender.

"A Sprite on a Friday afternoon? Most people need something a little stronger. Can I buy you a real drink?" asked the man that Kristen could now see was definitely not James.

"Thanks, but the Sprite will be just fine," said Kristen, as the beat of her heart, the disappointed beat of her heart, was restored to a smoother pulse.

When she returned to the table, Kathy was as lively as before. Teaching was as important to Kathy as blood to a vampire. The life could be sucked out of her by the walls of her house and the dispassionate man she had married and was now trying to divorce, but with thirty-five desks in front of her filled with the fickle energy of youth, she was a dynamo, erecting minds of passion and possibility. Not all minds, but more than enough to make students eager to find themselves, uncomfortable in their desks but pleased with how their teacher took their minds and challenged and stretched their gray matter into new shapes and

178

sizes. Kathy fed them doses of Shakespeare and Donne, of Chaucer and Keats, of Kafka and Camus, medicine that students would never take by themselves, but soon, many would be cured of the apathy that seemed to inflict them each year.

"What was that all about?" asked Kathy, as Kristen sat down with her Sprite. "Did you know him?"

"Yeah. I thought I did. But it wasn't who I thought it was."

"Who did you think it was?"

"I thought it was this guy I knew before Ken. But it was so long ago. Just the way he walked. I'd have no idea what he would even look like now," said Kristen placing her Sprite on the table and raising her hand for the waitress to bring something stronger.

"By the way, Frank finally signed the papers. Good God. Over two years. I really don't know why I ever married him. At least we didn't have any kids. I won't make that mistake again."

Kristen cringed with the word "mistake." Her hand was still in the air, her heart on the ground.

Chapter 23

When James and Noe pulled up to Trevor's, the red and white rose bushes were in full bloom, the liquid amber in the middle of the front lawn was filled with green leaves, and the white bricks lining the driveway were all in place, each laid at a sixty-degree angle, except for one that lay prone on the manicured front lawn. When they entered the house, little was in place.

"I don't get it? What the fuck? How do you do that to someone?" wondered a distressed Trevor. "On our second anniversary. I bring home flowers and she's gone and half the house is gone and the bank account is wiped out."

"Have you tried calling her?" asked Noe.

"Yeah. Like every fifteen minutes," said Trevor, checking his phone once again.

"Looks like you got fucked by Victorville this time," said James, reflecting on the irony of the situation. Trevor had married Madlyn McNomber two years before. They had met four months before the wedding, and during those passionate months, Trevor was on top of the world. Madlyn came from a strict religious family. She attended high school at Victor Valley High during the same time that Trevor was the king of the school, the hunk of all hunks, the most desired of all, the cock that strutted in glamour and approval and desire. She, on the other hand, was attending church on Tuesday and Thursday nights and, of course, on Sunday. She was in charge of the youth group at the church, the kids from kindergarten through the second grade. She didn't have time for the frivolity of most of the student body, just time to study and to pray. Madlyn was disgusted by the tales and stories of the other girls at the school and at the same time a little curious about all the sexual anecdotes she had heard.

During Madlyn's second year of college, her ultra religious father severed at least two of the Ten Commandments. He was found with his penis in the mouth of Delores Perkling, one of the choir members of the church. Mr. Perkling accidentally caught them when he entered the men's restroom. There he encountered his wife's knees on her white cardigan sweater and her mouth around an organ that played no music, but could be finely tuned. A memorable church scene, much more memorable than any nativity that had unfolded over the years. Madlyn was thrilled to have missed the damaging scene. Over the following years, she weaned herself from the sanctity of the church, searching for something she could trust. For years she was unsuccessful in her quest. When she arrived in Burbank a little more than two years earlier, she found herself employed by Virgin America at the Bob Hope Airport, working with none other than Trevor Rogers, God of Victorville, the Hunk of all Hunks, and even though it had been more than fifteen years since she had graduated from high school, she was eager to jump into the arms of this famous Sex God and reach the heights of orgasm that she had heard so much about.

Trevor loved the role of Sex God, and for the first time since his glorious senior year in Victorville, he returned to the role that he had been cast to play. During those heated few months and even during the first few months of their marriage, they were eager

181

to spend a lifetime together, but then the headlines of high school fame started to fade, and soon, for Madlyn, the headlines had turned to the obituary page. The only thing Trevor ever talked about was his fast times at Victor Valley High, but that wasn't a topic Madlyn wanted to listen to, and so there was no reason for him to ever bring up the subject. They had even less in common than Ken and Kristen, who at least had children to keep them happy. And the more Trevor talked about wanting children, the more frightened Madlyn became of being trapped with someone she didn't love.

Two days before, Madlyn had left work, feigning illness, and while Trevor was throwing luggage on the conveyor belt at Virgin America, she and most of the furniture in the house disappeared, never to be seen again.

"She even took the sixty-inch television?" questioned Noe in amazement. "How'd she do that?"

"You wanna come stay with us for a few days?" asked James. "Molly doesn't mind. You just have to deal with the kids."

"Your kids are cool, James, but I'll be okay."

"Hey, you can stay with us, too," said Noe.

"She kept telling me I was a fraud. You're just a lie. I didn't want to be the Romeo of Victorville. It just happened. I was chased by every damn skirt, but man, this skirt hurts."

"Did she leave a note? Did you have any clue?" asked James.

"Mostly it was the usual unhappiness. I wasn't who she thought I was going to be. Yeah, but there were a couple of things, now that I look back. The sex had gone from sizzling hot to the North Pole. The last few months were nothing except for one night when we were drunk. She always had some excuse but insisted it wasn't me, that it was her. She went to the doctor a couple of times, at least she said she went to the doctor. Now I don't know if that was true. She always had some excuse. Then about three months ago, she started going to church again. Every Sunday morning, but what am I supposed to do when the NFL is

182

on? If it was during the summer, it wouldn't have been a problem, but my Sundays are locked on the couch. So she looks great, kisses me goodbye every Sunday, and then off to church. She always gave me a rundown on the sermon and who she saw, so I never had a reason not to trust her, but a week ago she tells me the sermon is on material possessions and how they can't buy happiness. That if you have a roomful of things, they don't mean anything without love. But randomly I run into this minister at the airport Tuesday morning who is flying back to Des Moines. We start talking and he explains how he is here on an exchange program with Madlyn's church. He says he gave the sermon on Sunday. Spoke about your home being where the love is or should be. I asked if he talked about materialism. I went over all the details she had told me. That was two days ago, and I came home to find this."

"Maybe she'll come back. Either way, you're a good dude, Trevor. You'll find your woman. I thought I had the perfect woman ten years ago, and then the day before I was supposed to take her to Los Angeles, she was killed." James reached into his wallet and removed the worn newspaper article and carefully unfolded it. He handed the article to Trevor. "Molly and Noe both know the story. I never told anyone else."

"I never knew. You never said anything," said Trevor reading. He didn't remember his callous behavior when Kristen had died. Now, he was relieved to find someone else with a loss like his.

"It was a sign to get my life moving. Either fall down and dig myself into the dirt or start waiting for the dawn to light up the room."

"I've made a mess of thirty-seven years," said Trevor, as he continued reading the article before handing it back to James.

"This is the line that always gets me," said James, as his eyes found what he had long ago memorized. "'I can't believe so much life left so quickly.' You'll be okay, Trevor."

"What should I do?"

183

"I think it is time to kick Victorville into the trash and to start making some new stories," said James. "You can live in the past for only so long."

"Hey, Trev. I gotta agree with James. First, let's find out if the meatballs from Biagio's are really an antidepressant," said Noe. "Then we'll come back and put this place back into shape."

Chapter 24

"C'mon, Mom! I gotta get the book on my mission before someone else checks it out," said J.A., waiting by the door, the wrist of his handless arm nervously beating against his thigh.

"Can you grab a snack for Jake?" asked Kristen, as she scampered around the rooms looking for Kimberly's sweater, discovering it hidden under the morning paper still opened on the dining room table.

J.A. poured Goldfish, the cheddar cheese-like crackers, into two plastic lunch bags and snatched an apple from the fruit bowl on the counter. "Got it. Now can we go?"

"What mission is it?" asked Kristen, as she and Kimberly and Jake made a serpentine trail to the car.

"San Juan Capistrano," answered J.A., as he secured his seat belt in the front seat.

Kimberly and Jake were busy fishing the Goldfish out of their plastic bags as Kristen headed toward the mountains on Magnolia Boulevard. "Mom, can we go see our old house on the way to the library?" asked J.A.

"I thought you had to get to the library before anyone else? Wasn't there just the biggest rush in the universe like two minutes ago?" said Kristen with a smile.

"Two minutes is a long time," said her wise-beyond-his-years son of ten years. "Besides, a library must have more than a few books on each mission. Otherwise, why would it be a library?"

"Yeah, mom. Let's see our old house," said Kimberly, still nibbling on her bait.

"Let's see the hows," echoed Jake not sure what he was talking about other than supporting his siblings. If it was good enough for them, it was good enough for him.

They turned right on Glenoaks, passed the library parking lot on Orange Grove Avenue and then turned left up Olive Avenue toward their old house. When they reached Sunset Canyon, Kristen paused at the stop sign where James had missed her by a matter of seconds ten years ago, unbeknownst to either of them. They started the climb up Country Club Drive until they passed their house where Kristen traveled another hundred feet and turned the car around and parked. J.A. was six, almost seven, when the bank seized the house as one of their assets.

"Remember that time we were playing catch, and you missed the ball and you had to run so far down the street before you could get it?" said J.A. nostalgically.

"Or the time you hit the ball that broke your dad's headlight?" said Kristen.

"I know. I shoulda listened."

"I only told you five times," said Kristen.

"Dad wasn't very happy. But when is he?"

"Which one was my bedroom?" asked Kimberly, finished with her feeding frenzy of the edible Goldfish. "I have to go to the bathroom."

"You can't see it from here. You could see the whole Valley from your room. I thought you went before we left the house?"

186

"I didn't have to go then. Why'd we have to move?" asked Kimberly. "Mom, I really gotta pee."

"We'll be at the library soon. Things just happen sometime," said Kristen, not about to get into the real reasons with her seven-year old daughter. The crooked employee and the subsequent lawsuit that had bankrupted them and their law firm. How a multimillion dollar settlement had made the Porsche and the fine scotch and the designer clothes and luxurious travel and the twenty-nine-foot boat and their outstanding reputation and their spotless character disappear under the magic wand of a judge's gavel and enough bad headlines in the business section to send any company into the hospital with little chance for a cure. One bad seed in Ken's firm had poisoned everything they had reaped in one fell swoop. Ken and his father were left with the stump of the tree they had once seen bloom and bear fruit, and now there was no hope of leaves or limbs or blossoms again. Ken had enough left to buy the house they now lived in and a decent couple of cars, but the life of luxury that Ken had been accustomed to had disintegrated, and there was nothing to nourish Ken's moneyed appetite.

For J.A. the move to their current house was a blessing, with Verdugo Park less than a half mile from their house, where he could play baseball or basketball or football or any game he decided upon. During the summer, Marco Polo in the Community Pool or Capture the Flag on the large field at the end of the park. And the yards around his house were on flat ground, where his mother didn't have to run four hundred yards down a hill to catch up with an errant throw. He might have been able to see a ton of lights shining at night from the backyard of their old house, but if he wanted a Slurpee from a 7-Eleven, it was four miles and a long fifteen minutes to get there. The new house was a stones throw or a baseball toss away from everything. Five minutes at the most to satisfy a kid's ludicrous cravings. There in no time. Much better than a waxed Porsche sitting idly in a garage.

187

In the driveway of their former house, a vintage 1965 white Ferrari rested silently under the shade of two eucalyptus trees. An oak door had been replaced and widened with a pair of white French doors, and the driveway had become a puzzle of concrete and artificial turf. Kristen couldn't help but wonder how the revisions to their house had transpired, like the owners had reached into a closet and pulled out a new hanger of landscaping and architecture. The wardrobe of life was an individual choice, with so many possibilities from which to choose.

Kristen eased the car past the house until they reached the stop sign at the bottom of the hill, where she turned right on Sunset Canyon Drive and then left on Orange Grove Avenue, where the parking lot of the library awaited.

"Mom, I gotta pee," reiterated Kimberly, as Kristen drove down the street.

"We're almost there, Honey," said Kristen, turning to reassure her daughter that the library was only a couple of minutes away.

It happened so fast Kristen barely had time to react. A minivan was parked along the side of the street, blocking Kristen's view, and when she looked behind to reassure Kimberly, she didn't see the little boy run into the street or his father sprinting madly to grab him just one moment before Kristen would have hit him. At the last second, and with a blood curdling scream of "Look out" from J.A., Kristen swerved just enough to miss them both by inches, maybe even grazing the gray sweatshirt of the father. She hit her brakes after passing and could see them both heading toward the sidewalk safely, the father squeezing his son tightly. She thought of stopping to see if they were both okay, her own body trembling from a moment that could have transformed a tranquil early evening into a day never to be forgotten. A couple of seconds. A couple of feet. A slower reaction. Her body shuddered with what could have been. She slowed the car toward the curb and could see in the rear view mirror a gray, sweatshirted hand, wave a comforting sigh of relief. There was almost something familiar in the man's wave.

"Mom, I gotta pee!" said Kimberly, completely unaware of the events that had just unfolded.

"You okay, Mom?" asked J.A. "That was close."

"Too close," answered Kristen, barely able to get the words out. "I should really stop."

"Mom!" said a squirming agitated Kimberly.

"You were great, Mom. I thought they were dead. You missed them. You saved them," said J.A. "Kimberly be quiet, we're almost there."

Kristen didn't feel much like a savior, as she continued slowly down the street toward the library. She had prided herself on her defensive driving skills, always being ready for what might materialize, always being prepared for the unexpected, and always being primed to stop a moment from lasting a lifetime. One second of checking her daughter in the back seat and then one second of action, of quickly turning the wheel, was all she needed to pounce and swerve out of the way.

Except for Kimberly's bathroom success, the library was uneventful. Three books on the Mission San Juan Capistrano, founded less than four months after the United States of America's own Independence Day in 1776, were just waiting for the eager hand of J.A. Anderson to snatch them off the shelf and for another pair of young eyes to read and understand the story of Father Serra and his travels through California. Kristen Anderson's voyage down Orange Grove Avenue with her three children in the car was enough of an adventure, an adventure she hoped she would never face again.

Chapter 25

"**Did** you make an appointment?" asked James.

"They said they could see me in two weeks," added Molly, pulling frozen hamburger meat from the freezer.

"They didn't have anything sooner? Two weeks seems like a long time."

"They said if they have a cancellation they'll call. I told them I would like to get in earlier, like today, if they get an opening. The doctor isn't even there on Friday. What has happened to people working five days a week?"

"I'm sure the lump is going to be nothing," said James.

"I feel good except for that. I hate not knowing," said Molly, placing the hamburger meat into the microwave to thaw.

"Yeah, me too. I can call if you want and make a stink. I'm good at stinking."

"Tell me about it. They'll call if they have an opening. I don't think two weeks is going to make a difference," said Molly. "Amber should be home from dance pretty soon. Will you be able to take next week? I think I have a meeting."

"It shouldn't be a problem. Next week is open for me."

"Do you want to take her to the library when she gets home? She has her mission project due soon."

"Can't she just use the internet?"

"No. The teacher said they needed at least two books as sources," said Molly, as she retrieved the thawed ground beef from the microwave. "And your sweatshirt..."

"I'll change before we go, but I am really good at stinking."

"Probably an hour and a half until we have dinner."

"Where's Christian?"

"He should be kicking the soccer ball around. Did you look in the backyard?"

"Yeah. Didn't see him. I'll try the front."

James opened the front door. At first he didn't see Christian, but then he noticed his short legs running down the driveway after his soccer ball that was rolling toward the street. A nightmare formed in James' mind as he screamed at Christian to stop. A car was coming down the street. Like Usain Bolt in the Olympics, like a speeding bullet, like lightning released from a bottle, James sprinted toward his son, his six-year-old son, who went to sleep each night at eight, who couldn't even watch a movie rated P.G. yet, who couldn't throw a baseball more than twenty feet, who was the epitome of innocence, and who was now, almost at the end of the driveway, now passing their minivan parked in the street, their minivan blocking Christian from a driver's sight, hiding his little body from the approaching car. James swiveled his head and could see the car oblivious towards his son. As he raced with every ounce of adrenaline pumping through his legs, James snatched his son, grabbed one of the two best presents he had ever received, a second before the swerving, screeching car would have hit him. James felt the side of the car graze his thigh, as he twirled like a ballerina, and then watched as the car slowed toward the curb in front of him. Christian started to cry with the intensity of his father's hug, knowing that he had

191

broken the rules of the street. But they weren't hurt. James waved to the slowed car. He could see it was a mother and her children, that they were fine, that they weren't hurt. He watched as the car slowed and edged toward the curb and then continued slowly down the street. He hugged his son with the passion of knowing how close they had come to death or at the best a serious injury. He remembered a day ten years ago, and a tragedy he would never forget. He looked at the crying, innocent eyes of his son and remembered 'How so much life can leave so quickly,' and sank to the ground and sobbed, a waterfall of tears, a waterfall of thanks. His son broke the tears as only a small child can.

"Daddy, can you get my soccer ball?" asked Christian, looping his arm and his tears around his dad's neck.

Christian waited on the front steps of their house as James retrieved the ball from across the street where it had rolled up his neighbors' driveway and stopped on their lawn. He crossed the street and rolled the ball toward his son, who promptly kicked the ball right into his father's stomach. James grunted as he caught the ball. "Good kick," he said thankfully, and the world resumed turning on its axis.

When they both entered the house, the almost tragic events were downplayed. How does one tell his spouse that their child was possibly a second from disappearing from the earth? How does one explain a mistake that could have led to tragedy? How does one explain the importance of a second?

"Molly, I think we need to talk to Christian again about playing in the front yard," said James, as Molly approached the boys in the living room.

"Why? What happened?" asked Molly, drying her hands.

"I almost got hit by a car," said Christian, starting to cry.

Molly put her arms around her son. "You have to be really careful. I thought we said no playing in the front yard? He almost got hit?" she questioned James.

"Yeah, I grabbed him just in time."

"Someone was speeding down the street?"

192

"No. A mother and her kids. He was chasing the ball and ran right in front of their car."

"Christian, no dessert for a week."

"But Mom," and Christian's wails hit another decibel.

Amber walked through the front door into the hysteria of the living room. "Did something happen to Peaches?" she asked with fear in her eyes, worrying that her Scotch Terrier had been run over.

"Everything is OK, Honey," said Molly, reassuring her daughter. "Your brother and you really need to be careful when you are crossing the street."

"Can I go to the library?" Amber asked, quickly shifting the gears of her life.

"Your dad will take you as soon as he changes. Just be careful when you are crossing the street. There's a lot of crazy drivers out there."

Minutes later James and Amber drove down Orange Grove toward the library.

"What are we having for dinner?" asked Amber from the back seat.

"Hamburgers or spaghetti. I can't remember which mom said she was making."

"Nancy said my pirouettes and my plies were really good today," added Amber with pride. "I don't know why we have to do a mission project. I don't want to make a mission."

"What's your mission?"

"Mission San Juan Capistrano."

As James' car entered the parking lot at one end, another car filled with three children and a shaken mother exited the lot from the opposite end and drove up the street.

In the 979.4 section of the library, James and Amber found hundreds of books on the missions of California, but as much as they searched, they couldn't find any on San Juan Capistrano. The missions at Santa Cruz and Santa Barbara and San Jose and San Buenaventura and Santa Clara were well

193

represented on the shelves, but the Mission San Juan Capistrano was nowhere to be found.

At first the librarian was little help in aiding James, and when she viewed her screen to see when the books had been checked out, she chuckled that they had just missed by a few minutes the person who had gotten to them first. This time of year was always a scramble to find enough books on each mission and the Mission San Juan Capistrano was one of the most popular. She hinted that the library five miles away on Scott Street might have some, and then grabbed the initiative and called ahead and successfully had them hold two books at the main desk until James and his daughter could arrive.

In twenty minutes James and Amber were headed home, hungry to bite into dinner, with two Mission San Juan Capistrano books lying untouched on the floor of the car.

Chapter 26

"**I** think this was the house," said Kristen, as she pulled to the curb.

"I think you're right, but I don't see the car anymore," said J.A., examining the front yard for any clues.

"I never should have just left. I almost .."

"Mom. You saved that kid. He never should…"

"It doesn't matter. I just feel terrible." Kristen stopped the car and lovingly ran her hand through J.A.'s hair. At ten years old he was a real man. She walked up the driveway and then to the front door of the house she hoped belonged to the father and son she had almost hit.

Molly opened the front door and Christian hid behind her. "Can I help you?"

"I just wanted to stop. I think, I know I almost hit…" and Kristen could see the little hands holding the dress of his mother. "I'm happy you're okay." Kristen tried to peek behind the grasped dress. "Is he okay?"

"Yeah. He really got a scare. It is really nice of you to stop and check. I guess it was a close call."

"I have three kids," said Kristen, her eyes starting to well with emotion.

"Tell her you're OK," said Molly, but Christian wouldn't come out of hiding.

"And your husband is …"

"He's fine. He just left but should be back soon. I'll tell him you stopped. That is …"

"I should've stopped before. That was my mistake. I'm just happy everyone's OK," said Kristen, as she turned to join her own priceless gems waiting in her car.

Chapter 27

"**I** can't believe my mission got a 'B,'" said J.A. as he climbed into the car, removing his backpack and placing it on the seat. "She said I forgot the cross and that the grounds needed to be bigger, or something like that. I think everyone else got an 'A'. I don't think she likes me."

"A 'B' is totally acceptable. And J.A., trust me, she likes you. I think everyone likes you," offered Kristen as she checked her mirror for cars.

"I'm hungry. You forgot the cookies in my lunch today," began Kimberly, climbing in behind J.A. and adjusting her seat belt.

"We'll be home soon, Honey. You can grab a snack when we get there."

"Dad was up early today," added J.A. "He was really happy. I don't get it. I thought he was going to be mad about my room, but he even made us waffles. I was at school so early today. I even played four games of dodgeball with the little ball and pegged a couple of fifth and sixth graders. I wish he was up early everyday."

"That's just your dad. He tries the best he can."

"I love playing in the morning. Johnny has been talking about how good he is at kickball and I can't wait to play him," said the competitive J.A. "He always kicks the ball toward Marcie, but everyone knows Marcie can't catch. I don't know why he would do that? She's really nice."

"Is she your girlfriend?" chided Kimberly.

"No way. Wow! Looks like Dad is home already."

"That is a change, isn't it?" said Kristen, a little uneasy about the oddity of Ken being home before six-thirty.

The car emptied and feet and projects and backpacks made their way through the front door, and into the kitchen where they were greeted by a black sport coat, gray pleated slacks, blue and white pinstriped shirt and a solid blue tie.

Kristen's arms were filled with the papers of the day and a Tupperware dish stained with the remnants of two-day-old lasagna. She dumped her goods on the kitchen table and kissed the cheek of the stranger in her house. "What's going on?" she asked suspiciously.

"I think I got a job."

"You look good." said Kristen, impressed with Ken for a change, but still cautious.

"One of my dad's friends. Remember Bill Thomas, the guy with the car business?"

"Don't tell me you're selling cars? A car salesman?"

"No. I'm not selling cars, though some car salesmen make a decent living."

"But you're not used to a decent living."

"I was a lawyer and a damn good one," started Ken, more effusive than he had been since his exterminator debacle. After the lawsuit that ended his law career, his first attempt back into the world of work was killing pests, but the picture of the giant roach on the hood of his car destroyed his confidence and ability. "And you know that after Bug Dye, I wasn't too eager to get back to work."

"You never should have been putting tents over houses, Ken. I told you that, but you insisted," continued Kristen, as she retrieved a bottle of Coppola Vineyards Cabernet.

Ken found the wine opener in the drawer and eased the bottle from her hand and then the tightness of the cork from the neck. He poured her a glass and set the bottle on the counter. "I am the new auto finance manager at Burbank Lexus."

"Good for you," said Kristen, not about to throw any dirt on this newly lit match that might light an actual fire. It is a terrible thing to lose one's reputation, and with the fall of Anderson, Anderson and McClure, names that now were synonymous with fraud, Ken had an almost impossible task of reestablishing a name of value and trust. Even though Ken was held partly responsible for his firm's failure, this step into auto finance seemed to be a move in the right direction. Reputation is strange. It can cover some undeserving soul in gold. On the other hand, it can smear an innocent person through vicious rumors of misdeeds that never happened. Maybe through the small office in the back of Burbank Lexus, Ken could return the shimmer to the name of Anderson.

"Within a year, they said, I should be able to double my salary."

"What're they starting you at?

Ken shook his head negatively and took a deep breath, "Fifty K plus commission. That's where the real money is."

"That'll help. You're really good with numbers, and you know how to make people believe in you." Kristen felt a pang of appreciation for Ken's reaching under his king-sized bed of expectations and his willingness to, for once, take off the belt of entitlement he had worn for so long. When your father and your father's father have been such big players in the game of life, you don't have any expectations of being taken out of the game and thrown out of the league. An automobile financial manager was a title he would never have seen in a crystal ball.

199

"Jack Boston, the guy that interviewed me. The guy can talk like most people walk. He introduced me to Herb Likken, sounds like a money guy, the guy who's leaving. Pretty cool office. Classy dark wood, maybe mahogany, last stop for the person who has just bought the car. And then it's up to me to get a few more dollars out of his wallet. Just like in court, I'll have to make my case. But I'll get to be judge and jury and convince the poor sucker to buy the extended warranty on his car, or the best interest rate that he can get is a six point nine percent, or he better make sure his paint is protected." Ken was in salesman mode.

"When do you start?"

"On Monday. I'm feeling good, Kristen. I know I've been a burden for the last three years. I know you do more than you should have to with the kids. I've gone through about ten new leaves that I keep turning over and then I step on their edges and they turn brown. But today the leaf is staying green for good. Hey kids, let's see what they're selling at Farrell's."

As the children reacted predictably, Kristen poured herself another glass of wine, the red liquid spilling into the glass, running up the side and then settling, its surface smooth, a red calm ocean of alcohol, waiting for the waves to form and crash on the shore.

Chapter 28

"Mrs. Brand," said the nurse, as she opened the door into the waiting area of Dr. Saki's office.

Molly grabbed James' hand tightly, as they walked past the nurse toward the doctor's desk. "Please take a seat. Dr. Saki will be with you shortly," the nurse continued with little warmth.

As the door closed behind them, Molly and James sat anxiously. They knew the results of the tests were in, and now it was a matter of waiting for the news. James looked at Molly reassuringly. "No matter what the news is," he started, squeezing her anxious hand, "we are going to take care of this. Besides there was nothing there two months ago, so this is the beginning stages of whatever it is, and it might be nothing. We don't know. It could be just some fibrous growth that is not cancerous." His words did little to lessen the apprehension that Molly was feeling. She was an iceberg, a smile to reassure James, but underneath her smile, a continent of ice was chilling her soul.

Wearing a white lab coat, Dr. Saki entered the room, and after greeting James and Molly warmly, took a seat behind his desk. He clasped his hands below his chin and then just as quickly started talking. "Thanks for coming. The tests came back positive for cancer."

Molly started to cry immediately. Dr. Saki's lips continued to move, and despite Molly's sobs, the room became deafeningly silent as James put his arm around his wife.

"Molly, I think you are going to be fine," assured Dr. Saki. Remember this isn't the dark ages of cancer treatment of ten to fifteen years ago. The lump they found was small, very small. The research shows that a case like yours reacts exceptionally well to a new drug, THX21, from the Center of Genomic Regulation. With just three doses of THX21, I expect you to have a full recovery. One dose a week for three weeks, not even a month of treatment. There has been a ninety percent success rate in the past year with patients suffering from the same cancer that you have."

"What is THX21? We read about it. We read about some side effects," said a still icy Molly, wiping the tears out of her eyes.

"It's actually named after Dr. Thukix, a Welsh scientist, who used the spines of sea urchins found off the coast of Scotland to create a serum that has proven unbelievably powerful in destroying the cells found in breast cancer. In your case, the size of your lump was under two centimeters. Also in your case, the cancer cells are not the aggressive cells I see quite often. I am extremely optimistic."

"What can Molly do? What can we do? Will there be any side effects? Will she lose her appetite? Will she have to have a mastectomy?" asked James, leaning forward still gripping Molly's fingers.

"She can do anything she wants. And she won't lose any of her hair either. Some patients complain of nausea and insomnia, but the overall results have been excellent. The THX21 should clear things up for good. We will bring her back in for tests in three months, and I expect the tissue in her breasts to be one hundred percent healthy."

"Thank you, Dr. Saki," said Molly. "Thank you so much." She lifted her cold, calmed frame from the chair, confident, as confident as she could be that she would be cured.

"If you have any other questions, don't hesitate to call."

"I'm sure we will," said James.

After they left the office, they quietly walked through the hall, Molly's hand draped over James' arm.

"You, young lady, are going to be better than ever," said James optimistically.

"Yeah. I think you're right," whispered Molly, reflecting a few rays of sunshine off her iceberg. "And I'm going to be here bugging you with honey-do lists that never end."

"Are you sure you like Dr. Saki? Maybe we should get a second opinion?"

"Are you trying to be funny? Not funny, James."

"Yeah, you're right. Not funny at all. You make that list longer than the Dead Sea Scrolls."

"Never read them."

"I don't think anybody has."

"Then how do you know how long they are?" asked Molly, her ice melting, noticeably devoid of the anxiety that had invaded her fifteen minutes before in the doctor's office.

"Google. Said they were a mile and a half long."

"I don't think you should believe everything you read on the internet."

"Well, I asked Google if we should have more children and about our future."

"What'd Google say?"

"Said if we had another child, it would be born as only a head."

"Just a head, huh? We wouldn't know what sex it was?" wondered Molly.

"That's where Google told me the future of the head. Said we would name the head Pat, so maybe it was a Patrick or a

Patricia. Just play it safe. And the kids would take Pat to school under their arms," said James.

Molly smiled at James and continued his story, "And then after it graduates from high school and goes to college the kids carry the head under their arms like a football, to Scully's on Pat's twenty-first birthday and they drink and Pat sprouts legs and arms and a body, and then they have one more drink, just one more, and Pat dies, right there on Scully's floor. What a mess. And the bartender looks at dead Pat on the floor and then at the kids and says, 'I guess he should have quit while he was a head.'"

"You've heard it before?"

"You told it to me at least twice. James, I don't know why you try to be funny. You're not," said Molly smiling. "Stop Googling the future, for Christ's sake."

"Did I ever tell you about the lady who wanted a chocolate ice cream from 31 Flavors?"

"They were probably out of chocolate," said Molly shaking her head at James' old jokes, wondering if the fear of her cancerous iceberg would ever melt away.

Part 3 - Fifteen years later – 2029

Chapter 29

Twenty-four-year old Amber steered into the parking lot of Biagio's restaurant and spotted her father standing behind his fifteen-year-old Ford 250.

"I don't know how these new fangled cars drive. It is five times worse than playing video games back in the day, with all those buttons," said James approaching his daughter's car, waiting for the doors to close automatically. "It's good to see you, Honey. You look great."

"I can't wait for lunch. Every time I come back, I want to taste the good ol' days. And let's get this settled right now. I'm paying for my father," said Amber, as she inhaled the nostalgic Italian aroma she knew so well.

"You've gotta tell me about your new job. You interned for the Dukes and now they've hired you? Sports medicine is a tough field."

"I feel pretty lucky. You should get a new car, Dad. You can afford it."

"I still don't see how a person can take a nap while the car is driving you. I don't think I could ever get used to it. I'll have to drive my old truck until I die. I actually went down to the dealership and took the new version out for a spin and just about scared the hell out of the car salesman."

"Dad, things change."

"I know. I bought myself a Bathroom Bot. A machine to clean the toilet and shower. Now, that is progress."

"To flux or not to flux."

"Shakespeare must have said that."

"My dad is still the coolest guy around. So is she a hottie?" said Amber, as they were seated at a booth and handed menus, a remnant of the past in most restaurants. "Gotta love the feel of a menu."

"Your mom was the hottest," said James.

"Where are you going on your date? It's about time you got back out there."

"I'm taking her to dinner and then I have three options. The new and improved paintball is making a comeback, or I thought maybe we would do the African Interaction in the Serengeti, or the old school midnight drive to the beach after watching a movie. I hear the remake of *One Flew Over the Cuckoo Nest in 3D* is supposed to be pretty good."

"I like the paintball. The new weapons are outrageous and the new Paintball Playgrounds, especially the one that is a replica of the Fermi Crater on the far side of the moon. My friends played Fermi, a few months ago. They have one in Texas, and they said it was awesome."

"That's probably where I should take her, but it's tough to teach an old dog new tricks. I'm probably just going to do the movie and then drive to the beach."

"Christian called and said you finally broke down and bought one of the new roll up entertainment screens. Have you taken it to the beach, yet?"

"I'm not going to do that. The beach is for umbrellas and bodysurfing and skimboarding and suntan lotion and sunglasses and making castles. I still can't get used to people unrolling their entertainment system at the beach and watching reruns of *The Simpsons*. It's ridiculous. Watching shows at the beach."

"Dad, now you can get a tan and not miss your favorite ball game either. The Super Bowl at the beach instead of inside some stupid house. That is so much better."

"I guess you can't stop progress, but could we slow it down a little," said James sarcastically.

"I'm happy you're going on this date. You know Mom would be pushing you out the door. It's been four years."

"I've been busy. Disneyland has been going through all those renovations. I haven't even taken a vacation in the last three years. Welding has been good to me. Kept me out of trouble."

"It kept you out of fun, too, if you ask me. You're the one who always said a person's gotta live 'cause everything could be lost in a second. Mom said you always kept a newspaper article with you for motivation. Why?"

James wondered if this was the proper time to share his past with his daughter. Did it really matter what had happened in his life so long ago?

When James hesitated, Amber asked again, "Did you always keep some article with you? Did you?"

"A long time ago," started James, as he was interrupted by the waitress, a welcome interruption to take their orders, as he struggled to find the proper words to explain his past. "I thought my life was going one way and then. Pow! Life is…" James struggled, collapsed, "…unpredictable."

"Do you still have the article? I'd like to read it," persisted Amber, not ready to let her father off the hook.

"Honey, it really doesn't say much."

"Then why do you carry it? What happened?"

"Someone died and you and your brother lived."

"Who died?"

"Amber," started James awkwardly.

"When I was growing up, we never really talked. I was always so into me, that you and Mom were just Mom and Dad.

207

Now I don't get to see you as much as I would like and Mom's gone. I want to know more. Until Mom died, the two of you were my inspirations of how to live. You went places. You tried new things. You weren't afraid to fail. The two of you. I really miss Mom. And then you just seemed to stop."

"I wasn't very good at taking my own advice."

"So what happened so long ago?"

The sandwiches arrived at the table. "Let me take a couple of bites first, and then," said James, as he unwrapped the paper from the dripping meat sauce and chewed thoughtfully.

"Well you heard the story of the black eye at least a thousand times. I didn't think there was much chance of your mom and me ever working things out. I was obviously wrong about that. But before I found out your mom and I had a chance, I met this woman who swept me off my feet. I really thought she was the one. It was cosmic, that feeling of a lifetime that you maybe get once or if you are lucky, like I was, twice. And then one day, she was just walking down the street looking through store windows, when a car went out of control and ran up on the sidewalk and killed her instantly. Just like that, gone. Her death has always reminded me just how fragile life can be."

"That must have been heartbreaking. I guess if that didn't happen, though, Christian and I might not be here."

"I was crushed when it happened. But from every thorn grows a rose. Yeah, you and Christian are pretty damn good roses. And I get to break meatball bread with my daughter today. Do you still want to see the article?" said James, reaching toward his back pocket.

"No, that's okay. I'm just happy I'm here. Did you ever think how different your life would have been if she hadn't been killed?"

"Not really. Since that day I haven't worried too much about what might have been. If you ask me, it is a waste of time to think how life would have been different. No sense living in the past. The past isn't going to change. I wish I could bring your

208

mom back to life, but I can't. I wish she was here to see you get married and have children. I'd give my left arm to have your mom sitting at the table with us right now, but my left arm isn't going to bring her back. It is what it is. And if, what is, isn't what you want, and you can actually do something to get what you want, then you better get busy and start throwing fastballs at the red circle in the middle of the target. Speaking of fastballs, I still want to hear about your new job."

"I have six days off, now that the Dukes are paying me, and then I rejoin the team here. They're playing out in the desert. Remember that kid that set all the records in high school and only had one hand?"

"Yeah, J.A. Anderson. I followed him through UCLA, but I've lost track of him lately."

"They think he is making it to the big leagues. He is the number two starter in Triple A. He plays for the team that hired me. For the first two months, we didn't really talk, but lately I've been working on his arm."

"Tell him your dad is a big fan. I think it was your Uncle Noe who first told me about him. He struck out Aaron on two pitches when he was really young."

"Aaron played little league? Don't you mean three pitches?"

"He was so good he only needed two pitches," said James with a grin.

"The team is coming into town this weekend. You should come out for one of the games."

Chapter 30

"**Are** you sure you want to enlist?" said Kristen.

"Mom, no. I don't want to enlist. I think it is a stupid idea, really," said Jake, across the kitchen counter from his mother, still in the same house on Whitnall Highway.

"Then don't go. Get your general classes out of the way at Valley College at least. Don't go unless it's what you want."

"Mom, we have been over this," said Jake, with a little frustration.

"You'll turn it around."

"I was never J.A. And I was never Kimberly. And everything I have ever tried has always gone into the shitter. I mean my brother's almost in the Big Leagues and here I am with another possession charge against me. I'm just lucky I haven't had a felony."

"We all mess up. I made a mess of your dad and me."

"I think Dad made a mess of things."

"It takes two to tango."

"Yeah, but you didn't get drunk three nights a week and use windows for your basketball backboards."

"But I should have done something. I don't know what, but I should have done something."

"All those teachers used to look at me when they found out J.A. was my brother, like they couldn't believe it. Like, what happened to you?"

"Everybody has their different talents, Jake."

"Ya wanna tell me what mine is, besides getting into trouble?"

"I always loved your art, but after middle school you never wanted it anymore."

"That's why I want to enlist. I've always done what I wanted. It's never worked. Maybe if I do something I don't want to do, then maybe, this time it will work. I'm tired of jumping into the dumpster of life. How's J.A.'s arm? I heard he was going to be out for a couple of days."

"You should call your brother. He's coming to town in about a week, I think."

"He doesn't want to see me. Ever since I was asked to leave that game a year ago."

"Your brother wants to see you. Didn't he always stick up for you?"

"That was a long time ago, before I started hanging with the wrong crowd. Sorry about some of the late nights."

"I'm sorry about all the fighting you had to see. Every time we were in the car together we were two ugly human beings. You never should have had to watch us wage our stupid wars."

"Mom, you are a beautiful lady, despite a couple of the gray hairs I gave you. Was Dad a lot different when you first got married? I just never saw the two of you in love and it kinda scares me to think I could end up like that, too."

"Awwww Jacob, that was a long time ago. You think you know what is right and wrong and you try to do the right thing and think that it will be good, but you just never know. I was always picking the wrong guy. Maybe if I had enlisted things would have been different."

"I just never saw Dad as charming. As some white knight. I always saw you as the beautiful princess."

"Your dad was a really good lawyer. But you know how that one guy that he hired turned out to poison the whole company. Your dad lost more than just his work. He lost his identity, and no matter how hard he tried, he never got it back. Maybe he should have enlisted, too."

"Mom, one of these days I'm going to make you proud."

"I've always been proud to be your mother. You've pissed the hell out of me, but you're my son and will always be my son."

"You deserve someone, Mom. I'm the last one at home and I'll be gone soon. You're way beautiful. Wouldn't you like to meet someone?"

"Maybe my sixth grade boyfriend, Kyle Carnes, will reappear, and we can reminisce about tetherball and how we used to share Hostess Twinkies at lunch. Or maybe James will come back," said Kristen with a sudden jolt of memory, "and kiss me again, like nothing has happened for the last twenty-five years, and explain why he left me standing in my room, throwing my phone into the wall, like an idiot."

"You see, there is still a chance for you," said Jake. "Who was James?"

Chapter 31

When you haven't been on a date in twenty-five years, the only basis for your actions is the antiquities of the past. James hoped the yellow store-bought roses that smelled like cardboard would be the appropriate introduction for an arranged date with Patty, a friend of Noe's wife. The first step was always the most difficult, and James wasn't looking for a home run, just the chance to swing at a few pitches and maybe, if he was lucky, make contact.

Patty had worked with Noe's wife for over ten years. For the last two years she hadn't dived into the waters of dating. After fifteen years of marriage, Patty's unexpected divorce from her traveling-salesman husband had left her squeamish about sticking her feet back in the water, but Noe's wife had insisted that Patty get her feet wet and she knew just the person, James.

Meanwhile, Noe's wife told James that Patty was beautiful and could make him laugh if he would only accept her idiosyncrasies. Her idiosyncrasies, James realized, were a large red flag flying over the high dive of dating, but Noe was still his best friend, and his wife had comforted James through the difficult time of Molly's passing. He had to say yes.

"Hi, James. Come on in," said Patty as she opened the door. "James, you shouldn't have. These are beautiful. Let me put them in water right now." She took the flowers immediately to the kitchen as James followed.

"You have a nice place," said James as he watched Patty perform with precision in the kitchen, removing the paper, trimming the stalks, filling the vase, and drying the bottom of the glass, before placing the finished product in the middle of the kitchen table. James wasn't sure what Noe's wife's definition of beautiful was, but he knew it didn't match his. She was pleasing to the eye, a few pounds overweight but at this age who is counting, and the red, not ginger, but red streak through her dirty blonde hair, would have been better placed in a rainbow than on her head.

"Let me grab you a glass of wine."

"I would have brought some if I had known."

"I usually drink too many alone, so it's nice to share. Red okay?"

"Yeah, that'll be fine." The first few minutes were over, and James presumed this was the process of dating. The meaningless introduction. The commonality of pleasantries spread, whether meant or not, before the main dish of the evening was served. And then the nibbling at the entree, being polite with bites and smiles. Of savoring the flavors. Of deciding if this menu item was indeed inedible after all. The true and false question of how the evening went would only be answered in the morning. Although it had been twenty-five years, James couldn't help but think about his chance meeting with Kristen at Scully's. Two tumbleweeds blown together by the wind. Two separate roads that converged into one. Two raindrops that fell randomly on the windshield of life and then ran together. Their meeting had been pure poetry. Now he was standing in the living room, wondering if there would be any words that rhymed with Patty.

High in the hills of Burbank stood the latest "in" restaurant, The Clouds, the trendy buzz of where and what to eat. Their filet mignon with Beárnaise sauce was praised with salivating words. The restaurant changed owners and names more frequently than Taylor Swift had changed husbands. Seven at the last count. James assisted Patty out of his truck and toward the receptionist who led them to their table overlooking the city.

"Did you just touch my shoulder?" queried Patty, as they were seated.

"Yeah, I think I grazed it, when I pushed the chair in."

"Oh. You didn't mean for your fingers to leave ..."

"What do you mean?" asked James.

"Why'd you touch my shoulder?" asked Patty, her eyes scrutinizing James for a reason for breaking her law of the shoulder.

James didn't know what to say, wondering if maybe she had had a few bottles of wine before he had arrived. "I wanted to see if it was real," attempted James, hoping levity would relieve the pressure of a swelling shoulder.

"You don't think my shoulder is real?" asked Patty, with too much realism in the face of absurdity.

"I never questioned that for a second. What do you think you might want to order?" said James, trying to redirect the traffic jam, trying to hit the brakes of this conversation, as he lifted the menu screen in front of his face.

Patty, thankfully, left the world of the shoulder and lifted her screen. "Just coffee, if you don't mind."

"Just coffee? The steaks are supposed to be some of the best in all of Southern California. You can't order just coffee."

James could see the wheels turning in Patty's transparent head, realizing she was about to drive this date over the side of the road and down into a ravine. "Maybe just the mashed potatoes. Do you think they have any Jello?"

215

The city lights stretched for miles, as James shifted his eyes away from the streak of red hair toward the night. Jello? He wondered. Strawberry or lime or lemon or orange or maybe even a restaurant like The Clouds would have mango with a hint of pineapple. He reminded himself not to judge and that if Patty wanted mashed potatoes, he would hope they were the best she would ever taste. "I've heard their mashed potatoes are excellent. You sure you don't want a steak."

"No. Just the potatoes. And some coffee."

After they had ordered and the waiter gave James a look of bewilderment about his choices, James looked for a positive avenue of dialogue.

"Have you traveled very much?"

"All over the world. I love traveling."

"What were some of the places you liked?"

"Benny took care of everything. He would do the packing. He ordered the flights. He chose the cities. Benny left me, James. We were in Denmark when he left. He just left. I had to figure out how to get home. He just left."

James was wishing Noe's wife would walk through the front door of The Clouds and rescue him. "But you made it home, didn't you?"

"Not before landing in Portugal. Did you know they speak Spanish in Portugal and speak Portuguese in Spain?" said Patty, brushing the streak of red hair behind her ear. Patty moved her water glass to the side, as the waiter carefully placed a plate with a mound of mashed potatoes in front of her. "And the Portuguese man-of-war lives in the ocean and helped Portugal win the war with Spain in 1960, I think." She inched the plate of mashed potatoes close to the edge of the table.

As his steak knife slowly cut through the filet in front of him, James tried to comprehend the nature of the universe spinning around his axis. He noticed Patty taking an imaginary forkful of mashed potatoes as he took a bite of steak that had lost the flavor of the circumstances. She chewed as if there was

216

actually something in her mouth. His teeth weren't tasting the lifeless meat in his mouth. James watched as Patty placed an infinitesimal amount of mashed potatoes on her fork and slowly brought them to her mouth. He cut off another piece of the steak and raised the fork to his lips.

"Have you ever been to Paris?"

Before she could answer, Patty started choking on her mashed potato. The bite she had taken was actually too small to say it was really mashed potatoes. She coughed again with uneasiness and then took a sip of water. When James asked if she was all right, she quickly tried to bring a hand to her mouth, but it was too late, and she awkwardly spit the contents over the table and quickly excused herself to the bathroom.

"James, I'm really sorry, but I just don't feel well," she said upon returning to the table.

"I am so sorry, Patty. We'd better get you home," said James, hastily rising from the table, joyfully leaving his half-eaten dinner behind, as he summoned the waiter to clear the bill.

The fifteen-minute ride home was filled with Patty's explanation of the night. A river of "hows" started flowing from her mouth. How she had always been nervous when she first met someone new, and especially one as handsome as James. How coffee is her comfort food, and how she suffers from dysphagia, a problem swallowing. How she is not sure of the cause, that nothing physical has been found, and she is sure it is nothing psychological. How when she saw James look at her after she forked a small bite of mashed potatoes into her mouth, the dysphagia hit with a vengeance. How, if he wanted, he could come in and have sex with her if he didn't have anything else to do, and how Benny said she was great in bed, and in fact, all the men she sleeps with, all say she is really a "hot mama" when it comes to "you know." James was thrilled when the car stopped at the curb and she kissed him on his cheek, when he said he couldn't come in. The river of "hows" was finally dry.

After dropping Patty at the Ponderosa, he reflected on his luck. He was sure Kristen would have been perfect, and Molly wasn't very far behind. He had had eighteen good years with Molly, and two wonderful children, before she was taken from him. The doctors had been sure that she would be cancer free for life and that breast cancer would soon be eradicated with the treatment of THX21. Scientists were shocked to find that eight to ten years after THX21 treatments had been green lighted by the FDA, that the first patients receiving the cure relapsed, with the cancer returning with a vengeance, centered in the pancreas. Two years after so many were inflicted with this recurrence of cancer, scientists found the medicine that inhibited its return, but by then it was too late for Molly. For eight years Molly's yearly check-ups were a clean bill of health, but now James was driving home with the passenger seat empty.

In the last hour, James had been on a date he couldn't have scripted in a Hollywood movie. No wonder Ben left her in Denmark. James had no idea if that was even true. He had crossed the border, taken his first steps into the universe of dating and knew his next step could only be in a better world.

Chapter 32

"I'm just making sure you have next weekend off," said J.A. on the phone from Albuquerque.

"It's circled on my calendar," said Kristen reassuringly.

"We have a day game on Saturday; maybe we can go to Scully's that night. I haven't had their steak sandwich and steak fries in so long."

"Yeah, Scully's sounds great. I'll call Kimberly in San Diego. She's not that far away, so maybe she can join us. I know she'd love to see you."

"Jake will be there, right? Are you going to let him enlist?"

"It might be the best thing for him, but I just worry that something bad is going to happen. You know, the whole mom thing. Worry, worry, worry. I should have pushed your brother and his art more. He's a good artist. Life never lets a mother throw a perfect game. How's your arm? You missed a start?"

"We just got a new trainer about a month ago. She interned for the Angels. She was working on my arm last week and now it's feeling great. And she is pretty hot."

"Like in dating?"

"Not there yet, but maybe. You ever hear from Dad? I tried his number in Louisville, but nothing. He said he would go to a bunch of games this year, but I still haven't seen him or heard from him."

"He'll get there, Honey. He just needs to figure things out."

"He's been trying to figure things out for a long time, Mom. Whatever. How many things can a man do before he knows this is what he's meant for?"

"Your dad was meant to be a lawyer, and since that fell through, he has just floundered. Some people never find what they were meant to do. It's not as easy as you might think. You've been blessed in finding your passion. Trust me J.A., you are not typical."

"You've always been there for me, Mom. I can't wait to see you guys on Saturday. Maybe some day the ghost will reappear. Do you know what he's doing?"

"The last I heard, he was designing a package for portable entertainment systems, but I don't know any more than that. Turning over another new leaf."

Ken was always turning over another new leaf. The tree of life was almost bare with all the leaves Ken had torn from the branches. When the roots of his attorney days had died, the leaves started falling: car financier, where within two years the walls of his office became the claustrophobia that could only be cured by shots of Sapphire Gin and beer chasers; real estate agent, where in two years his skill at bullshit resulted in financial gain, but then the shit smeared over two questionably signed documents during escrow, and whatever trust he had with his clients soon disappeared; safety harness innovator, where for a year he was on the ground floor, only to find the floor crumbling under the stress tests performed by Consumer Reports and their subsequent negative rating; Costco Senior, only nine months, a steady job with a steady pay check, just not the employment for someone as earthquake prone as Ken; sewer cleaner, where in only four hours, he knew by lunch, that the job wasn't for him; and sporadic months as a house painter, everyone at some point paints houses, but not for long, as the ladders and preparation became as tedious as taking care of a newborn, and most men aren't ready to change diapers for the rest of their lives. His attempt at construction, though, turned out to be the leaf that broke the camel's back.

When Jake was in the third grade, Kristen knew she would leave Ken when the kids were out of the house. She could make it through another nine years, no matter how much dirt was stuck to the dishes. If she just soaked plates long enough in hot water, the dirt disappeared without much scrubbing. The kids gave her enough strength that she could deal with whatever dirt Ken had to throw at her, but she never expected the dirt that fell from the shovel of Conroy's Construction Company. Jackhammering through concrete, pickaxing through roots, and shoveling the earth contradicted the trial briefs Ken had expertly created as a lawyer. When the day ended at the construction site, his skin scorched, his muscles ached, and his fingers barely straightened for a job that required the physical brawn and physical attitude of youth, he looked for solace in the bottle and in the large breasts of the company's receptionist. Kristen had dealt with the bottle for many years, but the large breasts extinguished the chance of waiting for the house to empty before the divorce papers were signed. Ken promised to turn over many new leaves, but like George Washington had supposedly done hundreds of years before, Kristen chopped the blossoming cherry tree to the ground once and for all. After the breasts divided Kristen and Ken's marriage, he moved to Oregon where he worked for a subsidiary of Nike, and then to Idaho where he was a fly fishing guide along the St. Joe River, and finally to Kentucky, where he now resided. Ken's

221

attempts at parental stability were shaky even when he was living at home, but now that he was transient, rarely did he connect with his children.

"Maybe if I make it to the Majors and throw a no-hitter, he'll remember he has a son," said J.A. "He didn't remember I was family when I threw my perfect game at UCLA. He never said a thing."

"Listen J.A. Your dad never could accept or understand the imperfection in perfection. I'll try to find where he is. You never know what the future has in store for us. Maybe he will finally turn the right corner of life and find where he needs to be. I'll see you next week," said Kristen tenderly, her voice an ocean of serenity.

"See you then, Mom," said J.A. knowing it had always been his mother who had been there. She was the nurse and the teacher and the priest. She was there those few times that all the dirt had been excavated, and the shovel couldn't dig any deeper. She was the one, who handful by handful filled him with hope again. Those few times when he could see only the dark side of the moon, she was the one who stopped the ebb and flow of the tides, until he was ready to dive in again. She wasn't a ghost. She wasn't the Sahara Desert and the next day the South Pole. She wasn't a mirage as you drove to your destination. She was Mom. A hand you could count on for holding and touching and trusting.

Chapter 33

"Kathy, I'll be there," said Kristen, her hand fanning through a row of dresses hanging from a rack.

"I know it's a lot to ask, but the kids are out of the house now, and…"

"I'll be there. You're my sister and just because neither of us has the best taste in men doesn't mean that we shouldn't keep sampling the product."

"But you haven't taken a bite lately," said Kathy, picking a red dress from the rack and holding it before her.

Kristen shook her head no, "I still have a bad taste in my mouth. I don't know if all the Scope in the world can rinse it away."

"When was the last time you heard from Ken?"

"He sent a Christmas card and a little money, a very little money for the boys and Kimberly. The return address was from Buckner, Kentucky. About twenty miles east of Louisville."

"Talk about the fall of a tragic hero. Twenty-five years ago, he was on top of the world, and now he is living in Buckner."

"I would never have put him in the hero category. Tragic, yes, but Ken was hardly a hero," said Kristen.

"I think this one is the right one," said Kathy, eyeing a yellow floor-length gown.

"No. I don't see it," said Kristen her hand continuing the march through cloth.

"What's wrong with Howard?" said Kathy, stopping abruptly, a little shocked.

"There's nothing wrong with Howard," said Kristen, her hand exiting the dresses, and then realizing Kathy had mistaken her last comment. "I meant the yellow dress wasn't the right one. Not Howard."

Kathy was relieved, but still not sure, "You do think Howard fits me?"

"Kathy, I'm not exactly an expert on men myself. I thought Frank was a good fit. I admit I was wrong. He was about as bad as Ken and maybe even worse. Wilhelm, I thought was good. He liked to travel and knew history and knew literature and knew how to talk. I still don't know why he left so suddenly. I never saw that coming. On the other hand, Howard is kind and considerate and laughs, and he doesn't want a fancy wedding or a fancy car or a fancy menu to make him happy. He only seems to want you."

"He is pretty good, isn't he? You're right. It's like I was the Titanic and I kept hitting iceberg after iceberg, but I think with Howard, it's going to be smooth sailing."

"Yeah. I think you have finally found the one." An internal switch was triggered and Kristen felt an urge she had dispatched twenty-five years earlier. "Kath. I need to sit for a minute. How about a coffee?"

The wheels of confession slowly turned in Kristen's body, as the two sat with lattes in hand. The hard wooden chair didn't bring comfort to Kristen. She brought the mug to her lips, took a few sips of the truth serum, and deciphered the best way to begin. "I once thought I had found the one," started Kristen.

224

Kathy immediately sensed the seriousness of what Kristen was about to say, her gaze and tone well off the course of a typical conversation. "You mean you had an affair?" said Kathy, eager to listen to the depths of her sister's anguish. "When and with who?"

"No, before I married Ken."

"You're supposed to do that before you're married! We all try to find the one."

"No. I mean right before I married Ken. Three weeks before I got married, I went to Scully's one night, dressed like an earthquake because I didn't want anyone hitting on me, and this dorky guy walked in. He had a black eye and he wasn't looking for anything either. Just someone to talk to. Kathy, I started falling for him right away. I mean, Ken didn't talk to me. With Ken I felt like a piece of meat. Maybe not even meat. More like a dinner plate that gets used and washed. Anyway, I was talking with this guy and wondering why Ken couldn't be more like he was. And then I wanted him. And then the next week we met at Scully's again."

"Two weeks before you were married?" demanded Kathy. "You saw him again?"

"But this time I dressed up. That navy blue dress that I wore forever. Heels. Necklace. I looked good. And he walked into Scully's and just from having talked to him once, I knew. His being, his aura screamed adventure and contentment and sensuality. Kathy, I'd be lying if every ounce of me wasn't on fire. I wanted to jump on top of him right then, but I guess that's not my style, so we talked and talked and I felt love pour through me like water through a faucet. In two days he had swept me off my feet with his words and his character and that was on a Friday night. Ken was coming back into town so we made a date to go to Los Angeles on Tuesday. Kathy, I have never told anyone any of this. I was sure I was calling off the wedding. I was sure I was marrying this guy, James. I was sure he was the one."

"What happened in Los Angeles? Did you sleep with him there?" asked Kathy, with eyes wider than the moon.

"I'll never know what could have happened. I somehow missed his call on Monday, and when I listened to his message, he was crying into the phone that he was so sorry, just so sorry, and I just lost it. I really thought he was the one, and when I heard his crying voice, I just snapped."

"Oh, my God. You were that close to calling off the wedding?"

"If I had gone on that date to L.A., my whole life would have been different."

Kathy's latte lingered in the air, inches from her lips. "I can't believe it."

"Yeah. Weird how things work out. I never would have had J.A. or Kimberly or Jake. I can't imagine my life without them. Who knows? If this had been the guy, maybe we wouldn't have been able to have children. Maybe, I don't know, ... life is always filled with so much stuff you never see happening. Ken was a bum, but my kids, my kids are the best. J. A. is coming to town this weekend. We're supposed to have dinner on Saturday."

"Maybe he was already married," said Kathy, still processing all the possibilities of Kristen's confession.

"I don't think so. He had this whole black eye story that was pretty convincing. Maybe, though. He said it was his girlfriend that had punched him. Maybe it really was his wife. Though he seemed pretty single."

"You never saw or heard from him again? Did you have his number? Did you ever look him up?"

"I was so mad when I listened to his message. I went ballistic, and I mean ballistic. I started throwing things around the house and at Ken. Then Ken actually came around a little and I thought, like the moron I can be, that maybe Ken would turn over a new leaf. There was so much I never knew about Ken. Kathy, I don't know if your Howard is Mr. Right. I hope he is. I think

226

we both deserve Mr. Right. Please don't tell J.A. or Kimberly or Jake about how stupid their mom was."

"It's safe with me. Thanks for telling me. It means a lot. I haven't always been the best sister."

"No, you have been the best sister. I couldn't have asked for better. Now let's go find you a wedding dress."

They were out the door and two steps toward a dress for the future bride for the fourth time, when Kathy turned to her sister, "Let's sit for a little longer."

"Did you forget your glasses or...?" said Kristen as they returned to the empty table.

"I haven't always been the best sister," said Kathy, with her own truth serum surfacing.

"I thought we had already gone over this," said Kristen. "Do you want another coffee?"

"You know I have been teaching Stephen Crane's, *The Red Badge of Courage*, for almost twenty years in my American Lit class," said Kathy, slowly approaching her topic.

"I remember reading that. It was the Civil War, right, where the main guy dies at the end. Doesn't he?"

"Henry Fleming. But it is in Chapter Eight that he is walking with the troops when this soldier, the Tattered Man, starts walking with him and asking Henry where his wounds are. Henry tells him he hasn't been wounded, but the Tattered Man persists and keeps asking Henry. Henry gets so bothered by him that he finally just leaves him. What the tattered soldier is trying to do is to get Henry to reveal his internal wounds. I guess what I'm trying to say, Kristen, is that I haven't always been a good sister." A tear of confession rolled from Kathy's eye.

"What Kathy? What is it?"

"I slept with Ken. I'm so sorry," said Kathy, and an ocean of tears broke upon her cheeks.

Kristen stood immediately, walked to the counter and grabbed a handful of napkins before returning, not knowing how to respond.

227

"I'm so, so sorry."

"God, I can't believe it. How did this happen? Really, how could you have?"

"Remember four years ago when Wilhelm left me?" asked Kathy, her face contorted in anguish.

"Four years ago we were divorced," said a relieved Kristen. "You slept with Ken then? Why?"

"I don't know," said Kathy, regaining her composure. "No, I do know."

"Well, why Kathy?"

"I always thought he was so perfect, and here I was stuck with this hunk of golf clubs that sat on the couch and you had Mr. Everything. Looks. I always thought he was gorgeous. Money. A great house. I was jealous. I wanted to be you."

"He was a bum," said Kristen emphatically.

"I just couldn't see the forest for the trees."

Kristen shook her head. "I can't believe you did it with Ken."

"I can't believe I'm telling you. I've wanted to tell you for so long. I hate that I did that to you."

"What happened? Did you do it a lot? Was it like an affair?"

"It was just once. Really, it was awful. I met Robin and Donna at the Chick Touche, ya know, that dive on Magnolia."

"At the Chick Touche? Please tell me not there."

"They both left after a couple of beers and I was finishing up when he walked in. He was working for that construction company then. He always looked good to me. He looked dirty and rugged, and then about four beers later, the place was almost empty."

"Oh my God, Kathy."

"In the men's room, pushed against the urinal." Kathy started to sob. "It was the most disgusting thing I have ever done. For a couple of seconds of pleasure."

The pangs of conscience had finally opened this horrible wound, and tears bled endlessly from her eyes. Kristen could see the anguish she had held inside, could see the suffering oozing down her cheeks, could see the plague of sisterhood that she didn't know how to cure. She lifted her sobbing sister from the chair and wrapped her in the arms of a loving sister.

"I am so sorry. Every time I have taught that novel since then," stammered Kathy as her sobs slowed and Kristen still held her tightly, "I knew I was a coward, just like Henry Fleming, afraid to tell the truth."

"I love you, Kathy. Against a urinal? With Ken? Now that is disgusting."

Chapter 34

"**I** think Pegasus Will Fly has a real chance. Fifty-to-one on the morning line, but the last two races have been his best. If you throw out all of last year, he has a real shot," said James, as he became an expert on the horse races on the first Saturday in May, the day of the Kentucky Derby. For the last twelve years, when the Kentucky Derby rolled around, James and Noe and Trevor would drive to the Santa Anita Race Track and lose some money. Twelve years ago had been their inaugural trip to the track and beginner's luck had covered them in four leaf clovers as they walked away from the pari-mutuel windows with more than twelve thousand dollars in winnings. For the next ten years, they made this pilgrimage back to see if lady luck would shine on them again, but the sun never returned those golden rays of fortune, instead the cyclone of hooves on the racetrack left their pockets barren of cash. This year though was another chance at controlling the winds of fate.

"Just tell me how much money I need to give you and I'm ready to win," said Noe, not involved in who won or lost, more involved with the two friends in the car.

"Willie's Freedom and Sergeant Private and the favorite, Onetwomany, are the ones I like," said Trevor.

"How're Jessi and the baby doing?" asked Noe, who rarely saw Trevor anymore.

"They're good. Real good. Katie is starting to climb out of the crib."

"The kid wants some freedom."

"Yeah, she's figured out that when she is in high school, her dad is going to be about seventy. She wants to get the hell out," said James warmly.

"When you go to kindergarten with her, they're going to think you're her grandfather or the principal," said Noe jokingly.

"I don't give a shit what anybody else thinks, and I especially don't give a fuck what you two think," said Trevor, letting his Toyota Stiletto guide itself onto the freeway at Burbank Boulevard.

"Amber is coming into town tonight. I'm meeting her at Scully's," said James. "Either of you want to meet us there?"

"I'll have to see," said Noe. "It might be a possibility. Especially if we break the bank today at the races. You might have to upgrade from Scully's if you have mad cash hanging out of your pockets.

"Nobody says mad cash anymore," said Trevor, now an expert on linguistics.

"Whatever they say today, that is what I want in my pockets," parried Noe.

As Trevor's Toyota passed where the Five and the 134 converged, he glanced to his right toward Griffith Park as did James and Noe. He returned his focus to the road and brought the fingers of his right hand to his lips and raised the kissed tips to the picture of a mother and her two children clipped to the sun shield above him. Trevor and Noe nodded their heads in understanding as this was the place where Trevor buried Victorville and resurrected who he could still be.

231

For Trevor, he could count the most meaningful times of his life on one hand. The decision to move from Hawaii to Victorville before his senior year of high school had been one traumatic event. And then his unexpected year in Victorville where he, Trevor, reigned as the Sexual King of the school. Then, when he was almost forty he found a young woman from Victorville, who would marry him, only to find that she would leave him before the ink had a chance to dry on their wedding license. Of course the birth of his beautiful little girl, Katie, still a toddler, from his present wife Jessi, was a monument built to show that spots on a leopard can change, that a voice of idiocy can become a voice of reason. The resurrection, the spots on the leopard, the return from the ashes happened because of one remarkable day four years ago.

Noe's boss had called at the last minute with four box seats to a Los Angeles Dodger game that he couldn't use, and so the three friends, James and Trevor with Noe driving, had started the trek to Chavez Ravine and Dodger Stadium. Noe merged from the Ventura Freeway, the 134 to the Five freeway and was in the second lane from the right when he saw a car careening out of control. A red Hyundai traveled from the fast lane, directly across the lanes of traffic toward the Harding Golf Course and Horse Trail that paralleled the freeway. The car flew off the freeway, hit a tree stump that made it flip twice, and then came to a stop with small flames shooting from the motor. Without hesitation, Noe angled his Toyota to the edge of the freeway, and before the car had a chance to come to a complete stop, Trevor, in one motion, grabbed a crowbar from underneath his seat and ran toward the accident not like a man nearing fifty, but like a man possessed. James and Noe also exited the car and ran toward the disaster, as the flames started to grow larger. Other cars and passengers had also joined the scene with another man running with abandon, fire extinguisher in hand, toward the flames. Most had joined James and Noe with hands to mouths. Trevor was insane with action, his crowbar shattering the window of the locked door and then opening the door, with flames just inches away. First he dragged the mother, unconscious, from the front seat and laid her on the ground. James and a woman in a sundress broke free from the onlookers and went toward the injured woman and carried her to safety. Trevor then rescued the first of the two children from the backseat and then returned for the other, still imprisoned by her seat belt. The smoke was darkening inside. Hysterical screams were echoing eerily over the heads of the onlookers, as the fire on the ground began to singe the bottom of Trevor's jeans. Through the billowing smoke, Trevor found the latch for the safety harness that was holding her, and then carried the hysterical screams away from terror, ambivalent to the fire burning his pants. Noe stripped his Dodger jacket from his arms and raced toward the advancing Trevor and awkwardly wrapped it about his leg, as Trevor was lowering the saved child toward the ground. A fire engine arrived at the scene, its shrill siren, abruptly quiet.

"Let's go," said Trevor, his voice shaking, but strong, his hand covered in soot, his face blackened, a Dodger jacket around his leg, his hand barren of any crowbar.

There was no questioning Trevor's authority. He led them through the growing crowd that had gathered next to the side of the freeway, toward their car that was not blocked by the arriving emergency vehicles.

James couldn't explain what had just taken place. If anyone had ever asked him, who was more courageous, he or Trevor, he would have laughed at the stupid question, knowing the answer was himself. Trevor was the sex fiend who only talked about his past exploits of sexuality when he was young, who had never done anything substantial in his whole life, who had made a mess of his marriage, if a marriage less than two years could be called a real marriage, who had been a manager at the Ceiling Exchange for the last fifteen years, who seemed as brave as a puff of cotton. No one in his right mind would ever have said Trevor was more courageous than James. Yet, at the scene of the accident, Trevor hadn't hesitated, and James and Noe had become bystanders.

James thought about the mother and the two children that Trevor, by himself, had rescued. Without Trevor they would have died. Without Trevor there would have been no future. Without Trevor a mother would have lost her two most valuable treasures. It didn't matter what Trevor believed in. It didn't matter if he believed a woman had a right to an abortion. It didn't matter if he believed in capital punishment. It didn't matter if he thought the drinking age should be eighteen or if marijuana should be legal or if he had ever been arrested for a DUI. It didn't matter if he was a Republican or a Democrat. It didn't matter if he was a rabbi or a priest or a man without a home. It didn't matter if he was black or white or brown or Asian or Middle Eastern or from the first colony on Mars. It didn't matter who he was. It just mattered that he was. That he reacted. That he was in a place and his instinct told him he had to do something, and he did. James and Noe had been in the same place, but for whatever reason, their reactions had been different. Not wrong. Just different.

The next day in the newspaper, Trevor had been described as an unidentified bystander who had saved the lives of the Mendiola family, a mother and her twelve-year-old son and ten-year-old daughter. Trevor didn't stay unidentified for long, as every incident in the world seemed to be filmed by somebody. In a quiet ceremony at City Hall in Los Angeles, he received the city's award as Citizen of the Month, and the Mendiola family, aunts and uncles, and grandparents, and nieces and nephews, showered him with letters of gratitude, and a perpetual place in their hearts, and, most importantly, a picture of the Mendiolas, the three of them, mother and son and daughter, that he kept above the steering wheel in his car.

It was after the Mendiola rescue that the Trevor of old was laid to rest once and for all. The burial of that year of sex in Victorville. The last rites given to the stories that had spewed

234

from his lips, stories that life was only an exercise performed on a mattress. The birth of a new Trevor had been long overdue.

"So, how's the sex life with Jessi?" asked James sarcastically.

"Did I ever tell you about Deandrea from Victorville?" said Trevor.

Noe, not paying enough attention to the inflection in the voice, fell into the trap. "I'm sure you must have, probably at least ten times."

"I don't think I ever knew a Deandrea, come to think of it. No. Not that I can recall. I can't recall anyone from that time, a long, long, long, long time ago."

"Amen," added James and Noe.

Chapter 35

"**We** are the essence of femininity," said Kathy, kneeling next to the tilting white rose bush, a pickaxe resting on her shoulder before it made contact once again with the earth, her gardening gloves resembling the hands of Mickey Mouse.

"Sweat and the sweet smell of roses," added Kristen, her old blue jeans covered at the knees with the brown of dirt, her gray sweatshirt with each elbow soiled, and her Los Angeles Dodger baseball cap hiding the smudges on her face. Her black Chuck Taylor low top Converse left her ankles bare and also unprotected, as the two sisters continued severing the roots that fought hard against destruction.

"I agree with you. Roses are too much work. Aphids and thorns and pruning," said Kathy.

"If I had a green thumb, maybe. I think I'll like the succulents."

Kathy swung the pickaxe into the ground and leaned back, pulling on the wobbling plant. She swung the pickaxe again and a third time, and then, with both hands wrapped around the base of the plant, yanked the freed plant from its home.

"Did Ken plant these?" asked Kathy.

"Are you kidding? Ken never planted anything. I've been wanting to take these out forever."

A BMW pulled up to the curb in front of the house, and Kristen raised her sight from the roses, dried the right side of her face with the forearm of her sweatshirt, the only clean spot not stained with dirt and perspiration. "Hey! It's J.A."

The gardening gloves and pickaxes and spades and plants and dirt were soon abandoned, as the two sisters rose to greet J.A. Built like a middle linebacker, J.A. exited the car, his pressed charcoal slacks and navy blue golf shirt, the definition of masculinity and class. He opened the back door and retrieved his suitcase with his one hand.

"Looks like you're ready to go to Scully's right now," said J.A. with a laugh. "You need a little more dirt on your left cheek. Hey, Aunt Kath! What, no hug?"

"I'm a little dirty," said Kathy.

"Isn't everyone a little dirty, and aren't you forgetting I play baseball. We play in the dirt," said J.A., as he wrapped his arms around Kathy and then his mother.

"It's good to have you home, at least for a night. What time do you have to be at the ballpark tomorrow?" asked Kristen.

"About ten. Are you coming to Scully's with us? I think you should," said J.A. to his aunt.

"I don't think so," said Kathy.

"Mom tells me you're about to take the plunge. I'd love to meet him," said J.A.

"I'd like you to meet him. He said he had something special planned for tonight. Right now, everything is roses and champagne. If it weren't something special, I'd go to Scully's."

"Kimberly's going to be mad that she missed her Aunt Kathy."

"Your sister said she might be a little late," added Kristen as the three of them entered the house. "Jake's going to a concert tonight, but he said he'll see you in the morning."

"How's the arm?" asked Kathy.

"It's fine. My right hand has been giving me problems. I can't flip a coin anymore."

"Where did you find this kid, Kristen?" said Kathy with admiration that her nephew with a physical disability could joke so easily about it. Of course, J.A. never looked at a missing hand as a physical disability.

J.A. walked into his bedroom, still a shrine of pictures and trophies and ribbons won over the years. The ball signed by his teammates, when he threw his perfect game against the Cal Bears. His picture with the oldest remaining UCLA hall of famer, Gary Robson, also a Burbank resident, both holding the Forty-Two jersey of UCLA and major league Hall of Famer, Jackie Robinson. His picture with Jim Abbott, of the California Angels, J.A.'s idol and mentor, who has his arm, the arm with no hand, around the shoulder of J.A. The headline announcing J.A.'s selection by the Los Angeles Dodgers in the second round of the major league baseball draft. His CIF player of the year plaque, when he led Burroughs High School to the State Championship, next to his state championship ring. He wore the ring proudly for three months, until he stepped onto the campus of UCLA for the first time and realized he was now a collegian and that all things high school should be put on layaway and reclaimed only if needed in the distant future.

J.A. peeked into his brother's room, the antithesis of his. The walls were painted a psychedelic array of colors, mostly blues and purples and reds, with random moons and suns and stars. Rock posters littered the walls haphazardly, with disturbing images of contorted faces and dismembered parts of bodies. "When's Jake leaving?"

"Still three months before he reports," said Kristen. "You want something to eat or drink?"

"I'll just wait for Scully's," said J.A.

Chapter 36

Everything about Scully's had changed in the last twenty-five years except for the wall of pictures that made every new patron stop to peer closely at the faces that covered magazines around the world, and that at one time, at least once, these famous faces had also walked through the front door of Scully's, the same front door that welcomed every Tom, Dick, and Harry, Eileen, Mabel, and Jasmine to enter and sit at a booth or at the bar and taste the same food and knock back the same drinks as every other patron since the doors first opened in 1947, two years after the end of World War II. The new headliners, the new faces of fame, the new "it," the new heartthrob. These new faces of stardom were now mixed with the forgotten names and faces of yesterday. All gave thanks and best wishes to Scully's, an autograph pursued by the rest of the world, scribbled across their face. The long bar and stools where Kristen and James had sat twenty-five years before had been replaced with a circular revolving bar of alcohol. The Spanish tile roof was gone as were the faux leather booths that were now covered in brown cotton, treated by Incix, a new chemical product, making them impossible to stain or tear. One could choose his own table ambience, with ceiling laser lights that did not disturb other customers or tables. Now, customers ordered from the screen atop each table. The green felt on the pool table in the back was the only other relic that remained.

Everything does change in twenty-five years. Twenty-five years before there were no J.A or Kimberly or Jake. No Christian or Amber. Ken hadn't married Kristen. James' eye was healing from the onslaught of Molly's fist. There were no self-driving cars that took you to work. Twenty-five years ago people actually took phones from their pockets or their purse. Twenty-five years before, pictures were taken with cameras and not fingers. And during that twenty-five years, over nine thousand new days were crossed off of calendars, over nine thousand times the sun had risen and set, over nine thousand new chances to grab laughter, to snare intelligence, to fight lethargy, to drop to the earth in failure, to rise to the mountaintop in triumph, to walk in one's own shoes, to walk in the shoes of others, and to make a list of all the things you couldn't accomplish today but would find the time to accomplish tomorrow.

And ninety-eight percent of everything that happens during those twenty-five years is long forgotten, never to be remembered, never to be recalled. But it is that two percent that is the luggage that you pack and unpack the rest of your life. The arms of a two-year old child, hugging you with the strength of love, the gentle hand of romance caressing your cheek, the first taste of lobster, or brussel sprouts, or pizza, the first time you stood in front of the Eiffel Tower or Big Ben or Niagara Falls or Half Dome. The first day of school when you let go of your child's hand and they take those first unsure steps and look back over their shoulder for one more reassuring nod of approval. The day your child is born without a hand and the crushing feeling of guilt that there is something wrong with you because your child is missing something every child should have. And then the discovery that your child only needs one hand. The mornings of Christmas. The mornings of Easter. The meal at Thanksgiving when the oven wasn't turned on and the turkey never cooked. The day you served soup to the needy, and the sense of appreciation you received from that one man with the eye that drooped and the stained flannel shirt that was his only shirt. The day that was supposed to be sunny, according to the forecast, but the clouds had other ideas, and you were soaked to the bone by the unexpected downpour. The days of death when grief shook you like a rag doll and threatened to tear you to pieces. The days of Superman when you felt so good that nothing, that not even Kryptonite could stop you. The fright of a good Halloween story. The laughter of watching "that man" trying to carry the package as his pants were falling down, and the dance of pants and balancing packages that followed. The comfort of a shower after getting lost during an hour hike that lasted five hours. The cool breeze on a hot day. The smell of the ocean. The comfort of a bathroom. Over nine thousand days when you were the inventor. Where you devised your own plan. When you concocted a potion for the day. When you cooked the day's recipe. When you broke the shell of the egg and saw what hatched. Nine thousand days in twenty-five years.

...And today.

J.A. walked with pride toward the front door of Scully's, his arm draped around the shoulder of his mother. She had always been there for him, always trusted him to do the right thing, even if there was an occasional bad hop. She stressed there would always be bad hops, always curveballs in the dirt that got away from the catcher, always fly balls, the proverbial "can of corn" that would be misjudged and fall in for a hit. But don't blame the mistake. Take responsibility. Be a man. She was a little over fifty, but the last twenty-five years hadn't robbed her of her beauty, and the years had added strength and courage to her character. J.A. knew one element had been missing for many years, an element he wasn't sure she would ever find, the element of love. J.A opened the front door of Scully's, and his mother,

241

Kristen, walked inside, her thoughts inhabiting the same parallel universe as her son. She looked with admiration at the man her son had become.

"Table for three. Anderson," said J.A., raising his good hand with three fingers in the air as he approached the hostess.

"Just a few minutes," she said. "Anderson, three."

"Kimberly's stuck in some traffic around Griffith Park, but she should be here soon," said Kristen, checking the message on her iPhone20. "She's worried that she's not wearing the right shoes. I told her I was wearing flats. It's nice that they're back in style."

"She worries too much about the way she looks. It'll be nice to see her. I hope she can make it to the game tomorrow."

"What time do you have to leave in the morning?" asked Kristen, as she remembered a night so long ago, a night twenty-five years before when she was questioning her decision to marry Ken, that night when she dressed like a slob, to just sit by herself and contemplate the shifting gears of the world, whether to drive straight ahead or put the car in reverse. Kristen squeezed J.A.'s arm, realizing reverse would have meant the disappearance of J.A. and Kimberly and Jake. She laughed to herself. What would life have been like if she had married James? She couldn't imagine.

"They want me at the ballpark by ten, so I should probably leave about eight-thirty, just to be on the safe side."

Kristen and J.A. stepped aside as a man, Noe, and his son walked toward the hostess. The son stopped as his father continued on.

"We were supposed to meet a couple of friends. I don't know if they're here yet," said Noe. "It would be James, party of four?

The waitress checked her list, "They haven't arrived yet."

"We'll wait," replied Noe moving away.

"You probably don't remember me," said Aaron, Noe's son, to J.A. "But we played baseball against each other when we

242

were in Little League. I think you struck me out like twelve times."

"J.A. Nice to meet you," said J.A. reaching with his left hand.

"I'm Aaron."

"Twelve times, huh?"

"It was probably more like twenty to be really honest."

"This is my mom, Mrs. Anderson," said J.A., as he continued being a gentleman.

"My dad, Noe," said Aaron, finishing the greeting.

"This might sound stupid, J.A., but I always looked up to you. I always wanted to be like you," said Aaron, a bit embarrassed to admit his idolatry of someone his own age. "I would even get these really long shirts when I was in the fifth and sixth grade and always had the sleeve cover my right hand. I'd imagine that I only had one hand. I know. Pretty pathetic. But you always handled yourself with real class. Everyone knew you and talked about you. I never heard anyone say anything bad."

"I think you're going to be in the majors soon," added Noe, "I've tried my best to follow your career. I think you are the best player to ever come out of these parts."

"I appreciate that. I've been working hard to make it. And I've been pretty blessed with a bunch of good coaches."

"I imagine it's all in God's hands," said Noe.

"That lucky devil has two, and he only gave me one. I don't get it," joked J.A., as Noe changed color.

"I've gotta tell you this one thing," said Aaron, as Kristen stood silently, soaking in the waters of praise that Noe and Aaron were showering J.A. with. "I had struck out like eight straight times against you, but I was determined that the next time things would be different. It was always next time. There were two strikes on me and on the next pitch I connected like I had never connected before and hit a foul ball that went over the little league fence at McCambridge, and I heard this gasp from the crowd."

"I think I remember that," said J.A.

243

"To this day, that was my proudest moment ever playing baseball. I hit other home runs. I even drove in the winning run a couple of times. But hitting that foul ball off of you. I still remember that moment. Of course, you struck me out on the next pitch."

"Anderson, your table is ready," said the young lady at the counter.

"Good luck," said Noe, as he shook J.A.'s hand. "Nice to meet you, ma'am."

Kristen nodded to the gentlemen, as J.A. exchanged pleasantries, and then they walked to their booth.

"I remember that kid Aaron and that foul ball. It was weird. He could never hit me and then that one pitch and bam, I thought it was gone. Luckily it wasn't a costly mistake. That was probably twelve years ago."

"I don't remember them, but they remembered you. Do you ever hear from Sheila?" asked Kristen

"No, Mom. I know you really liked her. She was really sweet when she was around you. When she was around me, there was more lemon than sugar, if you know what I mean. Last I heard she was trying to join the Peace Corps. I think I told you that we have this new trainer, Amber. She is pretty cool."

"Have you been dating her?" asked Kristen, having forgotten J.A.'s mention of this new name.

"I haven't been around her long enough, but if first impressions are worth anything…"

"I don't know if I have ever heard you talk about someone else like this," added Kristen.

"I don't know if I ever have."

"She must be a knockout."

"She's cool. We had a game last week and I was running my sprints, sideline to centerfield, when I tightened up a little. I was trying to stretch it out when she came out of the dugout. I was on my stomach, and she starts massaging my hamstring, and this guy in the stands is heckling me, 'Hey, Hook. Hey, Five

244

Fingers. Hey, Bowling Ball Plus Two.' The usual garbage, when she goes bonkers and climbs into the stands to get to this guy. The trainer, trying to get in the stands and kick some drunk's butt, but one of the coaches grabbed her. I'd never seen anything like it."

"That's hysterical. So…?"

"We haven't even gotten a chance to really talk. I don't know where she grew up or anything. The coach made her go back to the dugout and cool down a bit."

"Take it slow, son."

"Like I said, I haven't even talked to her yet, so I don't know if I could take it any slower. But she was going after some guy to protect me."

"Just be sure."

"One thing I know is, I don't want a trophy wife. I want someone who is ready to climb into the stands, not someone who just sparkles under a spotlight. I have enough trophies to last a lifetime; I sure don't need another one that shines for a few hours and then only collects dust hoping to be polished soon."

"Then maybe she's the one."

"You gotta be shittin' me," said J.A., profanity spouting from his mouth for the first time in four years, his eyes a study in bewilderment. "I can't believe it."

"What?" said Kristen, starting to turn around to see what had amazed her son.

"No, Mom. Don't look. Please don't look. It's her. It's Amber. That's impossible. What are the chances? What is she doing at Scully's?" said J.A., as skittish as a rabbit being chased by a Doberman.

"The Amber you've just been talking about?" said Kristen, now eager to turn around.

J.A.'s eyes followed Amber and an older man that J.A. didn't know across the restaurant to where they were seated. The man was James.

"The guy we just met. What was his name?" asked an excited J.A.

"I think it was Aaron and…"

"Yeah. Aaron and Noe or something like that. She's sitting with them," said J.A., calming slightly, his head still swiveling.

"Well go over there and say hi," said Kristen, urging her son toward action.

"I can't go yet," he said, his mind spinning through possibilities as he watched the hugs of Noe and Aaron and Amber and James. He wondered, if maybe Aaron, his strike-out-sure-thing, was Amber's romantic interest. The irony was too sorrowful to contemplate. J.A. thought of Aaron at the plate, out of his element, without a chance to make contact, with only a prayer of a chance, a foreigner in the land of J.A., who was his executioner, who would send him back to the dugout to take a seat of failure on the bench. And now it was Aaron who might control the plate, who might be in love with Amber, and Amber in love with him, and it might be J.A.'s fate to sit on the bench, a strike-out victim of his own. J.A. had a moment of relief when James, the unknown man sat next to Amber.

"Oh my gosh, she saw me," said J.A, as he raised his hand in a wave. Amber had turned around and scanned the restaurant until her eyes had found his. Aaron must have told her that J.A. was in the restaurant. J.A. watched as James and Amber approached their table. "She's coming over," said an excited J.A., looking for a rabbit hole to dive into. Kristen touched his hand for comfort, his shaking hand that could control a baseball to fit into a space the size of a shoebox, that could control a bat of hatred to swing and only hit air, the hand that was about to face a line-up in Scully's that he hadn't expected to find walking toward his plate.

"J.A. What are you doing here?" said a bubbling Amber, obviously attracted to J.A. "This is my dad, James."

J.A rose and reached out for James' hand. "Nice to meet you, Sir. This is my mom, Mrs. Anderson," said J.A. as his mother, in her white dress, ascended like an angel from the table and turned toward James for the introduction.

There are those moments in life that one can only imagine how the person must have felt. How did Edmund Hillary feel in 1953, taking his last step to the top of Mount Everest? How did archaeologist Howard Carter feel in 1922 when he uncovered King Tut's tomb? How did Romeo feel the first time he set eyes on Juliet? How did Columbus feel when he spotted land? How did Neil Armstrong feel when he stepped foot on the moon? How did the city of Boston feel when the curse of the Bambino was finally broken in 2004? How did James feel when he saw the treasure of his life sink to the floor of the ocean, without a chance to ever reach the surface? How did he feel when his heart was ripped from his soul without the chance to be mended? How did he feel when the chance to taste the sweetness of life had been plucked from his tongue? And all that grief. And all that sorrow. And all that desire. And all that love. And then all that passion. And all that anguish. Became one.

Their eyes met at the same time. Kristen's eyes and James' eyes. The eyes that hadn't seen the other for twenty-five years. The eyes that had gently closed when they had kissed like no other kiss. Forget Antony and Cleopatra. Forget Romeo and Juliet. Forget Gatsby and Daisy. Forget Snow White and the Prince. Over twenty-five years had passed since James and Kristen's kiss had held a promise of an everlasting love. The eyes that had known they were meant for each other had been derailed by a misunderstanding and the deadly kiss of bad timing that had thrown them from their tracks of destiny and had delayed their love for almost three decades. Their two dots that could have been stuck together like glue for a lifetime, were thrown adrift by the winds of chance, two dots, that ran lives parallel to each other, almost intersecting over the years, almost touching. Two lives filled with accomplishment and happiness and achievement and grief and success and discovery and adventure and loneliness and pain and the elements that determine every life.

The voices of Amber and J.A. were muffled in the vision of their eyes. There in the middle of the aisle of Scully's, with a

247

waitress delivering a tuna melt and fries and a cheeseburger and cottage cheese to the table next to them, the eyes of James and Kristen were blind to the rest of the world, were blind to the past and the future. Their eyes were welded together. They were unable to speak. There would be time to talk. There would be time to discover the reason for James' sorrowful call, and Kristen's volcanic eruption. There would be time to laugh at James' attendance at the wrong funeral. There would be time to talk about Molly and to talk about Ken. There would be time for James and Kristen to meet again at Scully's on a Friday night, just the two of them, over a glass of cabernet. There would be time for James to show Kristen the article he carried with him his whole life and the phrase that had motivated his actions, "I can't believe so much life could leave so quickly." There would be time for James to embrace so much life in his arms and ensure it would never be taken away again.

Kimberly opened the front door of Scully's and walked inside. She spotted her brother, J.A., first. He was standing in the aisle of the restaurant. A young lady had her hand on his shoulder. She didn't know who she was. And there was her mother. Her mother's eyes were locked in a warm gaze with someone that was not her father. 'What was going on? Is Mom dating?' she wondered as she made her way toward the table.

J.A. had never seen his mother like this, had never seen her so lost in the moment, had never seen her so entranced. J.A. could feel Amber's fingers massaging his shoulder and then falling to his side where they entwined with his. Tomorrow he knew he would be taking the mound. Knew he would be as entranced as his mother, staring into the catcher's mitt for a sign. Fastball or curve or change-up. One step closer to making the Major Leagues. Each batter he faced would be a challenge. Each pitch he threw could be the one to determine his future. His hand was holding tomorrow.

Kristen, with an invasion of butterflies dancing in her soul, with a recapturing of lost passion, with a young girl's giddiness, ended the silence, ended the awareness of their eyes, ended the twenty-five years of being apart with an introduction, "J.A., I would like you to meet James."

Made in the USA
San Bernardino, CA
22 March 2018